PENGUIN
THE SAR

Rupa Bajwa was born in 1976, in Amritsar, where she is currently based. *The Sari Shop* is her first novel.

The Sari Shop

RUPA BAJWA

PENGUIN BOOKS

Penguin Books India (P) Ltd., 11 Community Centre, Panchsheel Park, New Delhi
110017, India
Penguin Books Ltd., 80 Strand, London WC2R 0RL, UK
Penguin Group (USA) Inc., 375 Hudson Street, New York, NY 10014, USA
Penguin Books Australia Ltd., 250 Camberwell Road, Camberwell, Victoria 3124,
Australia
Penguin Books Canada Ltd., 10 Alcorn Avenue, Suite 300, Toronto, Ontario
M4V 3B2, Canada
Penguin Books (NZ) Ltd., Cnr Rosedale & Airborne Roads, Albany, Auckland,
New Zealand
Penguin Books (South Africa) (Pty) Ltd., 24 Sturdee Avenue, Rosebank 2196,
South Africa

First published in the United Kingdom in Viking by Penguin Books Ltd 2004
First published in India by Penguin Books India 2004

This is a work of fiction. Names, characters, places and incidents are either the
product of the author's imagination or are used fictitiously and any resemblance to
any actual person, living or dead, events or locales is entirely coincidental.

For sale in India, Sri Lanka, Bangladesh and Nepal only

Printed at Pauls Press, New Delhi

In loving memory of two very special men:

Sardaar Piara Singh Goraya
and
Harvinder Jit Singh Goraya

PART ONE

PART ONE

I

Ramchand had overslept, waking up only when the loud noises of a brawl in the street below had jolted him out of sleep. He rubbed his eyes, got out of bed and walked to the window. He peered through the rusted iron bars at the two people who were fighting. One was a milkman, who had been cycling back after delivering milk. He had large, zinc-coated iron cans (that looked like aluminium) strung on either side of his bicycle, and one of these now-empty milk cans had bumped into a pedestrian on the narrow street. A quarrel had flared up, and the two were shouting loudly, red-faced and angry.

Ramchand sleepily brushed his teeth by the window, leaning against the wall. He watched the fight to its end, when the previously interested spectators began to get bored and calmed the two men down. It was just a ritual; people in street fights thought they lost face if they stopped before spectators intervened. The two finally went on their way. After that, Ramchand just forgot to watch the clock. He continued to stare vacantly out of the window for a long time, his mind still fuzzy with sleep. The morning was cold. His limbs and mind both felt frozen. He moved slowly.

By the time Ramchand looked at the little red clock on the table and realized that he was late, it was too late. He bathed and dressed in a hurry, dropping things all over the place, scalding himself when he warmed water for his bath on the kerosene stove, fumbling with the buttons of his shirt and spilling hair oil on the already dirty floor. Finally, he ended up misplacing the heavy iron lock, along with the key stuck in it.

He found both right under his nose on the table after he had spent fifteen minutes searching for them everywhere. He rushed out of his room and made his way towards the shop then, half-running and half-walking through the narrow streets of the crowded bazaar, hurrying past pedestrians, dodging rickshaws and nearly running into vegetable carts. He could feel his toes perspiring inside his grey woollen socks.

Even at ten in the morning, the bazaar was throbbing with activity. The halwai was already installed in front of the Mishthaan Sweet Shop, pressing jalebi batter into squiggly shapes that floated and simmered in the oil in a big iron cauldron. All the shops had opened for the day and, Ramchand noted guiltily, all the shop assistants were already in place, trying to sell things with fixed, attentive smiles on their shiny, bathed faces.

The older part of Amritsar, the original walled city, was full of bazaars – small ones that only the locals knew about, tiny bazaars that sold bangles and cloth very cheap but could be reached only on foot through tiny alleys; and the big, main bazaars where the streets were wider and the roads slightly cleaner. The bazaars of Amritsar were busy places where every day, throughout the year, transactions were made, prices were bargained over, shops were opened in the mornings and shut in the evenings. It was as if it had been so since the beginning of the world and would continue to be so till the end.

There were no empty spaces. Just a jumble of old red-brick houses, aged grey concrete buildings, shops, signboards, numerous tiny temples at street corners and crowded streets thronged with people, cows, stray dogs, and fruit and vegetable carts. There were no gates, doorsteps led straight from the streets into houses. Crumbling buildings ran into each other like cardboard boxes stuck together with glue. Their terraces overlapped, there were no boundary walls – you couldn't tell where one finished and the next began. Occasionally there

4

would be a gap in the mass of buildings, where a very narrow alley would nudge aside the unyielding walls and squeeze itself painfully through the solid structure, joining another similar narrow lane at some other end. It could take years to become familiar with the maze-like network of lanes and alleys and short cuts in the old city.

Money, congestion and noise danced an eternal, crazy dance here together, leaving no moving space for other, gentler things. The actual walls that had once surrounded the city had fallen away long ago, but the ghosts of the wall still separated the old city from the newer one that flourished outside.

The shop where Ramchand worked was one of the oldest in the city, tucked neatly between Talwaar Furnishings and Draperies and Chanduram's Fabrics. It was in one of the main bazaars, buried away in the heart of the city, yet with parking space for customers who came in cars. In this bazaar the shops were larger, older, with good reputations and old, regular customers, and the shop owners were all considered respectable people from old business families.

A large fading green signboard over the entrance of the shop said Sevak Sari House in flourishing red letters in old-fashioned calligraphy, both in English and Punjabi. The signboard was slightly misleading. The shop did not just sell saris. The ground floor stocked fabric for men's clothes as well. There were dreary browns, blues and blacks here. But very few people visited Sevak Sari House to buy Men's Suitings and Shirtings. There were other, larger shops that had a wider range devoted entirely to men – the Raymond showroom two lanes away, for instance. So the ground floor of the shop wore a dusty, jaded look. It was the first floor of the shop that sold saris.

Packed from shelf to shelf with crisp Bangladeshi cottons, dazzling Kanjeevarams, Benaras silks, chiffons, crêpes and satins, it was the first floor that pulsated with an intoxicating, rich life of colour and silk and brought in the customers and

5

profits. And it was because of the huge success of the first floor that Sevak Sari House had been known for decades as the best sari shop in Amritsar. The suiting and shirting cut-pieces in the ground floor cowered under the sparkling, confident dazzle above.

There was also a second floor that customers never saw. It contained a big storeroom and a small toilet that was used by Mahajan and the shop assistants.

Ramchand was one of the six shop assistants who worked in the sari section.

*

Ramchand stood uncertainly at the entrance of the shop, his palms cold with sweat despite the chilly December morning, thinking of Mahajan's rage that would soon descend on him. Ramchand peered in. Mahajan was talking to somebody over the phone. Making the best of it, Ramchand sprinted across the ground floor under Mahajan's disapproving eyes.

There was a Ganesha idol installed near the foot of the staircase that led up to the first floor. Ramchand would usually stop before this idol for a moment every morning, with folded hands and closed eyes, and then after an elaborate bow, would make his way upstairs. But today he just hurried up the shaky wooden steps as fast as he could. His heart thudded inside his chest. Any moment now Mahajan would stop him and give him a dressing down. But he climbed up to the first floor safely. In the small space on top of the staircase, and in the front of the big glass door that led into the sari section, he tried to get his breath back. Then he struggled with his shoes, first hopping on one foot and then on the other, trying to get them off. His hopping made thumping noises on the wooden staircase.

And then Mahajan finally bellowed from below. 'Trying to

break the place? Coming late? You think I don't notice? Am I blind? Stupid? Hunh? You think a shop can be run like this? You will come and go as you please? Are you a king or something? *Raja Ramchand*? Should we send an entourage and a bagghi to pick you up every day?'

Ramchand stopped immediately and waited. Silence. Then he cautiously took off his shoes, wishing his feet wouldn't smell so. He had taken a bath and worn fresh socks, and yet . . . He knew that the smell would become even stronger by the end of the day. Ramchand arranged his shoes neatly on the wooden shoe rack on the side of the wall, in the row assigned to the shop assistants. The other rows were for the delicate sandals, the kolhapuri chappals, the platform and stiletto heels of the female customers. Ramchand patted his hair and straightened his kurta to make up for the feet, and walked in.

He went to his allotted place and sat down cross-legged. The shop was an old-fashioned one and there were no counters. The entire floor space was spread out with thick mattresses covered with white sheets, and on these mattresses sat the shop assistants every day, facing the customers, and endlessly rolling and unrolling yards upon yards of important coloured fabric.

'Namaste Ramchand Bhaiya. Late again?' grinned Hari, sitting some distance away. Hari was the youngest among all the shop assistants. He was a careless, cheerful, young man with a cheeky face, who often got shouted at by Mahajan.

However, unlike the effect they had on Ramchand, these unpleasant encounters always left Hari completely unfazed. In fact, on slightly dull days, they even cheered him up. 'In from one ear, and out from the other,' he would always say, beaming broadly, after Mahajan had spent considerable time and energy telling him what he thought of him. Because of Hari's junior status, his inexperience and his indifference to

7

the intricacies of fabric, he had been put in charge of Paraag Daily Wear Saris and Paraag Fancy Saris for Occasions. One didn't need much skill or specialized knowledge of fabric to sell these. It would be a long time before Hari would be put in charge of anything else. Not that he cared.

Ramchand smiled back at him. 'What to do, yaar?'

'We could hear him shouting at you even through the door,' Hari said, still grinning.

'What to do, yaar?' Ramchand said again, this time more gloomily.

'Never mind,' said Hari comfortingly. 'You did a good deed for our Mahajan. If some people don't get to shout at someone early in the morning, they can't digest their breakfast properly. Now that raakshas Mahajan will have very good digestion.' Hari cackled at his own joke. 'For *that* is the sort of man our Mahajan is,' he added, winking at Ramchand, and cackled again. Then he sighed theatrically.

Gokul sat placidly folding some saris into neat rectangles. He was in charge of very expensive crêpes, and in the wedding season he also helped with ornate wedding lehngas and saris. He was a grave-looking man in his forties who took his work very seriously. Mahajan thought a great deal of his experience and his sincerity, but this still didn't save Gokul from occasional tongue lashes from Mahajan. About ten years back, Sevak Sari House had also decided to stock chunnis. For there were many Sardaarnis from old Sikh families, matriarchs as well as young women, who came in to buy saris and asked hopefully whether they had chunnis as well. For them, saris were necessary, they were fashionable, but their *real* clothes were salwaar kameez. And so, after many of them had wistfully enquired about chunnis, saying that Sevak Sari House was so *dependable*, and that it was so difficult to get really good quality stuff in chunnis these days, Bhimsen and Mahajan had put their heads together and had decided to stock chunnis too.

And Gokul had made it his business to know his chunnis very well. There were no ordinary chunnis in Sevak Sari House. They sold saris, so if some chunnis had to be there, they had to be special. All of them were two and a half metres in length, and of the required width. No well-dressed sardaarni liked a chunni shorter or narrower than that; they thought that those kind of chunnis were for Hindu women or for very young girls. Apart from the length, the quality was taken care of. There were pure chiffon chunnis, there were lovely white silk chunnis that could be dyed to match any silk salwaar kameez, there were gold-edged bridal odhnis in red, pink and maroon, there were white chunnis with discreet light-coloured embroidery at the borders for widows from good families, there were the colourful ones embroidered with traditional phulkari work – usually bought by Sikh women for their daughters' trousseau, and many others. And Gokul could handle all the customers who came in asking for chunnis.

Despite this, Gokul didn't swagger. He was in awe of Mahajan and was always warning Hari to be careful not to get into Mahajan's bad books.

Gokul now looked up at Hari and said, 'You be quiet, Hari! Calling Mahajan a raakshas at the top of your voice! You talk too much. Some day they will hear you and chuck you out. You have too long a tongue. That tongue won't earn you your living, boy.'

But Gokul was smiling when he said this. He had a small, benign face and a dome-shaped head sparsely covered with wisps of hair. Ramchand also gave him a wan smile. Chander was unlocking a cupboard nearby. All the walls of the shop were either covered with shelves, or had sturdy built-in cupboards that could be locked up with the more expensive or delicate stock inside. While the three were talking, Chander didn't even look up once. He was a quiet man, very tall, and with a very pronounced Adam's apple. He often did not turn

9

up for work, and maintained a melancholic silence whenever Mahajan shouted at him for this or for any other reason. He would just take in all the insults Mahajan hurled at him, staring into space all the while, biting his lower lip, not answering any of Mahajan's angry questions.

The two oldest shop assistants, Shyam and Rajesh, had been working at Sevak Sari House for a much longer time than any of the others. Shyam had greying hair, a thin face and a large gap between his two front teeth. Rajesh was plump, with slightly rheumy eyes. The two kept to themselves, confabulating in low voices about the rising prices, nought per cent interest home loans and where you could get the best bargains for household electrical appliances. They were paid slightly more than all the other shop assistants. Everyone knew this, but it was never mentioned, and the two men never admitted it officially. Shyam had a young daughter he was hoping to marry off to Rajesh's son. They lived in their own set, middle-aged world, went out for tea and meals together, and called all the other shop assistants 'boys', even Gokul, who was only a few years younger than them.

Ramchand spent the morning arranging new stock. Bhimsen Seth, the owner of the shop, came in at about eleven. The shop had been set up by his grandfather, Sevak Ram. Bhimsen had taken over at the age of twenty. That was when a fifteen-year-old Mahajan had come to him looking for work. Bhimsen had taken him in, and Mahajan had worked his way up in the business. He had, over thirty years, proved himself to be honest, reliable, enterprising and a hard taskmaster. Now it was Mahajan who looked after most of the practical affairs of the shop, though under Bhimsen's supervision. Most of the time now, Bhimsen Seth didn't need to come to the shop every day. He had some other businesses running that he also had to see to. Ramchand didn't know whether Seth was his surname or if it was just a respectful way of addressing him.

He had asked Gokul once, but Gokul didn't know either, and Ramchand didn't dare to ask anyone else.

On the rare occasions that Bhimsen Seth did come to the shop, he just reclined prosperously in a corner of the first floor, surrounded by a garish assortment of pictures of Hindu Gods, burning incense sticks and greedily counting hundred-rupee notes with his thick, stubby fingers.

Ramchand watched him out of the corner of his eye some-times. Bhimsen would intently flip the edges of the notes, and, if he happened to look up and catch Ramchand's eye, he would give him a slow, fleshy smile that chilled Ramchand's heart. He always found Bhimsen's benevolent manner a little sinister.

2

In another corner of Amritsar, far away from the old city, in an area where many government officers, doctors and a few businessmen had made new, spacious houses with lawns in the front and kitchen gardens behind, Mrs Sandhu stood in her kitchen and watched the milk boil and froth on the gas stove. She was a fat, fair-skinned woman with a clear, glowing complexion and long, glossy hair tied back neatly into a bun.

The kitchen she stood in was spotless and fixed up with the latest gadgets. The marble slabs gleamed clean and dry. Hawkins non-stick utensils were stacked neatly in a shelf, there wasn't a drop or stain on the LG microwave oven, and the floor shone. Mrs Sandhu's husband was Chief Engineer in the Punjab State Electricity Board. Many of his underlings came into his residence as cooks or gardeners to do domestic chores, and they kept the house spick and span. The Sandhus used to live in the Power Colony, in a government-allotted house, and had recently built and moved into their new house.

Mr Sandhu was intensely interested in the house, and had planned the construction as well as the furnishing very carefully. Only the best would do. Even after he retired, people ought to be able to tell that he had been Chief Engineer. So the house was big, with the latest fashionable architectural features incorporated in its design. The bathrooms had granite floors. There was a big arch leading into the drawing room, which was sunk into the floor down two or three steps. There were carpets that Mr Sandhu had ordered from Kashmir. All the doors were made of teak, the furniture and upholstery were expensive and had been personally chosen by Mr Sandhu.

Many people commented that it was strange that a government officer, no matter how high-up, had been able to afford such a grand house – but then the Sandhus had property, land in their village and, of course, they added with knowing glances, these days which government officer doesn't take in something under the table?

There was another Chief Engineer who had built a house close by, though he had built it step by step. First he had saved money for his plot of land. Then, over the next few years, he had saved enough to start construction. He had moved in with his family when the house was still incomplete. Five years later, he had hired carpenters to make built-in wooden shelves and cupboards to replace the two steel Godrej almirahs. He had a lawn and a kitchen garden too, but just a battered old Fiat, one ordinary carpet in the drawing room, old shabby furniture that his wife loved and refused to part with, and a not very large bank balance. He was a most impractical man, people said, most unwise . . . almost foolish.

Mrs Sandhu thought she was as good as anybody now. Never mind her weight, at least she was better than all those thin women with dark, rough skins and mousey hair. A beautiful house, status-family, a caring husband and good looks . . . what more could a woman ask for? Now, if only the children would do well . . .

She turned the gas off, and the milk subsided. She poured it carefully into a tall steel glass, filling it up to the brim. Her rolls of fat jiggled as she waddled to her son's room with the hot glass in her hands. The door was slightly ajar. She pushed it open and tiptoed to his desk, where he was working.

'Manu, beta, drink this,' she said encouragingly. Manu looked up at her. He was a gangly adolescent with the beginnings of a moustache and bony knees. He was soon to sit for his entrance exams to medical colleges. All eyes were on him. He was the P.M.T. boy, the pre-medical test boy. His parents were proud, anxious and loving. He took the steel glass from her languidly, leaned back and took a sip. Mrs Sandhu waited, her rolls of fat now still and expectant, her lips slightly parted.

'Chheee!' Manu made a face and pushed the glass back into her hands. 'Didn't you strain it? You know I hate cream in milk. Take it away.'

He returned to his work without looking at her. She went back to the kitchen and took out her steel strainer, the one her mother had given her when she had got married. It was still in such good shape, she thought with satisfaction. She strained the milk carefully into another glass. The offending cream remained stuck in the strainer. She took the new glass back to his room. He was bent once again over his papers, his lips moving in a silent murmur. He took the glass from her hands without looking at her. He took slow sips without a word. She slipped out of the room.

The phone in the drawing room rang. She rushed to it, hoping the ringing hadn't disturbed Manu.

It was her husband calling from work. He was in a good mood; he had just finished receiving a bribe that was politely disguised as a gift. He asked his wife gently what Manu was doing.

'Studying,' she answered proudly.

*

Two houses away, Mrs Gupta sat in her bedroom on a large bed covered with a peach satin bedspread. She was in her late fifties, though a careful diet and regular exercise made her look younger. Her skin was pale and translucent, but she had thin hair. To cover that up she had got it cut to shoulder length and tied it back with a hair clip. On another woman of her age it might have looked ridiculous, but it went well with her perky, overconfident manner, her smart walk and her trim waist. Her eyes were small, and her nose a little hooked. She didn't like these two things about her face, and the thin hair of course, but she knew that on the whole she looked good – smart, trendy, respectable and from a well-to-do family at the same time.

Crystal ornaments sat on a shelf in the wall – crystal was the latest, and she made sure she kept adding to the collection whenever she could. There was a crystal vase, with imported artificial white flowers in it, a miniature crystal violin and a statuette of a dancing woman among other knick-knacks. Though lately she had been wondering if she ought to shift the crystal to the drawing room. Hardly anyone saw it here . . .

The large mirror of the glass-topped dressing table reflected the well-kept room – the beautiful double bed with a red velvet headboard, the crystal pieces, the glass-topped side tables, the rust-coloured carpet, and the pleated curtains with the rust and peach check pattern. It also reflected Mrs Gupta, sitting resplendently among all this, deep in thought.

On the dressing table, below the room-reflection, stood a jar of L'Oréal anti-ageing cream, a bottle of Lakme cleansing milk, packs of deep-red bindis and a big bottle of perfume. There were also sleek, red cases of Revlon lipsticks standing in a row like identical dwarf soldiers in red uniforms. These were the things she used every day. All her other cosmetics were tucked away neatly in the drawers of the dressing table.

Mrs Gupta had recently heard of Feng shui at one of the kitty parties she had been to. She had told her husband about it. 'It is just like our Vaastu Shastra, but more modern. There are books and all in English about it and Mrs Bhandari has done it too. She has made a rockery just where the book tells her to.'

Mrs Gupta didn't have much time on her hands to read books, but she managed to ask a lot of people about Feng shui and now, apart from many other changes and additions to the house, wind chimes hung at the entrance to the room, quivering and tinkling every now and then.

She stroked the satiny surface of the peach bedspread absently, a satisfied smile on her lipsticked lips. Her elder son Tarun's marriage had just been fixed up, and she was completely satisfied with the arrangement. The girl's name was Shilpa. She was a demure girl, not exactly pretty – she had rather indistinct features – but she did have a fair skin and was slim. That was all that mattered, thought Mrs Gupta. The rest could be worked on. She seemed meek and eager to please, her shy manner completely unlike the brash way some girls behaved these days. Anyway, she could be moulded. The real thing, the most important thing, was that her father was a rich and respected industrialist. The status of the two families matched exactly, so there wouldn't be any adjustment problems between the couple or between the families. Maybe, at a later stage, Tarun could even form a business partnership with her brothers . . .

Mrs Gupta had a lot to think about, the whole wedding to plan, in fact. Her younger son, Puneet, a computer engineer in America, would also come down for the wedding. He would help, of course. Mr Gupta was a well-connected businessman. He knew how to handle things. He would do most of the practical stuff, like ringing up contacts and making people like jewellers, caterers and tent owners give concessions on everything, but she'd have to do The Shopping.

The Guptas had had a lengthy, honest discussion with Shilpa's parents, and they had all decided that there would be three 'functions' – Ladies' Sangeet which could be incorporated with the Mehndi Ceremony, the actual wedding, and a Reception Party.

So she'd have to get ready three sets of clothes with matching jewellery to wear at each of these functions. She'd also have to plan and buy Shilpa's clothes and jewellery for the

Reception, for, according to tradition, everything that Shilpa would wear immediately after the wedding, must be a gift from her in-laws. And they'd have to decide about Tarun's clothes too.

Mrs Gupta herself had already decided what to wear on the wedding day. She had an old jewellery set of kundan and emeralds set in gold. She'd buy a silk sari to go with it. She couldn't let her hair down, of course, though she knew she looked much younger that way, but it just wasn't the done thing for the bridegroom's mother.

Mrs Gupta sighed and turned her mind back to the shopping. To begin with she would get about twenty pairs of salwaar kameez stitched for Shilpa. She'd also buy as many saris for her. Then there would be saris for her own relatives, and clothes for the menfolk of the family too, of course. And cheaper saris for the maids . . . A lot of shopping to be done, Mrs Gupta thought exuberantly. She had spoken to Shilpa's mother over the telephone the other day. Both the families – the Guptas and Shilpa's parents – were planning to buy all the saris from Sevak Sari House. She hoped they wouldn't run into each other there – it would make it awkward to discuss prices.

It was no fun thinking these thoughts alone, thought Mrs Gupta. She had plenty of relatives in Amritsar, but there was another wedding in the family coming up in ten days, and her relatives would think her selfish if she started talking about her own plans till that wedding was over.

Mrs Gupta reached for the cordless phone that Puneet had got her on his first visit home and called up Mrs Sandhu's number.

Mrs Sandhu answered at the first ring.

'Hello, ji,' she said, when she recognized Mrs Gupta's voice. 'How are you?'

'Bas, I am all right.'

'Arrangements started?' Mrs Sandhu asked her, for she had been informed the very day Tarun's marriage had been fixed up.

'No, not yet. Hardly any time. You see, my niece is getting married after ten days. So the family is a little busy. I have already done all my shopping for her wedding, so fortunately *that* tension is out of the way.'

'That's what I admire about you, Mrs Gupta. One has to say, you are so efficient,' gushed Mrs Sandhu.

Mrs Gupta said self-deprecatingly, 'No, no, hardly . . .'

Then she came to the point. 'Actually I was thinking of going out to do some shopping. Will you come with me? There are so many saris to buy.'

This reminded Mrs Sandhu that she too would have to buy a sari as a gift for Mrs Gupta's would-be daughter-in-law.

When Mrs Sandhu's niece Mini had got married, Mrs Gupta had been invited to the wedding. Mini had studied to be a dentist and had married another dentist. The couple had opened a clinic together – the dentist's chair alone had cost one-and-a half lakh rupees. At the wedding, Mrs Gupta had graciously presented the blushing bride-dentist with a beautiful, heavily embroidered purple silk sari.

Pity that Mini had never worn it, Mrs Sandhu thought, but Mini had said she was a doctor, even if just a tooth doctor, and she ought to look smart and professional, and she felt she looked smarter in short, plain salwaar kameezes. But, anyway, now she must buy a sari for Mrs Gupta's daughter-in-law that cost the same, at least, if not more, for Mrs Gupta remembered these things, and told other women too.

'Of course, I'll come,' she said aloud to Mrs Gupta.

'Oh, thank you. You know how it is, you just *can't* shop for saris alone.'

'You don't have to thank me. After all, it is as if my own son was getting married,' Mrs Sandhu said piously, still desperately trying to remember exactly how much that sari had cost. 'And anyway Manu won't be back for three hours. He has gone to college. After college, he'll go to his Physics tuition, then to the Chemistry tuition, poor boy. And they are having the Sports Day at the younger one's school. So, he won't be back before evening either, though he –'

Mrs Gupta interrupted her. 'Okay, so you come to my place in half an hour and then we'll go,' she said.

'Okay. I am just coming,' Mrs Sandhu said, still wondering how expensive a sari she should give to the girl who was to be Mrs Gupta's daughter-in-law. The trouble was, the Guptas were the only business family in their neighbourhood. So the woman thought she had a lot of money, but Mrs Sandhu always made sure, in her placid way, to show that *she* was no less than anyone else.

'Okay, then. I'll tell the driver to keep the car ready,' said Mrs Gupta, before turning her new, cordless, Japanese phone off.

*

'Ramchand Bhaiya, I have a sudden craving for a hot samosa,' Hari said thoughtfully to Ramchand. 'Or two hot samosas,' he added.

A harassed frown immediately appeared on Ramchand's face.

'Look here, Hari,' he said, 'Gokul has gone to deliver some big order, and if you slip off . . .'

'No, I won't slip off, not really,' Hari said reassuringly. Then after a while he piped up again, 'Think of it. Just think of a big, fat, hot samosa. Crisp outside, and hot mashed potatoes inside. Spiced with chillies and coriander and onions. Oh, and the chutneys. The red chutney with imli in it, and the green mint chutney. With a hot and crisp samosa. Fresh from the

19

kadhai. Ah ha ha ha.' Hari closed his eyes in rapture. His words were making Ramchand's mouth water as well.

Ramchand tried to adopt Gokul's stern method. 'Hari, see, I tell you, you must not . . .'

'I am really hungry, Ramchand Bhaiya,' Hari said with pathos. 'I'll just run out, eat, and run back. That's what I think I'll do. These people, the Seth and all, are rich enough without me having to starve myself and slave. *And* I'll get a samosa back for you too.'

'Yes, but, Hari . . .' Ramchand tried again, but Hari had already got to his feet. He just winked at Ramchand and then made a big show of tiptoeing out, which was wasted, since there was nobody around. Ramchand sighed, and went back to work, feeling tense and edgy, cracking his knuckles non-stop, desperately longing for a cup of tea that would calm him down. Soon customers would start to come in. He hoped either Hari or Gokul would be back by then. Chander hadn't come to work, and Shyam and Rajesh had gone out to eat at a dhaba. He was all alone. If a customer came and bought something, he would have to go to the counter downstairs where payments were made and write it out on the pad with the carbon paper underneath. He had done it only once before when Mahajan was out, and had shown it to Mahajan when he had come back. Mahajan had nodded approvingly, but the whole procedure had made Ramchand very nervous and he didn't want to do it again.

In most shops shop assistants never took the payment, but Mahajan was sure that nobody could cheat in a shop *he* was the manager of, and always said that if any sari went missing he'd be the first to notice it and call in the police. Everyone believed him too, for his sharp eyes missed nothing. No one would ever try to sell a sari in Mahajan's absence without making out a bill for it. However, usually when Mahajan was out, it was Shyam or Rajesh who did it. Only Hari wasn't allowed to, not because Mahajan doubted his honesty, but because he said he doubted Hari's brains, if he had any, that was. 'I am not letting that monkey go near the billing counter for the next ten years, not till that monkey becomes a man,' he had openly said. At this, Hari had asked, 'And what if I am still a monkey after ten years, Bauji?'

'If I were in your place, Hari, I would be ashamed to be called a monkey at the age of twenty-two, but to you it is just a big joke. You really *are* a completely shameless monkey,' Mahajan said angrily before walking away.

Hari had burst into peals of laughter after Mahajan had left and said, 'The problem is, I might become a man from monkey in ten years' time, but I think Mahajan will still remain Mahajan. Now *that* is a real problem. I forgot to ask our Mahajan something. How does he tell the difference between a shameless monkey and a monkey with proper shame?'

*

Ramchand leaned back against the wall after Hari had left. He pressed his palms over his tired eyes. He didn't know why he had headaches so often these days. And there were days when he woke up at four or five in the morning and just lay in his bed, staring at the ceiling, thinking of nothing at all, and then he'd realize it was eight o' clock. Who was he during those three or four lonely hours? And why had the shop started to suffocate him? Why had he begun to get the feeling that something was wrong? A feeling that he was being told lies – big lies, small lies, by everyone, all the time, day after day after day. Always the horrible feeling, some gap, something missing, something that he didn't know, something that he couldn't see, something terribly important. And that something was the reason that he felt different in the shop, with all the people around him, and different when he was alone in his room.

And sometimes, he felt different from both these selves, especially when he woke up in the middle of the night, in the dark, floating between wakefulness and sleep for a few moments, before he drifted back to sleep again.

Then Ramchand heard the wooden steps creak. You could hear the steps only in the morning. Later, there would be women swarming all over the place, more saris would be shouted for, packets of saris would fly across the shop from the hands of one shop assistant into another's and one wouldn't even be able to hear oneself think, let alone hear the wooden steps. The door opened and Mrs Gupta appeared, with Mrs Sandhu panting in tow. Ramchand groaned. Did they *have* to come while he was alone in the shop?

They both talk too much, he thought unhappily.

The two women were talking even as they sat down.

'I told you, it's best to come before every shop becomes crowded. Later in the day, it is more elbows and less saris,' Mrs Gupta said.

'I know, I know. It is better to make important decisions with a calm mind,' Mrs Sandhu replied.

Ramchand gave them a watery smile and asked what he could show them.

'Good news, good news,' beamed Mrs Gupta. 'My son is getting married. So show me the best saris you have.'

Ramchand sighed. It had been such a lazy morning until now. He wished people wouldn't keep getting married left, right and centre. It made him very sulky. But he started taking out saris anyway. They continued talking meanwhile, apparently resuming where they had left off to huff and puff up the stairs.

'It is just the right time for him to get married. He has just opened his own factory, and, touch wood, it is doing very well,' Mrs Gupta said smilingly.

Mrs Sandhu folded her hands and looked towards the

heavens. 'It is all God's grace. You should thank God that your children are doing well.'

'Believe me, I do. I also feed some poor unfortunates outside the Shivalaya temple every Monday.'

Ramchand looked up, a little startled. The Shivalaya temple was where his mother used to take him when he was a very small child. The smell of marigold flowers came drifting back to him . . .

He continued to take out the saris and Mrs Gupta continued her chatter.

'I am such a lucky woman. I know I should also try to do something for others. I was talking to Mrs Bhandari, and she really encouraged me to do something for the poor. She has *very* high ideals. Always thinking of what she can do for the society. Only thing is . . . you know, I am sure you have also noticed it at times, I sometimes feel she is a little snooty, maybe because her English is so good, because the Bhandaris are certainly not very *rich*.'

'Oh, who cares?' Mrs Sandhu said, beginning to examine a beautiful pale yellow sari with a tasselled border.

Mrs Gupta nodded smilingly. 'Maybe she is insecure. Only a daughter, you know. And still unmarried.' Then the conversation moved on to other things.

Ramchand took another stack of saris to them. Mrs Gupta quickly pounced on a green silk sari that had an intricate border of dancing peacocks. She showed it to Mrs Sandhu, who immediately said she liked it. Mrs Gupta asked its price, and then kept it aside for herself. The two women continued to look through more saris. Hari came back and looked very amused at the glare Ramchand gave him. He showed Ramchand an oily paper bag that contained a samosa for him. Shyam and Rajesh sauntered in too. The two women spent the next two hours looking at saris, and by that time, Mahajan was back. He congratulated Mrs Gupta when he heard the news of her son's wedding and she left with three purchases. Mrs Gupta smiled at Ramchand before leaving, promising to come back soon for more. Ramchand was relieved when they disappeared down the steps finally, making their way gingerly down each step.

Ramchand thought Mrs Gupta had too shrill a voice. And he ate the samosa, even though it was stone cold by now.

This was just the beginning of the day. A steady trickle of women who wanted saris began to come in after eleven. Ramchand did not know whether it was true, or if it was only his headache that made him feel so, but everyone seemed extra-demanding today. They wanted *that* particular green, and a *thinner* border, please, *no, no, no*, they did *not* want such heavy embroidery on the pallu. There was no room for uncertainty or absent-mindedness, no room for anything in fact, and as the morning wore on, Ramchand felt the shop closing in on him. He began to feel that he was having trouble breathing.

He went out for a quick lunch at two. They were all supposed to go for lunch one by one, a rule that was often disregarded in Mahajan's absence. He gulped down oily puris at a food stall in the next street, sitting on a wooden bench that shook if one chewed too hard. He ordered tea at the same place. Actually, there was a tea stall right opposite Sevak Sari House, but that was the official tea stall. Twice a day – once in the morning and once in the evening – all the shop assistants as well as Mahajan had a cup of tea – elaichi-flavoured in summer and ginger-flavoured in winter. It would be ordered merely by shouting out of the window, and a boy would soon appear with a steel wire carrier that held up to eight glasses of tea. He would bring seven, and then come back later to collect the empty glasses. The bill would be brought in at the end of the month, divided into seven, and every person would pay up his share. Occasionally, Mahajan had an extra cup, alone or if a friend of his came to visit him, and then he would pay up for his tea there and then.

But Ramchand often had tea at other little stalls around the market, stalls in the nearby lanes that were out of Mahajan's range of vision and away from the demanding cacophony of Sevak Sari House, stalls where he could relax, be alone, and sip his tea, for Ramchand needed much more than two cups a day.

Now, after the oily puris, it was when he had a cup of hot tea in his hands that he began to feel slightly calm again. He sipped the hot, fragrant brew and tried to think why he was feeling uneasy. And this uneasiness wasn't new. It had always been there, but it had been growing on him lately. He imagined he could glimpse some reality. What, he did not know. He felt that if he really concentrated, really *thought*, he would be able to reach some sort of a final truth. He wasn't articulate enough, that was the problem. He knew it. Look at other people, look at how clearly they spoke. When Hari described a cricket match, or when Gokul gave directions to a passer by, or when Mrs Gupta had explained what kind of saris she wanted, look how clear and precise they sounded. And *his* own thoughts – they always fanned out, spiralled upwards and downwards unintelligently, rolled themselves up into random curls, chased their own tails and came to nothing. He was twenty-six, but look at the way his mind worked!

Ramchand finished his tea and looked down into the empty tea-stained glass.

Or was he just being silly? What had he been thinking about? What reality? Ramchand paid for the puris and the tea in utter confusion.

He returned to the shop with a worried, wrinkled forehead, just in time to attend to the two women who had just come in. He knew who they were. One was Mrs Sachdeva, Head of the English Department at a local college. She was a squat

25

woman with a hoarse voice and hair pulled tightly back into a severe bun. She was known to have actually written things that came out in the Sunday supplements of the *Tribune*.

The other was Mrs Bhandari, a haughty, beautiful woman, wife of the D.I.G. of Police. She had won a beauty contest in college and was now in her early forties. She did up her hair in an elaborate way, with tiny curls piled high on her head in a kind of bun. She called herself a social activist when she introduced herself to people, and often organized charity programmes at the Rotary Club. Everyone said how talented Mrs Bhandari was! Even women who disliked her grudgingly admitted it. She could bake the most marvellous cakes that could beat the cakes in Delhi's best bakeries, she could embroider every stitch that was known, the soups she made were heaven, and she could even make soufflés, which hardly anyone in Amritsar could. She spoke perfect English, had an unerring taste in clothes and any party that she organized was bound to be a success.

Both the women were regular customers at the shop but Ramchand had never attended to them personally before. He said an awed 'Namaste' to them. They both nodded graciously in reply.

It seemed to the anxious Ramchand that the Head of an English Department must be terribly knowledgeable and well read. He had read only a few books himself, bought from the second-hand book dealer behind Sangam Cinema near the City Bus Stand. And they hadn't even been in English. They were Hindi paperbacks – detective novels with revolvers and half-dressed women on the covers. He had read three of them and had thought that they were very good, very exciting and inventive. But after reading the fourth one, it had dawned on him that they were a little repetitive. In all four the villain had forced the heroine to sleep with him, in one he had succeeded and the heroine had drowned herself because she thought it was the only honourable way out. In the other three, the hero had come in with a pistol and had saved the heroine and her honour. Ramchand had felt cheated when he had realized they were all similar, and he had given up buying and reading them. And then one day he had passed a grocer's shop that smelt of jute sacks and gramflour. It had immediately made Ramchand think of his father, and he had decided to see if he remembered any English. He had gone to the same second-hand book dealer and had bought a children's English book called *The Magic Lime Tree* that was thirty pages long with lots of pictures in it. It had words like hearth, pixie, bashful, wither, wicked and toadstool in it. Ramchand had found it too difficult and had given up. He had given that book to the landlord's young daughter, who had then sat in the courtyard and coloured in all the pictures in the book. And she had coloured the leaves of the lime tree purple. That was two years back. Since then, he hadn't read a word or touched a book.

Mrs Bhandari cleared her throat. Ramchand realized he must have been gawking. He gave Mrs Bhandari an uncertain smile and asked what she'd like to see. He knew that she was intelligent too. He had heard lots of customers mention her, some with admiration, others with malice or envy. But women are women, Ramchand thought. He didn't really know that, but that was what Gokul always said.

At least these two were a pleasant change from the wives of rich businessmen who usually patronized the shop.

The two settled down comfortably facing him and asked to see some silk saris.

Ramchand suddenly felt very hopeful. They were both learned, talented – they were both woman who were different from the rest. He eagerly took out a few saris and displayed them. 'See, madam, this is our latest stock. See this plain orange with gold border, this one here is yellow with gold embroidery, and this one . . .'

Mrs Sachdeva interrupted him, fixing him with a cold stare. 'I want some decent colours, not orange and gold and all. Something to wear to college, not to a village fair.'

Ramchand considered this for a moment, slightly disconcerted by the cold stare. He knew very little about colleges and village fairs, and even less about what women liked to wear to either. He took out another sari.

'Yes, madam, bright red with a black border, madam. Everyone is buying these, madam.'

His heart slid tearfully into the tip of his toes at the hard looks on their faces.

'Nothing shiny, please,' put in Mrs Bhandari, scratching her nose with a fingernail painted pale pink. Ramchand, a little crestfallen now, took out a parrot green sari with a gold border. The women exchanged a look, and Ramchand heard Mrs Sachdeva mutter to Mrs Bhandari, 'You can't really make these people understand, you know.'

Ramchand felt the tips of his ears burning. Mrs Bhandari addressed him in her refined voice. 'Something, you know, well, something more subdued.'

Ramchand waited uncertainly. He wasn't sure what she meant. He felt awful.

'Some dullish colour, you know. Like brown or grey,' said Mrs Sachdeva condescendingly. She liked to look plain and business-like. *She* wasn't one of the vain, idle housewives that this city was so full of. She was a literate woman, Head of an English Department.

Ramchand stood up to take some more saris down from the top shelf. He could almost feel their eyes boring into the back of his head, expectant, impatient. He nervously showed them a few more saris. They took one glance at the saris he had spread out before them; Mrs Sachdeva rolled her eyes and sighed. He took down some more, his face red with shame.

The two exchanged an exasperated glance again. Then they

began to rummage impatiently through all the saris he had taken down while he brought them more and more. They finally chose a beige sari shot with brown silk thread, and left. Ramchand sat down with his head in his hands.

3

When the shop finally closed at eight in the evening, Gokul came up to where Ramchand was putting stuff away and said, 'Come, yaar, let's all go and eat at Lakhan Singh's dhaba.'

'Why Gokul Bhaiya, very rich man suddenly?' Ramchand said, making an effort to smile while he said this.

Gokul made a disgusted face at this. 'Arre nahin bhai, what rich man? My life is utter hell. Lakshmi went to her uncle's wife's brother's marriage. And the same thing happened that happens every time she goes to attend a wedding. Comes back with her head full of rubbish. Says, I want this, I want that, we don't have this, we desperately need that. And, mind you, it always happens. *Always*. I keep telling her, Lakshmi, when you see that others have something, don't let your heart burn. Be content. Learn to be happy with whatever you have. But you know these women. This time she comes back in sulks, and, mind you, this is after she had bought a new sari and blouse and bangles to attend the wedding. Even after that she comes back with her face all blown up in a sulk. She comes and tells me that Munna wants new shoes just like Jaggu's son's. Bata shoes with laces! Can you imagine? Even my elder son who goes to school has never worn Bata shoes. And he doesn't care either. He would go around barefoot if we let him. As if it matters what kind of shoes a little child wears. Isn't it enough for her that she has bangles and a new sari? But, no, these women can drive you mad. I knew the reason why she was saying all this. I told her plainly. I told her, Lakhsmi, Munna is three years old. He doesn't even know how to wipe his own nose properly. He doesn't want new

30

shoes. *You* want. Because your heart burns when you see Jaggu's wife putting new shoes on her son's feet in front of all the relatives. How can I help it? I am not a rich man like Jaggu. Jaggu has a small electrical appliances shop of his own. And he isn't a very honest man either. I am sure he cheats each of his customers over a rupee or two. I told her. But does she listen? No. Pretends I am not even saying anything. Going yak, yak, yak herself all the time. And in the end, she always curses my poor dead mother. Why *she* has to be dragged into all this six years after her death, I don't know. I am not going home till late at night,' Gokul ended with a sigh.

Then he asked Ramchand, 'Do you want to come?'

Ramchand was about to refuse. He had a headache and the vague uneasiness had turned into a sour taste in his mouth after Mrs Sachdeva and Mrs Bhandari's visit. He wasn't sure whether he wanted to hear Gokul grumble all evening. But then Gokul usually didn't grumble for long. And the thought of going back to his room and cooking a lonely, tasteless meal with the light of the kerosene stove illuminating the peeling paint on the walls made up his mind.

'Yes. Let us go,' he said.

Then Gokul turned to Hari and asked him, 'Hari, do you want to go to Lakhan's dhaba?'

Hari didn't hear him. He was on his knees on the floor, mopping up some tea he had spilled earlier. He was also singing at the top of his voice, his eyes shut in concentration, swishing the wet rag about anyhow. Gokul clicked his tongue in exasperation, went across to Hari and thumped his back. 'Hari!' he yelled. 'Come, let's go and eat.'

Chander was about to leave too. He was wrapping his woollen muffler around his head. 'Shall we ask him also?' Hari whispered to Gokul.

Gokul looked uncomfortable. 'No, no,' he said hurriedly.

'Why?' Hari asked, curious as ever.

Gokul looked exasperated but answered him in a low voice, 'He goes out every evening with other friends. Old friends from the factory he used to work in before he came here. They drink and all.'

'Oh.' Hari subsided. Then he took his own sweet time wrapping up. After he was done, the three walked out of the shop and started towards Lakhan Singh's place.

It was cold outside and the evening fog was building up. They shivered as they talked. Along the way they were joined by Subhash, Hari's cousin. He was a shrewd looking young man with a very raucous laugh. He worked at Ladies' Fancy Store nearby, which sold many things – parandees, bangles, lampshades, bindis, objects made of glass, brass and polished wood that came under the name of 'decoration pieces' – just about anything, as long as it was bright and colourful and glittering. The shop looked like its merchandise; it had polished glass counters, there were mirrors on every available surface on the walls, and the shop was lit by more bright lights than were necessary. Ladies' Fancy Store was doing very good business, and just last month Subhash had been given a fifty rupee raise.

Subhash greeted everyone cheerfully and immediately started recounting how a customer had fought with him in the morning. She had bought a red parandee the day before and had woven it into her long plait the same evening. When she had taken it off at night, she had left it on a wet bathroom sill. The colour had run, the parandee was ruined and she was very angry. She had demanded either an exchange or a refund. 'Can't tell you how much she fussed and fought. All over a silly thing that women like to wear in their hair! What kind of brains do people have?' said Subhash. 'Even if you leave a human being soaked overnight, it will be the end of him. What is a parandee?'

Hari nodded in agreement vaguely and they reached Lakhan

Singh's dhaba. It was warmer inside the dhaba because of the tandoor that was giving off a tempting smell of fresh baking rotis. The dhaba was full of shivering people sitting on low stools and on plastic chairs, warming themselves over hot glasses of tea. The comforting smell of elaichi-flavoured tea hung in the warmth of the room. In a corner was an empty table with two chairs on one side and a sagging charpai on the other. The group of four quickly claimed it.

When they had settled themselves in comfortably, Lakhan Singh, a tall, gloomy looking sardaar, came to take their order. He had been running the dhaba for the past thirty years and it was famous all over Amritsar for only using pure ghee.

He had lost two sons during Operation Blue Star in the Golden Temple in 1984. After that, he had knocked off Paneer Masala from his menu. He explained to his customers that it had been his younger son's favourite. He always added in a low voice that his elder son didn't have any favourites, he was such a simple boy. Lakhan had a big, protruding mole above his left eyebrows and wrinkled hands that shook sometimes. Ramchand ate at this dhaba often, and each time he came here he realized that he felt slightly uncomfortable in Lakhan Singh's presence.

They ordered Daal Makhani and tandoori rotis and then sat waiting. Subhash was still going on about parandees and bad tempered women. Ramchand's headache persisted, and though he felt warmer now, his hands were still numb with cold. Hari, who was rubbing his hands together and blowing warm breath on them suddenly caught his eye and asked him, 'What's wrong, Ramchand Bhaiya? Is your mood off?'

'No, yaar, just a headache,' Ramchand said.

'What headache and all, like an old lady,' Gokul said with a laugh.

Ramchand smiled and they began to talk. Food arrived, hot and fresh, and cheered everyone up. A small boy, a helper at the dhaba brought them onions and pickles in a small steel bowl.

Outside evening grew into night, and it got colder and foggier. The shops all over the bazaar closed one after the other. Shutters were downed, gates were locked and people began to make their way home. The din of the traffic and the shouts of rickshaw pullers got louder. The four inside the dhaba also grew louder and more raucous. They had cups and cups of tea and there was a lot of backslapping and bonhomie and telling of anecdotes.

Ramchand soon began to feel much better.

Hari did an excellent imitation of Bhimsen Seth. He lolled in his chair, he peered over imaginary glasses, he called for tea in a hoarse voice. In the end he pretended to count notes, eyes gleaming and fingers moving fast. At this Subhash laughed so much that he almost fell out of his chair.

Gokul talked about Lakshmi again, but in a very droll manner, as if she was the funniest woman on the earth – she was illogical, she brought up old fights when she was angry, quarrelled for no reason and then inexplicably made up. She had a fascination for talcum powder, loved to embroider useless cushion covers and was consumed by strange desires. He laughed indulgently as he talked and was completely unlike his angry self of earlier in the evening.

Then Ramchand related his morning encounter with Mahajan. He told them of the sound his hopping feet had made and how Mahajan had shouted up at him. Ramchand laughed a lot while relating the episode, as if he hadn't been scared at all.

In the end, amidst all the laughter, Subhash elicited a promise from all of them to go to Sangam Cinema the coming Sunday to watch a rerun of Hero No. 1. They all ordered more cups of tea and talked till late at night. Finally, at eleven, Gokul got up. 'I think I'd better go now. By now Lakshmi will have got down to cursing all my ancestors.'

Everyone laughed and Gokul left in a hurry. Hari and Subhash said goodbye to Ramchand and they left too, still laughing uncontrollably over something.

Ramchand had sobered up a little, though. He saw Hari and Subhash disappear in the chilling fog and then he began to walk back to his lodgings.

*

Now that he was alone, the gaiety that had been upon him all evening fell away. The evening fog had turned into the dense, opaque mist of the night. The roads looked deserted. Ramchand made his way slowly towards his lodgings. He felt uneasy. The old feeling that always lurked in hidden corners inside him, crouching between his lungs, swimming in his blood, now came upon him more hideously than ever. He despised himself for the frivolous, futile evening he had spent, and saw his own conduct during it as cheap and vulgar.

The way he had been slapping Subhash's back, and the way he had been laughing at Hari's jokes!

Why did he have to do all these things?

He thought of Mrs Sachdeva and Mrs Bhandari and felt disgusted. At them as well as at himself! He thought back to the events of the day. All the events seemed disjointed, the people were caricatures, the sounds were all hollow and far-away sounding, and he saw himself as an ineffectual, affected, half-baked creature trapped in a particularly bad, pointless movie. Ramchand suddenly told himself that enough was enough. What was all this madness? Where would it lead him, after all?

No, this wouldn't do. He had to take control. Tomorrow was a new day. He would change everything. He wouldn't lie about in a stupor that his thoughts always induced. He would start exercising so he'd be fit and healthy, he wouldn't be intimidated by anyone and he would stop watching those silly movies on Sundays with Hari and the others.

Ramchand quickened his pace. He would read some good books. He had heard that Mahatma Gandhi had written an autobiography. Yes, he would start with that. And he would decide once and for all whether he believed in God or not.

He had been walking fast and reached his lodgings sooner than he usually did. He took out his big iron key in the light of the street lamp and climbed up the flight of dark, narrow stairs that led straight up to his room on the first floor. He unlocked the old, wooden door and stepped inside. He fumbled for the light switch in the dark and switched it on. The naked bulb that hung from the centre of the ceiling came to life, casting its dim glow on the walls. Ramchand took a deep breath.

He would also paint this room, and get a 500-watt bulb. It would brighten up the room and, anyway, it was difficult to read by the light that his 40-watt bulb gave out. Yes, a brighter light and a painted room. And he would practise English-speaking in front of the mirror every day. At least for twenty minutes. You never know, he might even get a better job some day ... Tomorrow was a new day, after all. And it was with these thoughts that Ramchand changed into his kurta-pyjama, took off his grey socks and wriggled his toes into his old blue night socks that had holes in the toes, and crept under a pile of blankets and quilts to go to sleep. He woke up a little late the next morning. The old city of Amritsar had woken up before him. He could hear the strains of the early morning kirtan at the Golden Temple playing on somebody's radio. Bells were ringing at a nearby temple. A vegetable vendor was shouting that he was selling fresh tomatoes for six rupees a kilo. Another vendor was selling marigold flowers to freshly bathed, pious housewives for their morning pujas. The landlord's children on the ground floor had already switched on the television. Ramchand had a slight headache again and he found the morning noises unbearable. He struggled into a sitting position, pushing his covers aside.

The weak winter morning sunshine filtered through the barred window of his room and fell on the discoloured floor in golden stripes. Ramchand tried to recollect his thoughts of the night before but could remember only the cold words that formed them. He failed to recapture anything else. His mind went blank, and he sat for ages on his sagging charpai, on top of his untidy bedclothes, scratching away deposits of dirt and dead skin from the base of his toenails. He sat there for a long time before he realized that he was going to be late for work again today.

4

Ramchand had been born twenty-six years ago. At the time, his father ran a very small shop in Amritsar that sold, among other things, rice and pulses, candles and brooms, sugar and gramflour, fried groundnuts and homemade biscuits. Ramchand loved the gunnysack smell of the shop.

The small family lived in a smaller room behind the shop that had a tiny adjoining toilet.

One corner of the room was curtained off with an old, doubled-up red sari of Ramchand's mother's that had a pattern of large yellow flowers on it. In the curtained-off part, a small drain had been let out. A plastic bucket and mug were placed here and the family used this space as a bathroom. Another corner of the room formed the small kitchen, an area where Ramchand's mother cooked on a tiny stove, rolled out perfectly round chapatis, neatly chopped onions and tomatoes and arranged shining clean steel utensils in neat rows. She always told Ramchand to keep away from the stove. She had smiling, serious eyes and she wore a leaf-shaped gold nose stud on her tiny, straight nose.

One day, she had finished kneading dough to make chapatis and was about to get the kerosene stove going. 'Little boys should never go near fire, understand? Don't forget. Remember what happened to Choo Hoo?' she told the five-year-old Ramchand, who was hovering around her. Then, seeing him look a little mutinous, for he always liked to be as close to his mother as possible, she pulled out a lump of dough from the vessel she had been kneading it in. 'Here, take this,' she told him with a smile. 'Go and sit in that corner and make something really nice with it. Go and make the *most* beautiful thing in the world,' she told him.

He understood, because she often made sparrows and rabbits with dough for him. She would work on the dough deftly with her slim fingers, pulling here, pinching there, rounding at one place, flattening at another, till a shape emerged from it. She would make a sparrow and give it a nice, sharp beak, wings folded by its side and a tail. She told Ramchand stories about how the sparrow used her beak to fight with her husband, and how she fed her children by bringing them food in this very beak. She laughed at his surprised face. When she made a rabbit, she gave him a perfect bobtail and nothing else. Just a blob with a bobtail. 'Where is its face?' Ramchand asked in confusion. 'It is so scared of you, it is running away,' she said laughing. 'And when a rabbit is frightened, all you see of him is his little bobtail.'

Once she made a mouse and called her a Choo Hoo. 'Is it a girl mouse then?' Ramchand asked suspiciously.

'Yes, and a pretty one too.' She had made this mouse with special care, and had given her a nice tail, eyes and mouth. 'You see, she has no whiskers,' she told Ramchand, 'because her mother told her not to go near the kerosene stove and she was naughty and she did, and her whiskers got singed.'

Ramchand was very impressed by this story. It was okay for Choo Hoo, because she was a girl mouse, but what if he went near the kerosene stove and never grew a moustache like his father's when he grew up?

Sometimes his mother made a face with the lump of dough, using a matchstick to make two dents for eyes, one for a nose and then a series of dents in a smile-shaped line to make a toothy, smiling mouth.

When she gave him the dough and told him to make the most beautiful thing in the world, he rolled the lump round and round in his chubby fingers and thought and thought and thought. What *was* the most beautiful thing in the world? It was his mother, of course, or possibly his father. But he couldn't make them out of dough. Besides, they were not really things. He rolled the damp piece of dough around in his hands, thinking hard.

Then Ramchand's father called out to his wife from the shop. 'Please come here,' he shouted to his wife as courteously as one could shout. Ramchand's parents were old-fashioned – they never addressed each other by their names.

She turned the stove off, put the kerosene can and the matchbox safely away on an upper shelf and threw a sharp, anxious glance at him. She was terrified about the stove; she had heard so many stories of children having accidents with them. But ever since she had told him about Choo Hoo, he seemed to be keeping his distance from the stove. She hadn't even planned it, it had just come out when she had finished making a perfect little mouse and had realized it would be difficult to give it whiskers. She smiled, untucked the pallu of her sari from the waistband of her petticoat, spread out the pallu, adjusted it around her shoulders and looked at her son. He was still absorbed in the piece of dough. Feeling he was safe, she went out to the shop. Apparently, her husband needed her help to look for a new tin of black pepper that he had misplaced. They found it after about ten minutes and Ramchand's mother went back in to continue with her cooking.

She found Ramchand in the same corner where she had left him, with the piece of dough still firmly in his hand. But he was crying. And he wasn't howling or throwing a tantrum or weeping like children do. He was really crying, with real heart-breaking sorrow, gulping and sobbing, his eyes full of grief.

Pain tore through her heart. She rushed to him and scooped him up in her arms, hugging him, examining him to see if he had physically hurt himself. But he hadn't, and she sensed it anyway. His eyes told her that. She murmured to him, she crooned to him gently, and when he calmed down slightly, the sorrow and incomprehension still in his eyes, she asked him very, very seriously, the way one asks an adult, 'Tell me, why are you crying?'

He didn't answer at first. He just looked down at the piece of dough in his hand, the look on his face more confused than miserable. He looked at the beloved, familiar face of his mother. Her clear gaze met his with honesty. He trusted her. He could tell her. 'Ma . . . ma, you said . . . you said . . . you told me to make the most . . . most –' He gulped. She waited. 'You said, make the most beautiful thing in the world.'

'And?' she asked, her face still serious and enquiring.

'And,' and here Ramchand burst into tears again and wailed out, 'I don't know . . . I don't know what is the most beautiful thing in the world.'

She didn't laugh at him. And she never knew how grateful her son was to her for the rest of his life for not laughing, not even speaking or moving at that moment. She hugged him lightly and stroked his head gently.

Ramchand's father came in then, saw Ramchand's tear-stained face and, to his surprise, also saw tears glistening in his wife's eyes.

'What happened?' he asked.

And she didn't say, 'Nothing. He just fell down.'

With complete, perfect composure, she told him.

Ramchand looked at his father apprehensively, his own face tense, the tears dried, the lump of dough now dusty, its surface drying and forming little cracks.

His father looked straight into his son's eyes and said, 'But I don't know that either.'

The silence of his mother. The simple truth in his father's voice. These were things Ramchand never forgot. There was perfect peace in the room after that moment. Ramchand didn't know where that lump of dough went. It was forgotten by everyone. His mother washed his face and hands, dried them gently with a soft cotton cloth and gave him some warm milk to drink. His father brought him a sugar-coated biscuit from the shop. Ramchand knew it was one of the most expensive ones in the shop.

After that, nobody mentioned the incident again and, after the shop closed, dinner and bedtime were just the same. But from that day onwards, Ramchand loved his parents much more.

*

Ramchand's favourite pastime as a small child was to explore the maze of sacks and tins in the shop, open them to see what was inside and lose himself in the exciting, ever-changing, yet never-changing smells of the shop. This was allowed only when there were no customers around. When there was a customer in the shop, his father expected him to behave, and leave when he was told to. On such occasions, Ramchand always obeyed.

When the shop was empty, Ramchand's father would be at his most genial, and his mother would also come and sit by the counter. While his parents talked, Ramchand would open this, touch that, run his fingers through rice, sit on top of sacks and declare that he was the king and plead with his mother to join him inside big cardboard boxes in which a local brand of washing soap was supplied to the shop. She would refuse, his father would laugh and Ramchand would emerge smelling of soap. Then he would go and tickle his own chin with the tips of the brooms and gurgle with laughter. His mother would laugh too and the air would turn very happy, full of shop smells and the laughter. His father would also laugh sometimes, but most of the time he just smiled benignly at his little son.

It was only rarely that Ramchand's father was in a bad mood. It usually happened on days when he had been dealing with too many customers, or when mice had found their way into one of the sacks. On such days, he would growl impatiently at his son.

'Go away, go away. Go and study. Try to become something in life, unless you want to continue to measure out besan, pack up sugar and haggle with housewives for the rest of your life. And deal with suspicious customers who think you cheat them while weighing things out, who want to check your weighing scales for themselves.'

Ramchand didn't understand much of this. He would just smile adoringly at his father, whom he considered to be the best man in the world, and sooner or later his father would take him in his lap and feed him salted nuts, saying, 'I am going to send you to an English-medium school, okay? You will work hard there, won't you?' The five-year-old Ramchand would nod obligingly, with no idea at all of what an English-medium school was.

Ramchand also loved to accompany his mother to the Shivalaya temple every Monday morning, carrying sweet-smelling marigold flowers in his upturned palms to offer at the temple. Before she got married, Ramchand's mother had fasted rigidly on Mondays to appease Shiva, so that she would get a good husband. Now she had a husband who was a good, honest man, who made her happy, who never even raised his voice while speaking to her, let alone hit her like many husbands did. Having found such a husband, or having been granted such a husband by Lord Shiva, she continued with her fasting, afraid of annoying Shiva if she stopped abruptly.

Ramchand looked forward to the temple excursions with great pleasure. He also thought that his mother was the nicest woman in the whole world. With her, however, he could dare to misbehave more than he could with his father. She was quick to lose her temper, but was also quick to regain it. Then she'd pick up her son, nuzzle his neck, hug him and kiss him, and call him a precious star. Ramchand often took advantage of his precious-star status.

At the temple, he would get excited the moment he was surrounded by the jostling, chanting crowds, with the brass bells ringing loudly and the smell of incense, marigold and sandalwood in the air. It would all go to his head and then he'd start to run around in energetic circles, pushing everyone who came in the way. His mother would first snap a warning at him. Her nerves would already be frayed because of hunger and she couldn't handle Ramchand in such a crowd on an empty stomach. But he usually took no notice of her warning, which was strange, because on most days he was well behaved. It was just the Monday excitement at the temple that made him hyperactive. After a couple of warnings, she'd feel like crying. Why did he go mad in the temple every Monday morning? Then she would give him a couple of tight slaps and he would subside.

And after being slapped, he would solemnly promise each time not to misbehave next Monday. And he always did misbehave. And got slapped again. It had almost become a matter of routine for both of them.

Except for these Monday mornings, the small family lived peacefully and was fairly happy. However, soon after Ramchand turned six and started going to an English-medium school for which his father had been saving up, the gunnysack and marigold smells abruptly went away. Ramchand's parents were killed in a bus accident while going to Haridwar on a pilgrimage. Their bus was overloaded with pious people, and it just toppled over. Ramchand had been left with his grandmother in the family village near Amritsar. The six-year-old Ramchand's first feeling was that of great astonishment at

44

the fact that a mere toppling over of things could take all smells away for ever.

Horror followed later.

Everyone expected the child to cry and ask for his mother at night, to ask where his father was, or why he wasn't living in his own home. His grandmother had anxiously framed suitable answers, ready to be used when he asked her any of these questions. But he never did. He became very quiet and resisted all physical contact with the grown-ups around him. He did cry occasionally, but not like a child. His eyes would grow cloudy and tears would trickle slowly down his cheeks. If anyone tried to pick him up or wipe away his tears, he would howl in anger and kick them with his small feet.

At last, Ramchand was sent back to Amritsar with a distant uncle's family so that he could go to school. He had never met this uncle before. Uncle worked as a craftsman in a jeweller's shop. He lived with his family in a one-roomed house too, though they had many more things than Ramchand's parents had ever possessed. In the room there was a dressing table with some cosmetics on it. There was a wooden cabinet for plates and glasses and they had a steel almirah in which there were hangers for clothes. Ramchand had never seen hangers before. His parents had kept all their clothes folded in a trunk. Everything seemed alien. Uncle's wife was fat and irritable, and often stayed in bed all day with a chunni tied tightly around her head, complaining of a headache. She had two children of her own, both boys, younger than Ramchand. When she was in bed with a headache, her wrath descended on anyone who dared to make a noise and disturb her. Often, when one of the children made a slight noise, she would rush and slap all the three children hard, once on each cheek and then go back to her bed, pulling a sheet over herself. Her own children were used to it, and dodged and giggled when she tried to hit them, incensing her even further, but Ramchand had never been slapped before, except on Monday mornings, and he knew he had asked for those slaps. His aunt's random slaps bewildered him completely. He sorely missed his good-humoured father and his temperamental, but loving mother. At nights, he dreamt of the red sari with yellow flowers on it that was doubled up and used to curtain off their 'bathroom' at home.

Ramchand was put into a new school, along with Uncle's children. New home, new school, new smells. No more marigold-gunnysack smells for Ramchand. Ramchand started growing up.

Every summer Uncle dutifully took his family for a vacation to his wife's parents' house in Old Delhi. At this time, who was family and who was not, was made very clear to Ramchand. He would be sent to spend his holidays with his grandmother in the village. Year after year, he spent long summer afternoons alone by the river, and it was here that Ramchand first came face to face with solitude. In the hot, sleepy afternoons under the trees, where only the gentlest sunlight filtered through, with the river lapping coolly, all thoughts became a rustly, swishy, ripply, secret blue-green. And Ramchand came to know the other being in himself, the secret blue-green shadowy Ramchand, who either thought things that did not make sense, or who sometimes thought things that came so dangerously close to making sense that he backed off from them, the way one does from a slavering, mad dog.

The actual Ramchand-of-the-world gossiped, laughed, attended Mundan ceremonies, and bought new, shiny polyester shirts on Diwali with great pleasure.

But the knowledge that the blue-green Ramchand waited inside him changed the Ramchand-of-the-world gradually. He grew quieter, withdrawn. Waiting. In the same way as a man who has a tumour in his brain, or a hole in his heart waits.

When Ramchand was fifteen, Uncle decided that a boy like him did not need any more education. It was more important that he should be settled in some trade. Ramchand was taken out of school and sent to Mahajan, whom Uncle knew through a mutual friend. Even though Ramchand intensely hated his school, he was tearful throughout the last day. When the bell rang and the children left noisily, chattering and laughing and swinging their water bottles, it was with a heavy heart and dragging feet that Ramchand walked out slowly. He left the life he had known as a schoolboy, thinking uncomfortably of a vague memory he had of his father measuring out sugar into 200-gram packets and telling his mother that he wanted Ramchand to study in an English-medium school. He also remembered the times when his father would take him on his lap and make him promise he'd 'become someone and not remain a shopkeeper like your father'.

With his eighth standard certificate lying at home in his trunk in a green polythene bag, Ramchand entered the shop.

Four years later, his uncle had died of a sudden heart attack. He had been at work, making a necklace in gold and pearls. He had just keeled over and died. Twenty days later, when it was long past the official mourning and all the guests had left, Ramchand's red-eyed aunt, looking unfamiliar in a white sari without her bindi and bangles, like a tree that had shed its leaves, had politely asked him to leave and find his own way in the world, so as not to add to her already increased responsibilities. She had sent him off with all his belongings in a tin trunk and her blessings. It was then that Ramchand had, with Mahajan's recommendation, managed to rent the small room with the two windows facing each other, the peeling paint on the faded walls, and a strange, musty smell.

Years later Ramchand had realized many things. He realized that his father had once had a shop. A very small one, true, but a shop nevertheless. And by rights, that shop should have been Ramchand's. Instead, it now belonged to Uncle's sons. He also realized that the leaf-shaped gold nose-pin that his aunt wore had once adorned his own mother's nose. He realized that after his grandmother's death, her house in the village had been sold off by his uncle, not only depriving Ramchand of any share in the house and an assured home in the family village, but also depriving him of any more serene afternoons by the river.

Ramchand also understood now, years later, why he had never been introduced to Uncle when his parents had been alive, and why Uncle had never visited them though they lived in the same town. But by now, perhaps, it was too late. Or maybe Ramchand just couldn't be bothered to fight for what was his any more.

*

Clouds hung over the city and blocked out the sunshine. A cold wind blew gently and people longed for the sun. By afternoon, it had begun to drizzle. Winter in Amritsar this year was already freezing cold, the drizzle made people shiver and retreat further into their mufflers, shawls and woollen socks. People moved around in the cold city with stiff joints, chapped lips and icy palms. They caught colds, noses became red, eyes watered. Dogs searched for warm, dry corners with their miserable tails tucked in between their legs. The wind became stronger and chillier, blowing the light drizzle this way and that, so that the rain danced about crazily in the air, wantonly lashing people's faces and bodies and buildings sideways, instead of falling straight on the ground as decent rain should.

Inside the shop, everyone shivered and felt the glumness of the grey winter day. Everyone except Ramchand. He never found the rain depressing; he just could not. No matter what the discomfort, it was never the cold, the dampness, the mud and the puddles that he noticed. Rain had filled him with exhilaration even when he was a child. It did so now too. Rain always sustained him, even if it was the gloomy drizzle of a winter afternoon.

Hari groaned and grumbled till everyone around him began to feel gloomy. 'This inhuman cold is giving me a body ache,' he said. 'And it has made every joint in my body so stiff that I just feel like an old man. Can't move at all.'

Gokul snapped at him, 'Hari, boy, all these aches and stiffness of joints that you have been complaining of since morning, they are not at all because of the cold. They are a result of laziness, of idleness, of not moving your joints at all till you are forced to do so. If you *had* moved your joints, the new batch of satin would have been put away neatly by now.'

'What, Gokul Bhaiya?' Hari said, stretching lazily. 'Why is everyone always after my life? I think for the past one year I have been working myself to the bone.'

Gokul snapped again, 'There is a lot of work to be finished, Hari. So just forget your joints and don't tell me about your aches and pains, okay? Just sort out the satin immediately.'

Hari got to his feet with a martyred air, sighing wearily.

Gokul continued to frown.

Chander remained sunk in a depressed silence, speaking only when he was asked something. Shyam sat away from the others, sunk deep in thought.

Rajesh was talking to Mahajan in a corner. From the black looks they were giving each other, they were evidently disagreeing about something for a change.

Ramchand was the only one who was not in a bad temper.

He looked dreamily out of the window at the misted world outside, where all shapes and images were beautifully distorted by the raindrops floating in the air. He was sorting out some new stock and he hummed lightly to himself.

Aa chal ke tujhe main le ke chaloon
Ek aise gagan ke taley
Jahan gham bhi na ho
Aansoo bhi na ho
Bas pyaar hi pyaar pale
Ek aise gagan ke taley . . .

A few raindrops clung to the outside of the glass window. They gripped the glass, trembling a little, shining like fragile pearls. Ramchand smiled at them, his fingers busy at folding and unfolding and checking the price tags. He continued to hum the same song over and over again. He was happy.

And of course, he thought bitterly, you couldn't even sing in peace in this shop. For he saw Bhimsen Seth come waddling up to Mahajan. These days he rarely came right up. His weight was making it increasingly difficult for him to climb the flimsy stairs.

Everyone snapped to attention at once. Chander looked up, Ramchand stopped humming, though he continued to hum in his mind. Hari began to sort out the different shades of pink satin and Gokul took the frown off his face and tried to look pleasant but busy.

Bhimsen was panting when he said, 'Mahajan! There is some important news. Ravinder Kapoor's daughter is getting married.'

A gleam appeared in Mahajan's eyes.

'When?' he asked, rubbing his hands together. Ramchand cracked a knuckle absently, watching the two men talk.

Mahajan turned to him and gave him a glare.

Ramchand stopped cracking his knuckles, went red and immediately got back to his work.

Mahajan turned again to Bhimsen Seth, his smile back in place.

'In January,' replied Bhimsen. 'The exact date will be fixed in a couple of days.'

Mahajan nodded, pursing up his lips in concentration. Bhimsen said, 'They are naturally not coming to the shop. They are so big. So send them stock at home, Mahajan, the best stock you can.'

He stopped, looking a little worried.

Ramchand looked up from his work again, intrigued. Bhimsen Seth rarely looked anxious.

Seth continued, 'Send them saris every day, whatever they say, whatever they want. Send them the best lehanga-cholis too. Keep them happy, especially the women. They have a younger daughter too, you know. Two more years perhaps, or maybe even one, and then they'll marry her off too. Big orders –'

Mahajan interrupted him, 'Don't worry, Sethji. I'll take care of everything.'

Then they walked to a corner, where they discussed things in low voices and soon went out together, looking serious and preoccupied. Soon Hari reported that the two were not downstairs either. They had stepped out of the shop for a while.

Everyone was relieved, especially Gokul. 'I forgot to bring my lunch today,' he confided to Ramchand, 'and I don't even have enough money to eat from a shop or something. I have been hoping and hoping since morning that Mahajan will go out. Now I can go home and eat.'

He hurriedly left for home, promising to be back in half an hour.

But after a whole hour, Gokul still hadn't turned up. This was very unusual for Gokul, the supreme stickler for rules. He came to work on time every day. Only an emergency like a forgotten lunch could induce him to break free of Mahajan's authority.

He finally came in limping a couple of hours later.

'What happened? You are late?' asked Hari. 'Got into a street fight?'

'Don't be silly, Hari. Of course I didn't. You just shut up. I am in no mood for your stupid talk,' Gokul said savagely, sinking down into the mattress with a groan.

'Why, what happened?' said Ramchand, wondering if Lakshmi had finally gone off her head and had beaten Gokul up.

'A vegetable cart rammed into my bicycle on my way here,' he said.

'Or you rammed your bicycle into a vegetable cart . . . ?' Hari said cheerfully, and then added hastily, as Gokul turned to glare at him, 'From his point of view . . . maybe.'

'My foot is hurting,' Gokul groaned, pulling up his right trouser leg to show them a swollen foot.

Hari's face immediately contorted itself up in deep concern. 'You just sit quietly. We'll do all the work today,' he said. 'Or for as many days as it takes for your foot to heal,' he added magnanimously.

'Yes, of course, Sethji,' said Gokul sarcastically. 'So nice for me to have a boss like you who tells me to take it easy.'

'These days, even if you try to help . . .' muttered Hari.

The glass door opened and Mahajan appeared suddenly, without warning, as he always did. Hari often said that it was a mystery why the wooden stairs did not creak when Mahajan climbed them.

'Gokul, drop whatever you are doing at once. I have a very important job for you. You'll have to take some stock to Ravinder Kapoor's house . . .' he began, and then took in Gokul's pained face and the swollen foot he was still displaying.

'*Now* what has happened here?'

'Nothing, Bauji. Just got hurt,' Gokul said shamefacedly.

'How?' Mahajan asked suspiciously.

Gokul just hung his head down.

'How, Gokul? Can't you answer a simple question?'

In a burst of honesty, Gokul admitted his crime. Mahajan

just stood there and lectured Gokul for a while on what responsibility meant. Then he asked, 'So you can't pedal, I suppose?'

Gokul didn't answer.

'Who am I going to send to Ravinder Kapoor's house with the stock tomorrow?' Mahajan muttered. He looked uncertainly first at Ramchand and then at Chander.

Hari piped up, 'I could go, Bauji.'

Mahajan's nerves were already frayed. He turned his wrath on to Hari. 'Yes, you could go. You are such a sensible creature that I'd gladly hand over saris worth lakhs to you. Yes, you could go. And break Gokul's bicycle, your own neck, stop somewhere to eat a kulfi like a schoolboy and let a cow chew up saris worth lakhs of rupees.'

Hari looked surprised. 'I don't eat kulfis in the winter, and I don't think cows eat saris in summer *or* winter. Goats do.'

Mahajan's face went red, and Hari quickly said in a polite tone, 'I'll order your evening tea for you, Bauji,' and scuttled out.

Mahajan looked at Hari's disappearing back with malevolence. 'Thankless job, mine,' he said, in an uncharacteristic fit of frankness, and then he turned to Ramchand, who had gone red on Hari's behalf. 'Ramchand, you borrow Gokul's bicycle tomorrow, and take some good stock to Ravinder Kapoor's house.'

Ramchand was stunned. He, Ramchand, was to do this? To think that he was being given such a big responsibility! Such expensive stock! And he had heard Ravinder Kapoor was the biggest industrialist in Amritsar. He was supposed to have a huge, palatial house with soft carpets, air-conditioned rooms and four cars. And he'd have to go there. His stomach lurched with nervousness.

'Gokul,' Mahajan continued, 'you supervise the selecting of stock. Send only the best saris. Also pick some pieces from the latest silk consignment. Maybe some of the raw silk lehngas too. Also the ones with silver ghungroos at the hem. And let me see first what you are sending.'

But Ramchand wasn't listening. His mind had shifted to other things.

An errand like this would probably take many days. He knew how these things worked. He would take to the Kapoor House a collection of saris in a big bundle. Hours would be spent by the bride-to-be and by the other women in her family to select a few out of them. More demands would be made. Tantrums would be thrown by the bride-to-be. Then they might change their minds about a sari and call up Mahajan. Then he, Ramchand, would go there again to offer a replacement for that sari. This way he would probably have to cycle many times to Ravinder Kapoor's house with saris.

After years of being cooped up in the shop, week after week, month after month, except for Sundays and the three days last year when he had sprained his ankle, he would now have a chance to be out in the open, cycle in the sun, look around, and maybe even sneak off to see if he could buy some second-hand books. Maybe he could also have some mossambi juice at Anand Juice Shop.

Mahajan turned to him. 'And, Ramchand, make sure you dress well before you go there. They are big people. We don't want anyone from our shop going there in rags. You should be dressed decently and look bathed.'

Ramchand immediately curled up his toes, to stop any smell that might be emanating from his feet from reaching Mahajan's flared nostrils. Was Mahajan making a dig at his shirt with its frayed collar and at his old trousers?

Well, he'd show him then. Enough was enough. Who did Mahajan think he was? He'd dress well and he'd also have a good time.

Ramchand was distracted all day and got into trouble with

Mahajan. He misplaced a light yellow cotton sari that a customer had ordered, and spilled water on one of the white sheets that covered the mattresses. Mahajan insulted him, saying that he was as bad as Hari. Hari just grinned at this, but Ramchand felt the rain was spoilt for him. He wished he could have taken the day off. He could have sat by the window in his room with a cup of tea watching the soft rain caress the guava tree in the courtyard below.

In the evening, he feigned a bad headache and left early. He went to a garment store nearby, and bought himself new black trousers and a crisp, sparkling white shirt. He felt extravagant and reckless. He hadn't bought new clothes for over two years. Rags, indeed! He would show Mahajan!

Then he bought a bar of Lifebuoy soap and new socks. Finally he stopped at a vegetable vendor's cart and asked for a lemon.

'Just one?' the vendor asked in surprise.

'Yes, just one,' Ramchand replied firmly. The vendor gave him a lemon with a disgusted look on his wrinkled face.

Ramchand put it in his pocket carefully and paid for it. The landlord's wife, Sudha, read *Sarita* and *Grihashobha* often, and sometimes Ramchand would ask Manoj, her eldest son, to see if his mother could lend him some old copies. He remembered once reading in one thus obtained issue of *Grihashobha* that rubbing lemon on the skin took away bad odour. He decided to try it now.

With all the purchases safely in a big paper bag under his arm, he went to the barber and asked for a haircut. The barber hummed and hawed and said he was about to close shop for the day. Ramchand wheedled and whined and requested, till the barber agreed. Ramchand got himself a neat haircut and then went back home.

He went to bed feeling excited about the next day. It was December, almost the end of the year, yet tomorrow would be the first day of the year when his routine would vary from the usual.

The last thing he felt at night was a quiet excitement in his heart, and a prickly feeling on the back of his neck, because he hadn't taken a bath after his haircut and sharp little bits of cut hair clung to the skin. When he woke up in the morning, he got out of bed groggily and remembered that today was the day. He wouldn't be spending the day in the shop. He was going to dress up, he was going to cycle through the city and go to the Kapoor House. He felt adventure looming in the day ahead.

He climbed out of bed, stretched and walked straight to the table. He seized the lemon, cut it in half and started rubbing his feet vigorously with one half of it. He'd make sure his feet didn't smell *today*, at least. A seed from the lemon clung to the space between his big toe and the next one.

Then, with his feet covered in lemon juice, Ramchand went into the tiny bathroom.

By the time he came out, his hemmed-in excitement had spilt over. He moved quickly, picking up this, dropping that, smiling broadly.

All the other shop assistants took leave sometimes. Ramchand was the only exception. Mahajan was quite stingy about giving anyone time off, but there were times when he had to. They all had to go off sometimes – they had places to go to, in their lives they had people and occasions that required their presence. Relatives died, there was a wedding in the family, wives had to be escorted to their parents' places in some other town, children fell ill.

With no relatives, no family, nowhere to go to, Ramchand could never ask for leave.

Ramchand had never even been seriously ill. Only once, when he had sprained his ankle badly the year before, Mahajan had sent him home. He had examined Ramchand's ankle and

told him, 'It should be fine in three days. Come back then.'
And Ramchand had.

He couldn't even feign illness because Mahajan knew where each of the shop assistants lived, and had a nasty habit of sending someone to check up on them when any of them took the day off claiming to be ill.

And anyway, Ramchand had often thought gloomily, even if he did manage to get leave, what would he do? Where would he go?

So he went to the shop, day after day after day. But today would be different. Ramchand felt like dancing. He couldn't control himself any longer and burst into song. It was just a hum first, then his voice broke out clearly, and soon he was trilling at the top of his voice:

> Yeh dil na hota bechara
> Kadam na hote awara
> Jo khubsoorat koi apna
> Humsafar hota

His voice reached a crescendo as he danced around in his room in his old white vest and pyjamas, immune to the cold.

The landlord yelled from the courtyard, 'Ramchand, be quiet!'

Ramchand pretended not to hear. He started again, his voice shriller and higher than ever. 'Yeh dil na hotaaaa . . .'

'Ramchand!' screamed the landlord.

'Kadam na hote awara . . .'

Ramchand ran across the room and jumped over the low stool in exuberance. He landed with a thud on the other side.

'He will break the roof,' wailed Sudha, the landlord's wife.

'Raaaamchand!' the landlord bellowed, his thin frame shaking in anger.

Ramchand quietened down. He switched songs. He bowed

charmingly at his reflection in the flecky mirror, tilted his head to one side and sang softly.

'*Tum bin jaoon kahan*,' he hummed softly to his own reflection.

And then a new madness seized Ramchand while he was shaving. He suddenly, and with great resolve in his eyes, lathered his upper lip.

And then he shaved off his moustache!

Thin and wispy, but a moustache nevertheless!

He splashed water over his face and looked into the mirror. He looked so different! Very few Bombay film stars had moustaches. Well, Anil Kapoor did, but then, he was Anil Kapoor. Ramchand studied his new face in the mirror. It wasn't bad, he thought, but his clean-shaven look would have suited him better if his name had been Vishaal or Amit or Rahul, instead of Ramchand. But despite this, he secretly felt very pleased.

Then Ramchand took a bath with the red Lifebuoy bar, scrubbing himself thoroughly and washing the lemon juice off his feet. Then he towelled his thin body dry, put on fresh underwear and a washed vest, and got dressed in his new clothes. He proudly tucked his new white shirt into the waistband of his black trousers. Usually, he either wore a kurta over his trousers or old shirts that he never tucked in. He put on an old but clean sweater, combed his hair neatly and peered into the mirror. He was looking neat and tidy, and his face somehow seemed more resolute without his moustache, and, like it or not, clothes did make a difference.

He wasn't looking shabby at all. He was looking quite respectable. He did not remember ever looking so good.

5

'There you are,' Gokul said, packing the last sari into a huge bundle. 'Take good care of them. They are very expensive. And be very polite to the Kapoors.'

Ramchand nodded.

Hari came up behind him and put an arm affectionately around his shoulder, 'You could pass off as the hero of a superhit film. Waah, what a change.'

Ramchand blushed. Then he hoisted the bundle of saris on his shoulder and went down to where Gokul's bicycle was parked. He put the bundle on the carrier of the bicycle and secured it firmly with rope. He threw a leg over the bicycle, settled himself on the seat, and pedalled off exuberantly, freedom breathing through each Lifebuoy-scrubbed pore of his body.

The sun shone down gently on him, with pleasant warmth. Ramchand meandered through a crowd of bicycles, vegetable carts and pedestrians, and made his way out of the old city. Just at the edge of the bazaar, he stopped at the noisy Anand Juice Shop. He parked the bicycle, but did not move away from it. A small boy came out and asked what he wanted. Ramchand ordered a glass of mossambi juice, with one hand placed protectively on the bundle of saris on the carrier. The boy brought him a glassful. Ramchand sipped at it.

The orange liquid slid down his throat smoothly.

He threw his head back and drained the last drop into his mouth.

Grey pigeons flew overhead.

A single drop clung to the corner of his mouth, caught the sun's rays and glinted quietly. Ramchand wiped it away, paid up and cycled off again, feeling more free and happy than he had in years.

After half an hour of serene cycling, Ramchand reached Green Avenue where Ravinder Kapoor lived. Gokul had told him exactly how to get to Green Avenue. Now Ramchand took out the piece of paper on which Gokul had scribbled further instructions clearly. He had to turn left when he saw a phone booth. Ramchand spotted a shiny new-looking glass booth with the letters 'P.C.O.' written on the smooth glass in bright red, and turned.

He was in a broad lane shaded with leafy trees and a proper pavement. On his right side there was a row of big houses with high boundary walls, on his left there was a big park, a large open space that Ramchand would never have imagined existed in Amritsar.

'The third house on the right,' he murmured to himself, wobbling a little. He passed two big houses and stopped at the gate of the third.

The high iron gates were of an intricate pattern, with brass knobs shining here and there. The top of the gate was spiked, so were the walls. A large granite nameplate had two words engraved on it. Ramchand stared at them, murmuring the letters that formed the words. Then he found, to his delight, that he had managed to read them. The words said 'Kapoor House'. The granite nameplate looked very impressive.

Through the grille of the gate, Ramchand could see a driveway lined with potted plants, a chauffeur polishing a long blue car, and a well-kept lawn. A gardener wearing a blue kurta was bending over some flowerbeds.

Ramchand rang the bell nervously. The chauffeur came and opened the gate. He was a hefty man. He had his sweater sleeves rolled back and Ramchand could see his muscular forearms.

'Yes?' he asked suspiciously.

'I have brought them,' Ramchand said nervously.

'Brought what?'

'Saris.'

'Which saris?'

'For memsahib's wedding. From Sevak Sari House.'

'Oh.' The chauffeur looked Ramchand up and down appraisingly and then moved to one side. 'Come in,' he said.

Ramchand wheeled his bicycle up the broad driveway. He was asked to wait in the porch. A big wooden 'Om' hung above the main door. He waited, cracking his knuckles swiftly, one after the other. He could see now that there was a red car behind the blue one and the garage door was closed, maybe there was another car inside the garage. The driveway was wide enough for any of the cars behind to be taken out without having to move the blue car.

After a minute or two, a surly looking maid in a mauve sari opened the door and ushered Ramchand into a big room with grand-looking sofas lining the walls and a glass-topped table in the middle. A thick blue carpet covered the entire floor space. There were paintings and brass antiques hanging on the walls. Ramchand nervously sat on the edge of one of the soft sofas with his huge bundle of saris sitting beside him, feeling like a fish out of water. There was complete silence, except for the loud ticking of a very fancy looking clock on the wall. He waited for fifteen minutes. Then a boy appeared through the door with a glass of chilled cola on a tray. He was blushing. Ramchand also blushed.

He took the glass self-consciously, and tried to look as if he sat in plush rooms every day receiving glasses of expensive soft drinks from domestic help. When he picked up the glass, he noticed that the tray was made of frosted glass with a pattern of dancing peacocks engraved on it. It reminded him of the embroidered peacocks on the blue sari that Mrs Gupta had bought for her daughter-in-law.

Ramchand stared at the tray.

The boy stood there uncertainly, shifting from one foot to the other. Ramchand suddenly asked him, 'Are you new here?'

The boy stared at him dumbly. Ramchand switched from Punjabi to Hindi and asked again, 'Are you new here?'

This time the boy nodded. 'From Himachal?' Ramchand asked.

'Yes,' the boy said, his eyes lighting up. 'From Lachkandi village, near Simla. Are you from the hills too?' he asked excitedly, in a voice that was surprisingly clear and beautiful.

Ramchand shook his head.

The boy's face fell. He looked at Ramchand uncertainly for a moment, then he suddenly turned and walked out of the room. Ramchand waited another fifteen minutes. Finally, a middle-aged woman dressed in a blue silk salwaar kameez and an expensive-looking shawl walked in. Gold and diamonds glittered on her ears and her wrists.

Ramchand stood up politely. 'Ji namaste,' he said with folded hands.

'Rinaaaa!' she shouted, startling him. 'The sari-wala is here.'

When she shouted, you could see the red inside of her mouth and her large, even teeth. Then she said, 'Namaste,' and sat down opposite him.

A young woman with permed hair walked in, the high heels of her shoes sinking into the soft carpet. She wore blue jeans, a slinky blouse with a purple and blue floral pattern and a black woollen cardigan. Silver bangles jangled at her wrists.

'Yes, mama.'

'Sit, let's take a look at these saris.'

Ramchand looked at both of them. So these two women were Ravinder Kapoor's wife and daughter. He had heard that the wife had once, at one go, bought pashmeena shawls worth ten lakhs. He looked at her curiously.

'What are you waiting for? Show us the saris,' she suddenly said to him, her voice imperious and harsh.

'Mama, let's have one of the servants here,' said Rina. She had a husky, languid voice.

'Okay,' replied her mother. 'Raghuuuuu!' she yelled, the red, cavernous opening of her mouth yawning wide again.

The door opened once more and Raghu, a tall young man, came in. He stood deferentially by the sofa watching the proceedings.

Ramchand, still sitting on the sofa, bent down and opened the knot that tied the bundle. But he was feeling uncomfortable, and his fingers fumbled awkwardly at the knot. Finally he excused himself, walked to the edge of the carpet, stepped off it, took off his shoes and came back. Then he hitched up his new black trousers and sat down on the carpet cross-legged, feeling back in his element. Rina caught her mother's eye and sniggered, but he ignored it.

Now, he swiftly undid the bundle and confidently began to take the saris out one by one, but what followed was completely outside of all his previous experience.

Ramchand had been working at Sevak Sari House for eleven years now. He had watched innumerable women choose saris. Though women were otherwise strange, alien creatures to him, there was one part of them that he knew intimately – the way they chose saris.

He had learnt to read their expressions and their moods very accurately. He could guess when they were definitely going to buy a particular sari. He could tell when they were in two minds and had to be pushed into buying one.

He could immediately sense when they had made up their minds not to buy anything and were just pretending to be interested.

He well knew the look on a young girl's face when she came to the shop with mothers and aunts and sisters to buy saris for her wedding trousseau. There was the glow on her face, the light in her eyes, the quiet nervous excitement. She would drape a pallu of a sari over her shoulder and look into the mirror intently. While the women accompanying her critically assessed how the sari suited her, she looked at herself with the eyes of her would-be-husband-and lover. Her moist lips would quiver and part in a virginal excitement. She would smile, and in the end she would be quite incapable of making up her mind. She would blush and nod when the women accompanying her asked whether she wanted this sari or that, creating a lot of confusion. On certain occasions, Ramchand had also seen such girls look into the mirror with melancholic eyes, as if the *sari* was quite all right, it was the idea of this particular marriage that wasn't so happy. This happened rarely, but when it did, it would tug terribly at Ramchand's heart, though he would later tell himself that it must have been his imagination.

He had seen vanity, he had seen envy, he had seen despair. He knew well the bitterness of a plain woman, who could see in the mirror that a sari could, after all, do only so much, and he could recognize the quiet, wordless triumph of the beautiful ones.

Ramchand had also noticed that women rarely, almost never, bought saris alone. They had to be in twos and threes to be able to decide, and to derive the maximum pleasure from the process of purchasing a sari. Buying a sari wasn't just buying a sari – it was entertainment, it was pleasure, an aesthetic experience. They would always come at least in pairs, if not in groups. Then they would talk about the sari, discuss its merits and demerits. They would make faces if they didn't like a sari, and shake their heads ruefully at each other, quickly saying that the sari would have been all right, had it not sorely lacked a good pallu, or a better designed border, or a *slightly* different shade of colour.

Ramchand had learnt to be patient while women talked and pored over a sari endlessly. They would peer at it closely, running their fingers lightly over the fabric, scrutinizing the pattern, as if trying to decipher faded handwriting on an old parchment.

He had also come to recognize the covetous expression, followed by a resolute look on a woman's face once she had decided that she *must* have a particular sari, no matter what happened.

If the women were from the same family, family hierarchies would come into play sometimes. The eldest, usually a grand-mother or a mother-in-law, would finally decide things, especially if the shopping was being done for a wedding in the family. She would make sure that nobody got saddled with the cheapest sari, lest the sari wars carry themselves danger-ously into kitchens. But on the whole, women from the same families were also pretty amiable and happy while buying saris together. They would ask each other anxiously, do you remember, do I have another sari of the same colour, are you sure? They would drape saris over their shoulders, sometimes even cover their head with the pallus, and ask each other how it looked on them. It was perhaps the one time when women were at their most honest, open and sincere towards each other.

And in every case, there would be the bargaining – the gentle bargaining that regular customers did, knowing they'd get their way eventually; the loud haggling that aggressive women did out of sheer habit, the sort that ended with head-aches on both sides; the coaxing, cajoling kind of bargaining that inexperienced customers indulged in hopefully; and the aristocratic requests that women from rich families made (please price it reasonably, they would command with an imperious wave of their hand). It happened in different forms. But it always happened.

But today, in the drawing room of the Kapoor House, there was no bargaining and very few questions were asked. In fact, they did not even bother to ask the prices, even when he unpacked the most expensive lehngas that were available at Sevak Sari House.

They exchanged very few words with each other, both women absorbed in picking out what they wanted. They ignored Ramchand completely. They chose expensive saris and went through the few lehngas he had brought with him without batting an eyelid and kept them aside, and carelessly tossed the ones they did not like into another pile.

Rina picked out two sheer saris, one in a delicate salmon pink edged with silver thread, and another that was a light blue, almost white, heavily covered with embroidered silver butees. Mrs Kapoor chose a blue crushed tissue sari with a brocade border without the slightest hesitation. A bottle green, almost black, tussar sari with brown and gold thread embroidery followed. And so they went on, while Ramchand sat there feeling awkward, useless and left out.

The few questions that were asked were by Mrs Kapoor, and they showed her to be quite an expert about fabric. Ramchand tried his best to answer them without getting visibly nervous. There was a certain ruthlessness in the way the two picked up a sari, ran a sharp eye over it, took in the border and the pallu and then felt the fabric between their thumbs and forefingers. Then, with a hard glint in their eyes, they made up their minds. There was no hesitancy, no doubt, about anything at all. In the middle of all this, a girl of about nineteen came in. She wore black jeans and had

66

short, cropped hair. When she spoke, her voice was even huskier than her sister's. There was an air of confident vitality about her.

'Rina Didi, I am going for a swim,' she said in English. 'I'll meet you at the hairdresser's, okay?'

'Okay. Seeya, Tina,' said Rina carelessly.

Tina was about to turn when she saw the saris strewn about everywhere. 'Hey, what is going on here?' she stopped and asked. 'I thought we had bought all the saris we wanted from the designers in Bombay. What are you doing with these?'

Rina looked up at her. 'You know, Tina?' she said earnestly. 'I was thinking I must be very careful while buying both clothes and jewellery. I don't want the usual conventional bridal trousseau. I want a collection that is *me*. A collection that is a mix of traditional and contemporary styles. You know, that way you don't get a fixed image and you can experiment with your looks.'

'Yeah, great idea,' said Tina, slowly. 'I suppose you are right. Really, Rina Didi, you do think of the most original things.'

Rina smiled. Then she held up a golden-yellow sari she had just chosen. 'Just take a look at this. It is an Orissa silk with real Palghat folk embroidery. You know, this shop does carry things from around the country. So, I thought, why not make a few additions to my Bombay collection.'

Tina examined the sari. 'Wow, that really has an ethnic look. I am dying to look at the rest of them. You might have called me.'

'Don't you look petulant now,' Rina said affectionately to her younger sister. 'You are the one who woke up so late. Don't worry, we'll go over them together tonight, okay?'

'Okay. Great. I'll just take a quick dip in the pool and then head straight for the hairdresser's. So you'll meet me there later then?' Tina asked, handing the sari back.

'Yeah,' Rina said, turning to the saris again.

Tina waved at her mother, who nodded. Then she turned briskly and walked out with bouncing steps.

Through the window, Ramchand watched her get into the driver's seat of a little red car, slam the door shut and drive off at full speed.

By now, the two women had gone through all the saris and had selected the ones they wanted. Ramchand started to make the bill in his head. It would come to about 80,000 rupees approximately, he thought.

Mrs Kapoor waved a hand at him. 'Bring the bill when you bring the next batch.'

Ramchand gaped at her. Mahajan would kill him. But if he made the Kapoors angry, Mahajan would kill him anyway. So he decided to let it pass. He wondered why nobody at the shop had told him what to do about the bill.

For a moment, blind panic seized him. What if they didn't pay? What if they denied buying these saris later? Would *he* have to shell out 80,000 rupees? His entire savings consisted of three thousand, four hundred and thirty rupees. Then Ramchand tried to get a grip on himself. These people *owned* factories. Eighty thousand rupees would be peanuts to them.

By that time, the two women had already left the room, talking excitedly about some jeweller who was supposed to bring some jewellery over in about ten minutes. Ramchand collected the saris in a daze, while Raghu waited to see him out.

The huge bill, the plush drawing room, Tina Kapoor's red car, the strange, self-assured women, the alien smells of the Kapoor House – all this had left him dazed, confused. He pedalled back to the shop slowly, the wheels of the bicycle rotated rhythmically, the new images played themselves over in his mind again and again. The moment

Ramchand got to the shop, the first thing he did was race up to Gokul.

'Gokul Bhaiya,' he said, agitated, clutching Gokul's arm.

'Ramchand,' Gokul said, springing up, 'I forgot to tell you about the bill.'

Ramchand almost died of shock. He said with urgency, 'Gokul Bhaiya, she said bring it later. I didn't know what to do. I haven't got the payment with me. I didn't make out any bill . . .'

Gokul interrupted him, with a look of relief on his own face, 'Thank God!' he said. 'You did the right thing. That is what I forgot to tell you. You did the right thing. I was so scared you'd start demanding the payment and create a scene and Mahajan would haul me up for not briefing you properly. Now, go and report to Mahajan. He has a list of all that was sent. He will send in the bill to Ravinder Kapoor who will give us a cheque. That's how it works with these big people, you know.'

Ramchand could have wept with relief.

It did not take long to report to Mahajan and put away the saris that the Kapoor women had rejected. Mahajan seemed quite pleased with Ramchand.

Mahajan said he could leave for the day if he wanted, because it was a tiring business cycling with that heavy bundle all the way to Green Avenue and back. 'But don't expect that luxury every time you go the Kapoor House, boy,' Mahajan said, when Ramchand thanked him, looking pleased. 'I'll speak to them over the phone. Maybe you'll have to take another batch tomorrow.'

Ramchand walked out. The evening was chilly and he hugged himself. The events of the day had thrown him into some confusion but the change had also stirred him. The long cycle ride, the sun and the breeze, the shops, the Kapoor House – all these were outside the routine and the world he had known for the last eleven years, and they had left his brain tingling.

The world was big, after all. He had just got into a rut – shop, room, shop, room, shop, room . . .

Once you got out of that rut, it was easy to see that there were endless possibilities in the world. There were the hills where the Kapoors' servant boy had come from, there were mountain streams on those hills that were as clear as the boy's voice. There was the swimming pool that Tina frequented – maybe it was like the one in *Baazigar*, with blue tiles and a board to dive from, at the edge of which Shilpa Shetty had writhed during a song, wearing a backless blouse and a thin yellow chiffon sari. There was the college where Mrs Sachdeva taught, there were the books that were written and read by many, there were cars and flowerpots and frosted glass trays with peacocks on them. Yes, it was a big world.

He began to feel exhilarated. He walked with a spring in his step, and then abruptly turned and began to walk in the opposite direction. He moved fast, unmindful of the cold now, sure of where he was going. Ramchand walked till he reached the cluster of small shops that sold second-hand books. These small shops were little more than wooden shacks, and were run by people who rescued old books from the kabaadi and then sold them at a profit. They mainly managed to get hold of old textbooks, but other books wandered in too.

Ramchand stopped at the first one. It was a little wooden structure, and there were piles of books and magazines inside, on the counter and even outside the shop.

Ramchand stood there and ran his eyes over them. He was determined to buy a few books today, but he had to choose carefully. He could not afford to spend more than a hundred rupees, which was a princely sum for him to put aside for books.

As Ramchand began to painstakingly look through the titles of the displayed books, he thought of his eighth-class school certificate, the certificate that still lay at the bottom of his tin trunk wrapped in a green polythene bag, the certificate that no one had ever asked to see . . .

Now, he had forgotten most of what he had learnt, and as he looked at the titles of the books, he realized he could read very little. He hadn't been bad at reading when he'd been in class eight, though. Not good, but not bad either. Only, he always tried not to think of class eight, or the day he had left it . . . or any part of his childhood, for that matter . . . But he wasn't going to let anything stop him today.

Ramchand stuck out his chin, narrowed his eyes and began to work at reading the titles. *The Complete Letter Writer* – he managed to read one out aloud, and immediately got excited. Yes, this was the one he needed. It would give him practice in reading, writing and communicating.

'How much?' he asked the shopkeeper.

'Thirty,' the shopkeeper said briskly.

Ramchand's heart gladdened and expanded and he clutched the book happily. He went through the rest. *Medical Dictionary*, *The Mayor of Casterbridge*, *Fat to Fit in Thirty Days*, *Wuthering Heights*. No, none of this made sense to him. He turned his attention to another pile. *Indian Vegetarian Cooking*, *Physics Text Book – Class 10+2 (C.B.S.E.)*, *Feng Shui Solutions to a Happy Life*.

Ramchand felt perplexed. Then he turned to the shopkeeper again. 'You have Mahatma Gandhi's autobiography?'

'No,' he answered, intently watching a lizard that was darting from the wall to the floor. 'Hoosh,' he said, flapping a duster at the lizard.

It was then that Ramchand spotted the *Radiant Essays – for Schoolchildren of All Ages*. Again the happy lurch in his stomach.

'How much is that?' he asked pointing, keeping his voice

casual. If the shopkeeper knew he wanted it badly, he would immediately quote a high price.

'Fifty,' he answered.

'Fifty?' said Ramchand, outraged.

'Fifty.' The shopkeeper's mouth was set, his voice was firm.

After a lot of bargaining, the two settled on seventy rupees for both the books. Ramchand handed the shopkeeper a hundred rupee note and waited for the change. While the man was rummaging for change in a drawer, Ramchand flipped through the books tentatively. And he discovered that though he had kept himself in practice by reading signboards in English and by trying to read the newspaper in which Lakhan packed pakoras if you wanted to take a few home with you, he could not understand most words in both the books. So, he asked, looking a little crestfallen, 'A dictionary? Do you have a second-hand, *cheap* English dictionary?'

The shopkeeper took out a tattered old copy of the Oxford English Dictionary and handed it to him.

Ramchand took the fat volume reverently and asked, 'How much?'

'Forty,' the shopkeeper said quickly.

'Forty? For this?' said Ramchand, holding up the dog-eared copy.

'Yes,' the shopkeeper answered firmly. 'It has all the words.'

Ramchand paid ten rupees over the hundred that he had meant to spend, but could not help hugging the books to himself as he walked home.

He felt armed to fight now. He hadn't done anything meaningful in such a long time. Suddenly reckless, he also stopped at a stationer's and bought a bottle of Camlin Royal Blue ink, a pen and a notebook. He wondered whether to buy whitewash for his room, but did not have the courage to spend so much money in one day.

He returned home feeling rejuvenated.

6

Ramchand put the packet of books and the blue plastic bag from the stationers on the bed and looked around at his room. It had two windows – one that opened on to the busy, narrow street and one that looked on to the courtyard of his landlord's house. These, in his mind, he had designated as the front window and the back window as soon as he had seen the room for the first time.

It had already been furnished with a string cot and a table when Ramchand had rented it. Apart from these two pieces of furniture, there was a framed poster hanging on the wall left behind by a previous tenant. It showed a thatched cottage with pretty wooden windows, the kind Ramchand had never seen in real life, with rambling roses growing over the door-way. There was also a chimney, and a cobbled path leading to the cottage. Behind the cottage you could see a bright blue sky and tall, snow-covered mountains. On the bottom right-hand corner of the poster were written the words, 'Home is where the heart is.'

Ramchand had not bothered to take down the picture of the thatched cottage, and it had been hanging there for the past eleven years. By now Ramchand had memorized every small detail of the picture – the two little stone steps that led up to the door of the cottage, the pattern on the curtain that hung at the cottage window, the pattern of the thatched roof. The red roses climbing the cottage had faded a little, and the blue sky was dimmer now, but the picture still hung there.

Ramchand had, in the course of the last eleven years,

73

acquired a chair, a low stool, two buckets and a mug, two plastic soap cases – one for Lifebuoy soap and the other for a Rin detergent bar – a doormat, and a small mirror on the wall that looked very old. He kept meaning to get curtains too, but hadn't got around to doing it. The money fell short every month.

He cooked simple meals in a corner of the room, where he kept a small stove and a few utensils. He rarely cooked anything more than daal and rice, and often made tea for himself. Occasionally he would buy the vegetable that was going cheapest in the market, chop it all up and drop it into the pot in which rice was cooking. This was as ambitious as his cooking ever got.

He had a saucepan, two steel plates, two steel tumblers, a few spoons, a ladle and a knife. When the utensils had to be washed, he had to carry them in a bucket to the bathroom and wash them there. Even if he had to rinse a knife to chop vegetables, he had to go to the bathroom to do it. The floor had been perpetually wet in the beginning, when he had just moved in. The steel utensils would drip while he carried them back from the bathroom after washing them, and Ramchand's rubber chappals would leave wet footprints on the floor. It was then that Ramchand had invested in the doormat.

His cot was by the front window. By the back window, which was very low, he had placed his tin trunk and covered it with a piece of cloth. He would often sit on the trunk, looking out of the open window at the washing fluttering below in the courtyard, the washing that had been scrubbed and rinsed by the lovely hands of Sudha, the landlord's wife. Now he looked around at the messy, neglected room. *This* was his world, he thought in disgust. No wonder his life was such a pothole. Shop, room, shop, room, shop, room.

In a fresh fit of energy, Ramchand quickly changed out of

his new clothes into an old kurta-pyjama, took up the rarely used broom and swept the floor, also clearing away as many cobwebs on the walls and the roof as he could reach. He swept all the broom-pickings, including the cobwebs, to the door, where he examined the whole collection with interest. A spider scuttled out from a recently demolished cobweb and ran away. Apart from the cobwebs and the dust, there were fluffs of wool that his old blanket had shed, bits of his hair, grains of uncooked rice that he must have scattered while screwing or unscrewing the jar lid, and little, black, tear-shaped lizard droppings. He then gathered up all these bits and pieces of his room, and tied them up in a plastic bag. He would throw it on to the rubbish heap on his way to the shop the next day.

Then he filled water in an old bucket, dipped an old rag in it and scrubbed the floor thoroughly, ignoring the chill that the wet rag sent up to his hands.

He cleared up the table, removing from it a bottle of mango pickle, jars full of rice and daal, a tin of Parachute coconut hair oil, a bright yellow tube of Burnol, a jar of Zandu pain balm (*Zandu balm, Zandu balm, peedahari balm. Sardi sar dard peeda ko pal mein dur kare. Zandu Balm, Zandu Balm*) and some clothes that he had dumped on top of everything else. He dusted the table, little clouds of dust flying into his face. Then he rubbed a wet cloth on the surface of the table. The round, oily stains made by the bottoms of various jars vanished. Ramchand lined a corner of the floor with the old newspaper in which his new clothes had been wrapped. He placed all the jars in two neat rows on this newspaper, with the bigger jars in the back row and the smaller ones in the front. This left the table bare and clean.

Then, feeling enormously tidy and virtuous, he pulled the table close to the bed so that he could sit on the bed and write at the table. This way, the bulb hanging overhead was exactly above the table.

Then Ramchand took out his new books and began to read haltingly.

He started with the *Complete Letter Writer*. To his dismay, he found that he could barely read. Any word that consisted of more than four letters caused him trouble. And even when he had painstakingly pieced together the letters and made the word, what it produced was only an empty sound to Ramchand. He rarely knew what it meant.

When he tried looking up a difficult word in the dictionary, first it took him ages to trace it, and when he finally did, he found that some of the meanings were as difficult as the words themselves.

Ramchand felt so disheartened at first that he almost burst into tears. He sat there staring at the open pages for a while, wondering if he hadn't just thrown money away by buying these books. Would he ever be able to read, write or remotely understand English? But, after a while, as the night noises grew fainter and the moon outside climbed higher in the sky, Ramchand set to work with an uncharacteristic determination, reading haltingly, constructing childish words in the new notebook, his head slightly aching with the effort. He dropped off to sleep at two in the morning, his tired head resting on the thick Oxford Dictionary. The next day was Sunday. Ramchand woke up resolute, and didn't let his mind wander at all. After a bath and a breakfast of banana and tea, he settled down to work. He stayed in all day, labouring at his new books. He took a short break in the afternoon to cook khichdi. It was so tasteless that he could only swallow it with lots of mango pickle. Then he went back to the books. By evening he found he could decipher the words at least, even if he had to struggle with their meaning. With a little practice the old forgotten skill was coming back to him, at least partially.

But even after he had got the meaning clear, and had managed to read a whole letter, he remained confused. He had opened the *Complete Letter Writer* randomly, and had begun to read a 'Letter Inviting a Girlfriend to Take Part in a Motor Tour', under the heading of 'Invitations and Their Replies'. Blushing a little at the word 'girlfriend', Ramchand had begun:

The Grey Towers,
Littlebourne,
Kent

1 July, 19—

Dear Peggy,
Will you come and join us in a motor tour? George is frightfully proud of a new car he has just bought and we want to have a really jolly tour through Wales. If you can come – and we are tremendously set on your joining us – there will be you, and George and myself, and my brother Frank. We ought to make a nice little party. We thought of starting from here about the first of next month. George thinks of mapping the tour beforehand; but of course it can be changed if anybody had any suggestions to make. Will you say which day you can come?

Yours with love,
Phyllis

What was that about a girlfriend then, thought Ramchand. He understood little of it, but the last line at least was clear. *Will you say which day you can come?* Yes, he understood that. It had taken him almost the whole day to read this one letter. Then Ramchand took a deep breath and started to read the next letter, which was a reply to the previous one:

Middle Cloisters,
Canterbury

3rd July, 19—

Dear Phyllis,
How jolly! And how good of you to ask me to join you! I shall love
it above all things! But do tell George to manage to get the Clerk of
Weather in a good temper! Tell me what clothes I shall want, and
about how long you propose to be on tour.

I should love to see Caernarvon and Bettws-y-Coed; but there
are so many lovely places in Wales that I shall be quite happy
to fit in with your plans. I suppose you will go to Tintern and
Chepstow and Raglan. If I come to you on the 28th, will that
suit you?

Yours, quite jumpy with joy,
Peggy

Ramchand was completely baffled by now. The second
letter had taken him three hours. It was dark outside now and
the muscles in his neck ached.

It had taken him almost all of Sunday to read the two letters
and now that he had managed to read them, he could not
make head or tail of them. From what he could gather, Phyllis,
Peggy, George and Frank were names of people, however
unlikely sounding they might be. Yes, 'Dear Peggy' must mean
that Peggy was a person. But what was a motor tour? He
knew what a motor was, and he knew what a tour was, but
what was all this? He tried to concentrate. He must not give
up so soon. Then he took another break, made himself a
strong cup of tea, and drank it squatting on the floor near
the stove. Then he went back to the mystifying letters and
underlined Caernarvon, Tintern, Chepstow and Raglan. They
were the difficult words that he had tried to look up in the

dictionary but hadn't found. Bettws-y-Coed he left out, certain that it was a printing mistake.

After he had figured out the phrase, 'yours, quite jumpy with joy', he found it very funny.

Ramchand still didn't really understand the gist of the letters, but he was tired now. So he went for a long brisk walk, then came back and got to work again. He kept to the letter-writing book, keeping the essay book for future use. He felt he would just get confused if he began on everything all at once. All the words and the phrases that he did not understand, or anything that he wanted to remember, he put down carefully in his new notebook with his new pen.

7

'Hmmm . . . la la la la a . . . hmmm, oh ho o o o.'

This was Ramchand going to work on Monday morning. Life was on its tracks, as it should be. He looked better, felt better, he had spent the weekend trying to learn. He hadn't wasted time loitering outside cinema halls or just lying on his bed, feeling depressed about nothing. He had exercised and got some fresh air on that long walk of his.

This was true strength of character. This was how life should be lived. The world was big, very big. You could do anything.

Today he was supposed to take another batch of saris to the Kapoor House, though the shop could ill-afford the absence of any of its workers. This was the auspicious time of the year for marriages, and the shop was doing such brisk business that no one had a moment of leisure, not even Hari.

However, the Kapoors could not be treated lightly, and so Ramchand went off whistling on Gokul's bicycle once again, with more saris for the Kapoor bride. This time he was dressed in old clothes, he couldn't afford something new for each visit to the Kapoor House, but he had still tried to look neat and smart.

Once again he loitered near bookstalls. He sat drinking chai at a tea stall for almost half an hour, watching people go by. He skipped the mossambi juice though. New clothes, books, pen, ink, notebook and what not. He had to be careful with money for a while now.

He finally arrived at the Kapoor House. Again he was asked to wait in the carpeted room. Raghu came in and told him he'd have to wait for a while, the elder memsahib was with a visiting jeweller and the younger memsahib was on the phone. Ramchand nodded and started daydreaming. Raghu left, leaving the connecting door open.

Ramchand never meant to eavesdrop, but she was speaking loud enough for him to hear. Maybe she thought he couldn't understand English. Well, he couldn't understand it very well, that was true, but he could follow bits and pieces of her conversation.

Her husky voice was unusual and attractive to Ramchand's ears. 'Honestly, sweetheart, I am not like the rest of the girls in Amritsar,' she was saying. 'I find them so *stagnant* sometimes, so content with the petty little lives they have made for themselves. I can't imagine being like that. I like to read, I like to explore new things, I like to take every day of life as a new experience. Now, look at me at this very moment. I have a stupid sari-wala and a greedy jeweller waiting for me, and still I am thinking of these other things. I think life is an adventure. And when you explore life, you also explore yourself. As you know,' she went on, 'my father is so wealthy that I never really need to work. Despite that, I made sure I finished my Masters in English Literature. *And* I have been topping my class. I am a creative person. My mind just can't be still, and it can't be content with all these things. Of course I like wearing good clothes, jewellery, living well and in comfort, because, after all, look at the family I belong to. But that is not *all*, it is not the end of the road for me. It is a means to an end, it is not the end itself.'

Here there was a pause in the conversation. She seemed to be listening to the person on the other end of the line.

Then she said triumphantly, 'Exactly! That is *exactly* how I feel too! What about my soul? What about my creativity? In fact,' she added, 'yesterday I wrote another poem. One of the poems in which I find that I can express the true meaning of life. And do you know when I wrote it? While a man who had brought over crystal bangles for me to see was waiting outside. I felt the urge and I knew that bangles could wait, but I needed to get the creative process going.'

There was a pause. Then Ramchand heard her voice again.

'In fact, I am even thinking of writing a novel. Someone had recently come from Delhi to a conference at the university and she said that I definitely have talent. And our own Mrs Sachdeva here, you know, has been very encouraging.'

Here she paused, and appeared to be listening to a reply.

'Well, I am glad you are supportive. When my father heard that I was in love with you, an army officer, he wasn't pleased. He always used to tell his friends, "When my daughter gets married, the whole city will watch." But, well, I convinced him. I am not one of those girls who'll just marry a rich man and go to kitty parties. Besides, I don't really need any more money.'

There was another pause, a longer one this time.

Then she said, 'Bye, poochie, have to rush now. I love you so much. I can't *believe* we are finally getting married. Just can't wait for us to be together.'

There was a click, and then silence after this.

Ramchand sat quietly, still trying to take in the conversation. Out of whatever he had understood, one thing was clear. She had called him a stupid sari-wala.

Ramchand reflected on this for a moment. But maybe that was just pre-wedding nerves, he thought charitably. And it must be especially difficult for someone like her, a person who sounded so different and sensitive. Ramchand felt torn up in two inside. He did not know whether to be annoyed with her for speaking of him insultingly or feel pleased that she was trying to find herself. 'To express the true meaning of life,' seemed impressive, though he wasn't sure what 'express' meant.

Then she walked in and he glanced at her warily. She didn't even look at him. Her mother followed her in and they were soon engrossed in choosing more saris, working their way through the huge bundle as avidly and quickly as they had done the day before.

*

Charged by Rina's converstion about writing and about 'expressing', Ramchand resolved to start on the *Radiant Essays* the same evening. This book, unlike the *Complete Letter Writer*, had been written by an Indian woman (Shalini, MA English, B.Ed.), especially for Secondary, Senior Secondary, C.B.S.E., Undergraduate students and Competitive Examinations. And Ramchand was delighted to find that though it was called an essay book, at the end it also had a few letters.

Ramchand began to read an essay for schoolchildren called 'An Indian Beggar'.

A beggar is a common sight in our country. You can find him outside a place of worship, at a bus stop, in the market, in the street, etc.

There are hundreds of varieties of beggars in India. Some are blind beggars. As they are unable to see or work so they start begging. Such types of beggars do deserve our pity. Also there are beggars who are cripples or lepers. They are unable to earn their livelihood. At the same time, there are beggars, young and stout, but have opted begging as their profession. Then there are beggars who look like sadhus, but actually they are not. Most of such type of beggars are drunkards, sinners and thieves.

This tired Ramchand out. He began to revise the paragraph slowly. He read the complete paragraph without halting even once. It filled him with immense pride. He had read a whole paragraph in *English*, and understood everything too. The language was much easier than that of the *Complete Letter Writer*, and he was pleased. However, the paragraph had also made him uneasy.

He didn't think that he would like Shalini (MA English, B.Ed) much if he met her. That night in bed, before putting on his blue woollen night socks with holes in the toes, Ramchand looked up 'express' in the dictionary. It had about ten different meanings, apart from an outbreak of *express trains* and *express ways*.

It took Ramchand about half an hour to figure what Rina had meant. 'Reveal, betoken, put (thought) into words'.

And then he spotted 'express oneself'. It meant 'to say what one means'.

This made it all clear to Ramchand.

He knew how difficult *that* was.

8

A few days passed. Ramchand was told that he needn't go to
the Kapoors for a while now. If they needed more saris, he'd
be told. He was distracted most of the time in the shop
and spent his spare time reading the essay book. After the
Phyllis-Peggy-motor tour confusion, he had become a little
wary of the letter-writing book. Yet he assiduously, though
suspiciously, went through it, making notes in his notebook
and looking up meanings in the dictionary.

He had hit upon a new idea, and he thought it was the most
brilliant idea he had ever had. If he started at the beginning of
the dictionary, and learnt the meanings of each and every
word, working his way from A to Z, one day he would know
all English, completely and irrevocably. The thought was so
mind boggling that it took his breath away. He wondered if
scholars had ever thought of that. It would take a long time,
of course, but nothing was impossible.

So it *could* be done. So Ramchand devoted half an hour
every evening – after he was done with the essays and had
been wading through the letters, perplexed – to learning words
and their meanings. In starting with 'a', he hadn't bargained
for the single lettered word 'a' that was the first one in the
dictionary. It seemed to have a million meanings, so Ramchand
skipped it. In six days' time, he had worked his way from
Aback to Altitude, spending every single spare moment he
had on the dictionary. He would even mutter the words in
the shop. However, after the initial fever went down a little,
he slowed down, and developed a steady pace.

*

During the evenings Ramchand sat at his table and worked, for the winter days were short and by the time he got back from the shop it was already dark. But on Sundays Ramchand would open the windows, and settle down on his tin trunk by the back window to read. From this window, not only could he see the landlord's courtyard, but also the living room and kitchen of his house. There were two tiny bedrooms too, and a bathroom, but they were behind the living room and the kitchen, invisible to Ramchand's eyes.

He often watched Sudha working in the kitchen. He had seen her there in all seasons, for the past eleven years, sweating and panting over the stove in the middle of summer, and happily making ginger-flavoured tea on cold winter days. He had watched her cutting paneer into neat little squares, peeling potatoes, chopping ginger, slicing French beans, pounding masalas in a little stone mortar, kneading flour to make chapatis with, stirring daal and various curries, boiling milk in a large steel pateela and frying pakoras for her family on some evenings. Sometimes, he saw her dusting the living room. She was a careful housekeeper and she'd thoroughly dust the television, change the bedspread on the divan once a week, and shake out the tablecloth every day. When the fifteen-year-old Ramchand had rented this room, the landlord had been a newly married man.

His young wife was slim and had a heart-shaped face that was somewhat spoiled by a flat nose. Though she wasn't very beautiful – apart from her flat nose, she had a rather short neck and close-set eyes – to Ramchand she was the most attractive woman he had ever seen. She smiled and nodded at him whenever she saw him.

As a newly wed bride, she wore shiny saris that left her beautiful, smooth midriff bare. At other times, she wore embroidered salwaar kameez with bright, sequinned chunnis. She had long hair that she coiled into a loose bun most of the time. She wore sindoor in the parting of her hair, a red bindi on her forehead and kaajal in her sparkling eyes. She wore gold earrings in the shape of flowers. The overall glowing effect enchanted Ramchand.

Her name, he learnt one morning, when the landlord yelled for her to get him his tea fast, was Sudha.

The landlord went to work every day, at some kind of a business, on a blue Bajaj scooter that he had received in dowry. Every evening before his return, Sudha would take a bath, put on perfume, and do up her hair elaborately using a lot of coloured hair clips.

Ramchand often got back a little before the landlord did, and on coming back, the first thing he did was open the back window with a quiet eagerness.

And there, in the courtyard, he would see her sometimes, taking the washing down, her silver payal tinkling at every step she took. Or sitting cross-legged, with a thali in her lap, cleaning rice, or chopping ginger and onions.

For the first few months of her marriage, she wore the bridal ivory chooda on her wrists. Then she had taken it off. In its place, on her right wrist, she now wore a thick gold bangle. A beautiful bangle with two elephant heads facing each other, their trunks raised high as if in salute to each other. She never took this bangle off, and two bright, shiny steel safety pins always dangled from its smooth, warm surface. The curved heads of the safety pins would always be wedged safely between the two elephant trunks.

When her hands and her forearms were wet, after she had been washing clothes or utensils, the bangle gleamed on the wet, golden skin of her arm.

On her other wrist, she wore glass bangles that she changed every day to match the colour of her clothes. When she chopped vegetables or cleaned rice, her bangles would tinkle and strands of hair would come undone from her bun. She would impatiently push them away, tucking them behind her ears.

Sometimes she sat in the courtyard to clip her toenails. Then she'd sit on the charpai, and concentrate on each toe, clipping the nails, according to Ramchand, to perfection. Then her sari pallu or her chunni would fall forward as she bent in concentration over her toes, and Ramchand would stare at the warm place between her neck and breasts – the place where her chains and necklaces rested snugly.

On Sunday mornings she washed her long hair with amla and reetha. Then she would sit in the sun drying it, the back of her blouse alluringly damp, running her slender fingers through her thick locks, while her husband assiduously washed his Bajaj scooter nearby, his pyjama rolled up to his knees.

Ramchand had begun to fantasize about her in his spare time. However, he had very little knowledge of the female body. The little that he had, had been gleaned from pictures in porn books covered with plastic that were sold on the pavements near the City Bus Stand. They usually had grainy pictures of nude white women, frolicking in the sea or kneeling, always with inviting looks on their faces. Once, Ramchand had seen a second-hand foreign colour magazine, in which women were not completely nude, but were pretty close to it. They wore glossy lipstick and their hair was red or gold or some other such impossible colour. But such magazines rarely came his way, and it was the black and white grainy pictures that he relied on the most. The latest he had seen had a picture of a naked white woman with huge breasts looking blankly into the camera, standing by a swimming pool, her legs slightly parted.

From the demure figure of Sudha in the colourful saris to the bare creatures in the porn books seemed like a very long and difficult journey to Ramchand, but he managed somehow.

He came across many women in the sari shop, with its

intense atmosphere of pervading femininity, but it was only the sight of Sudha, fully clothed, doing ordinary household chores, that could inflame Ramchand completely.

There was a tap in the courtyard where she usually washed the clothes. He loved to see her hitch up her sari, or the pauncha of her salwaar, and squat there, calmly scrubbing and rinsing clothes. She always seemed so unhurried, so calm, so different from the demanding customers and the neighbourhood women who were always quarrelling with each other in the streets. Many a time did Ramchand undress her in his imagination, stroking her midriff, touching her alluring pale ankle, running his hands through her long hair, biting her downy neck, unbuttoning the tight sari blouses she wore, slipping his hand under her petticoat . . .

His fantasies made him worry that he was not respecting her as he should. To make himself feel better, he was extra polite whenever he happened to meet her, but continued to fantasize about her when he was alone. But her newly wed self hadn't lasted long. In quick succession she had given birth to three children, two boys and a girl. She named them Manoj, Vishnu and Alka. Ramchand could never see the children playing about without feeling surprised that the slim, young woman he knew had produced all of them so efficiently, with the right number of toes and ears in the right places. The eldest boy, Manoj, had grown up to be a smart, sarcastic child who treated Ramchand with great disdain whenever their paths crossed. At the age of nine and a half, he was capable of completely intimidating Ramchand. No matter what Ramchand said, he was unable to quell the mocking air of superiority that Manoj adopted whenever he spoke to Ramchand. Vishnu was a friendly, boisterous boy. He was addicted to the new songs from Hindi films that played on the radio. He would dance energetically in the courtyard, copying all the dance steps that Shah Rukh Khan and Hrithik Roshan did in their films. Alka, the youngest, resembled her mother. She was a bit of a show off, preening in front of the living-room mirror whenever she had a new frock on, and reciting 'Baa-baa black sheep' in the courtyard loud enough for Ramchand to listen. Her eyes were like Sudha's, so was her flat nose. Ramchand almost felt a fatherly affection for Alka.

The landlord also surprised Ramchand by being very ambitious for his children. He had always struck Ramchand as a dull, uninteresting man. Yet now he was an energetic, eager, committed father. He bought bright-coloured clothes for his children himself – Mickey Mouse lime greens and Garfield fluorescent oranges. He fed them almonds through-out the year and cod liver oil in the winters to improve their brains and prevent colds. He sent them, including his daughter, to an English-medium school. His wife contented herself with cooking meals, cleaning the house and washing clothes, her placid manner intact, while he took over the responsibility of bringing up his children to be successful in the new world that was emerging – the world of English speaking jobs and passports and visas and big companies in Ludhiana, Chandi-garh and Delhi.

And once, when the landlord had come up to collect the rent, he had told Ramchand, 'This money that I take from you every month, this goes straight into a special bank account. Not a rupee will I spend till we have saved enough to move out of the inner city. Then my children can study in an even better school and become something. They will learn to actually *talk* in English, not just write essays and all. Maybe they can even learn to *swim* in a real swimming pool.'

At his words, Ramchand had remembered with a pang his own father's plans of sending his son to an English-medium school.

The landlord's family still hadn't moved, but Manoj could already *sing* a whole song in English.

9

Ramchand was once again sitting on the drawing-room carpet of the Kapoor House, with his bundle of finery. This morning Mahajan had told him that they wanted to see a few more georgette lehngas that came with gossamer net chunnis.

Mrs Kapoor and Rina had just settled down, and he had just opened his bundle when the servant, Raghu, came in and said, 'Memsahib, there is someone to see the younger memsahib. She says her name is Mrs Sachdeva.'

Mrs Kapoor got visibly irritated. 'Really, Rina, now these people have started to come to our home also. We are friends with the highest status families in Amritsar. Even in Delhi, people from top business families know of us. And just because of you, we have these ordinary, professor-type, service-class women coming here.'

Rina looked at her mother coldly. 'Mother, there are other things in the world besides money. You know, this is a big world, and out there, there are people who are considered very high status because of their learning, because of the work they have done. And it is not like this respect, respect from a few small towners, a few crass businessmen. No,' her eyes gleamed, 'it is respect from all over the world, from the academic, cultured world. It is recognition in its true sense.'

'It is wisest,' Rina said to her mother, 'to take the best of both the worlds.'

Then turning to Raghu, she said, 'Raghu, send her in, and please bring in some cold drinks or tea or something.'

Mrs Sachdeva was ushered in. She wore a muted rust and beige silk sari and a thin string of pearls around her neck.

There were tiny pearl drops at her ears and her hair was done back in a plain bun. She advanced to Rina with her hand outstretched. Rina got up, smiling.

They shook hands. Then Mrs Sachdeva said, 'I got your invitation card, my dear. So, so happy to hear the good news. I was passing by and I thought I'd just drop in to congratulate you.'

'Thank you so much,' Rina said. 'It is so kind of you.'

Then Mrs Sachdeva said a polite Namaste to Mrs Kapoor. Mrs Kapoor replied with a tight little smile.

'So, my dear, how are things going?' Mrs Sachdeva asked Rina.

Mrs Kapoor excused herself and went out, telling Ramchand she'd be back soon. That woman, speaking in English *on purpose*, just to show her up, she thought, as she left the room fuming. Well, they didn't even have their own house, they lived in accommodation provided by the college, so she wasn't going to bother about this sort of a woman.

Ramchand sat waiting. Nobody even seemed to notice that he was around. He sat on the carpet with his bundle of saris, watching the two women exchange pleasantries in English. He listened attentively. He should be able to make out everything now. This was like a test.

Now, Rina and Mrs Sachdeva, relieved of Mrs Kapoor's restraining presence, launched into an involved conversation.

'So nice for you, and actually, Rina, I am glad you are not marrying into one of those business families. I mean, I don't mean to be offensive, but a girl like you does need a more cultured atmosphere to explore her potential.'

Rina pursed her lips. Ramchand listened carefully. 'Explore potential' was difficult, but he persevered.

'Well, ma'am, as you know, there have been cloth merchants and jewellers in this old city for years, even before the Partition,' Rina said, 'so it is very difficult to break out of the commercial streak that runs through one's life. There are, of course, what we call the "service class" families. They look down upon us moneyed, uncultured ones, and we look down upon them, for they have no money, no big houses, though I must say that these days, with bribes and all, even they are doing quite well. Most of them have big houses at the outskirts of the city. Also ancestral property, I suppose. Some Sikh families, even the most ordinary-seeming of them, sometimes own quite a lot of land in villages.'

Mrs Sachdeva was listening intently.

Rina continued, 'But the chasm is great. Maybe in my own way, I am seeking to span that gap.'

Mrs Sachdeva gave a pleased sigh. 'Really, Rina, I do admire you. Maybe an MA in Anthropology would have been better for you. You even manage to place *yourself* and your own family in society with so much objectivity.'

Rina smiled. At this moment, Raghu brought in a tray bearing cups of tea and fried cashew nuts in a glinting glass bowl. Rina served the tea, and continued to talk, 'Well, literature and anthropology are closely connected. I just hope I can achieve something. Make sense of things. In our strange, multi-layered society that is a very, very difficult thing to do.'

Ramchand thought he understood some of this, at least the bit about trying to make sense of things, but then the two went into a lengthy conversation, talking about post-colonialism, paradigms of poverty, Indo-Anglian writing, and many other things. All these things went completely over Ramchand's head, he couldn't follow the conversation any more and he began to feel a little sad and sulky. Then he cheered up. After all, he still hadn't reached the letter 'p' in his dictionary. Once he did, he'd probably know as much about post-colonialism and paradigms of poverty as they did.

Then Mrs Sachdeva looked at her watch and said, 'Oh, my dear. I have been here for almost half an hour. Didn't mean to spend so long. And you were in the middle of your wedding shopping, I see,' she said, glancing at Ramchand, without recognizing him as the shop assistant who had sold her so many saris, and had got many a headache in the process.

'I do hope your mother won't be cross with me,' Mrs Sachdeva said, getting up and patting the pleats of her sari.

'Oh, no, not at all. I personally like these spontaneous visits more than formal meetings,' Rina reassured her with a charming smile. 'And you will be coming to the wedding, won't you?' she asked the older woman.

'Of course, my dear,' said Mrs Sachdeva. Then she placed a hand on Rina's shoulder. 'You know, Rina, sometimes teaching can become stagnant work. You ask yourself at the end of the day whether it is worth it, but with a student like you, it has been a real pleasure. I will watch your future progress with great interest. I do hope, Rina, that you will not let the mundane things of life take over the real things.'

'Never,' said Rina, with steely determination in her voice.

Then Mrs Kapoor came in. Mrs Sachdeva smiled at her and said goodbye, and then departed.

Rina resumed the brisk, business-like air that made her resemble her mother, and the two women quickly chose what they wanted. Ramchand cycled back, going over every word of the conversation he had heard that day, trying to fit the pieces together. On Saturday evening, Hari nodded and winked at Ramchand, motioning him to come over to the remotest corner of the shop. When Ramchand did, Hari whispered to him, 'I've got three tickets for *Kaho Na Pyaar Hai*, for tomorrow's matinee show. At Sangam Cinema Hall. They are running it again this week. I don't know why they can't show the latest films, but this one I do want to watch again. You, me and Subhash. Okay?'

Ramchand was about to refuse. Hadn't he resolved not to

waste any more Sundays watching films with Hari? But he *had* been studying his books regularly. It would be a nice break. 'Okay,' he whispered to Hari.

Hari said, 'For the morning show, Subhash and I are going to watch *Gadar*. That is a new release. You want to come for that too? It is supposed to be a super blockbuster. We haven't got the tickets for it yet, though. It is playing at Adarsh. It is too far away to go all the way there just for advance booking. We are just hoping we'll be lucky and will be able to get the tickets when we get there. You want to come for that?'

'Two films in a day?' Ramchand asked, his voice uncertain.

'Yes,' Hari answered gleefully.

Ramchand wavered for a moment and then remembered all his virtuous resolutions. Also, he knew most Sunny Deol films were very violent.

'No, no, both of you go for *Gadar* and then meet me outside Sangam for *Kaho Na Pyaar Hai*, okay? I'll just watch that one.'

'Okay,' Hari said. 'You are sure? *Gadar* is a big hit, and you have already seen *Kaho Na Pyaar Hai* once.'

'Yes, but I have almost forgotten it, I didn't watch it a hundred times like you did. And I really like the songs. And there will be too much violence in *Gadar*. I have seen the posters,' Ramchand said, resolving to spend the morning with his books before he went for the matinee show, so that he could watch the film with a clear conscience.

Hari shrugged, 'Okay, whatever you like.'

The next morning, Ramchand washed his clothes, cleaned up his room, took a bath and then sat down with the essay book. He carefully started reading an essay titled 'Science: A boon or a curse?'

He could read much more smoothly now.

Science has made great progress for mankind, he read. *Because of science, in fields of medicine and technology, there is great progress.*

Cures for many diseases have been found. Day to day facilities are many now, like household appliances. Science has solved many of our problems.

But every coin has two sides.

Science may be a boon, but it can also be a curse. Because of science, there is pollution and there are wars. Plastic bags and gases from factories are spoiling the environment. Toxic things are in our drinking water. So we must be careful how to use science.

One sentence in the paragraph struck Ramchand as very profound. *Every coin has two sides.* There are always two ways of looking at a thing. No one had ever told Ramchand that. According to Gokul, Mahajan, Hari, Shyam, Rajesh, and even the landlord (Chander hardly ever spoke to him), things were either good or bad. This new way of looking at things interested Ramchand very much. In fact, he berated himself – he should have been able to think this out for himself. There were many instances he remembered in the shop, when a particular sari, disdainfully rejected by one woman, would be eagerly pounced upon by another. He should have thought of this then. He had no originality! And what a nice way of putting it, every coin has two sides. He had never heard that before, so beautifully put. He noted down the sentence in his notebook in careful handwriting that was getting better every day.

Ramchand kept a careful eye on the clock. The show was at three in the afternoon. At two, he combed his hair once again, put some money in his wallet to pay Hari for the ticket, then slipped his jar of Zandu pain balm in his pocket, in case he got a headache. Then he locked his room and went downstairs. The mangy dog who lived in the street was sleeping right across his doorstep. Ramchand carefully stepped over him and walked to Sangam Cinema.

The bazaars were closed today. Stray dogs sunned themselves on the roads. A few families from the outer, newer city came in cars to the old city on Sundays, to visit the Golden Temple or the Durgiana Mandir and to later eat at one of the famous dhabas.

But outside Sangam cinema hall, crowds milled around near the ticket window, pushing and shoving. A huge hoarding of the film, in which Hrithik Roshan and Ameesha Patel's faces looked almost vermilion, had been put up outside.

Ramchand tried to spot Hari and Subhash.

He soon saw them both waving wildly at him from the middle of the crowd. He hurried to join them. 'You fools,' he said to them, 'why did you have to go and stand in the middle of the crowd?'

'You are the fool,' Hari said, 'if you think we did it on purpose. The crowd just crawled all over us till we were lost in the middle of it.'

They all grinned and called each other names and clapped each other on the backs, so that the right mood was set to watch the film together.

'Good we have the tickets,' said Ramchand, looking at the sea of fighting humans at the ticket counter.

'Yes,' said Hari, 'we really had to push and fight to get tickets for *Gadar* in the morning.'

'Oh, I forgot, how was it?' asked Ramchand,

'Zabardast! Great film,' said Subhash. 'And Sunny Deol is great, yaar. I really think he might *actually* bash up Pakistanis if he met them.'

'That's why I don't like him,' said Ramchand.

'Why, don't you think Pakistanis should be bashed up?' Hari demanded.

'Why talk of Pakistanis? Let us go and see if they are letting people in now,' Ramchand said evasively.

They were. The three made their way into the dark interior of the cinema hall. The walls were paan-stained, the floor was littered with peanut shells and empty packs of Ruffles chips.

97

The tickets had no seat numbers, so there was a general scrimmage for seats. The three settled themselves in comfortably soon enough and waited for the film to start. Hari sat between Subhash and Ramchand and he took out a bag of groundnuts from his packet. The three cracked open the shells, munching and talking happily.

Subhash and Hari put their feet up on the seats in the front, and Subhash regaled them with stories from the Ladies' Fancy Store.

'One day a woman came in to buy earrings. After a while, another came in to look at some bangles. And suddenly, at the same moment, they caught sight of this lamp shade, bottle green with a gold fringe. And they immediately asked how much it was. And would you believe it, when we told them we had only one piece, they fought each other like mad dogs. We just didn't know what to do. They started calling each other names. I was afraid they'd soon start pulling out each other's hair. And all over a silly lamp shade. Women!' Subhash said disbelievingly. 'They are capable of anything.'

'We don't have fights in our shop like that, do we, Ramchand?' said Hari. 'Must be something to do with Subhash's face. He is so ugly that after you have seen him once, you *have* to take it out on something or someone,' Hari said, giggling. Subhash punched him, and then he began to giggle too. Soon, Ramchand joined in and they laughed hysterically, Hari almost choking on a nut in his mouth.

'And there was this woman,' said Subhash, 'who leaned so far over to look at the hair clips displayed under the glass counter that she didn't realize I could see down her blouse and see everything.'

Hari roared at this, but Ramchand sobered up a little. 'Ramchand is a saint, don't talk like this in front of him,' joked Hari.

'No, I am not,' Ramchand said, smiling quietly, thinking of

Sudha. After all, there was no need to get crass about every woman one saw. For him, Sudha was enough.

Suddenly, the dim lights went off and the cinema hall became pitch dark. 'It's going to begin,' said Hari.

The titles rolled, people began to whistle and stamp. After all, *Kaho Na Pyaar Hai* had been a superhit a couple of years back. Hari and Subhash began to whistle and stamp along with the others in the audience. 'Please,' Ramchand urged them, 'what are you doing? Stop, both of you.'

'What, Ramchand Bhaiya? We have come here to enjoy. Don't we sit quiet and well-behaved in the shop for six days a week?' Hari answered.

Ramchand gave up.

Hrithik Roshan, the hero, played the guitar, he was poor. Ameesha, the heroine, was rich. There was a song where groups of young men and women danced on an ocean liner. All the women had flat stomachs and most of the young men wore trendy caps. Then the hero and the heroine were stranded together on an island, where they admitted they loved each other, and the title song followed. Ramchand sat enraptured. He leaned towards Hari. 'Hari, look at that ocean, so blue, so vast. What do you think it must be like, on an island, vast blue sky, vast blue ocean . . .'

Hari interrupted him, 'Shut up about the ocean, you fool, look at Ameesha Patel's thighs.'

Ramchand tapped his foot to the song, Hari and Subhash sang along loudly. Two women who sat three or four rows in front of them turned back to look at them in annoyance.

'Ay, Hari. Shut up, yaar,' Ramchand said urgently. 'Those women don't like it when men in the audience sing along. They think it is indecent.'

Hari stopped for a moment and said, 'What is your problem, yaar? Are they your daughters-in-law that you are so worried about them?' Hari began to sing lustily again, '*Dil mera, har baar yeh, sunne ko bekraar hai.*' And then the audience stamped and clapped and their voices rose to a deafening roar, '*KAHO NA PYAAR HAI . . .*'

Ramchand gave up again.

In the interval, they had tea and a samosa each. Ramchand went to the toilet. It was stinking beyond imagination. There he took out the jar of pain balm from his pocket and smeared some of it on his forehead, rubbing it in carefully. He had a slight headache.

The rest of the film was exciting too. Hrithik Roshan had been killed by villains, and had reappeared as a double, dancing wonderfully in a night club, wearing clinging black clothes. There were beautiful landscapes – mountains, green lush plains and clean roads that Ramchand loved. God knows where they were, he thought, and which lucky people lived in such places and woke up to such breathtaking beauty every day. When he got back to his room he felt indescribably sad. After the excitement of the film, the lovely landscapes, the catchy songs, the crowds, the room seemed very quiet and lonely. He had declined Hari's offer of loafing about till dinner time and then going to Lakhan's for dinner. Ramchand had said he had a headache and didn't feel like it. Subhash had called him an old woman. Ramchand had smiled and left.

Now he opened the back window and looked down. He could see the cosy living room of the landlord's family. The television was on, the landlord and the children were watching a film. The landlord sat in a chair, the children were huddled together on the divan, a quilt over their knees.

Through the kitchen window, he could see Sudha in the kitchen, standing over a pan on the gas stove. A gold earring she wore caught the light of the gas flame and twinkled on her ear like a firefly. Then, while he watched, she brought a tray into the living room and put it on the table. There were two cups of tea, one for herself and one for her husband,

and tall glasses of milk with Horlicks in it for the children. Ramchand knew it was Horlicks because he had often seen her rinse and dry empty Horlicks jars, and then store daal or salt or masalas in them.

Her warm body was covered in a thick salwaar kameez and she had a brown woollen shawl tightly wrapped around herself. How comforting it must be under that shawl, Ramchand thought wistfully. The landlord warmed his fingers on the outer surface of the cup of tea, before he took a smug, leisurely sip.

Ramchand shivered. The winter air was creeping into his room. He shut the window and sat down. His room felt horribly bare.

10

One day, Chander didn't turn up for work. Mahajan grumbled a little but then left it at that. Chander didn't turn up for the next two days either, nor did he send any message. By the third day, Mahajan was fretting and fuming. He snapped at everybody all morning, and told Hari that an uneducated monkey would do better work than him. Hari later said that one of these days they must ask Mahajan to introduce them to an *educated* monkey, perhaps one with an MA degree. Ramchand got nervous because Hari said this very loudly.

'Be quiet, Hari. You'll just drive him to lose his temper. The way you are grinning! I am sure Mahajan can see all your teeth gleaming from far away.'

Hari laughed and went about his work, singing *Aati kya Khandaala* to himself.

Ramchand was cautious all morning and tried not to catch Mahajan's eye. He crept about quietly, doing his work as noiselessly and inconspicuously as possible. But at the end of the morning Mahajan suddenly called him in his booming voice.

'Raaamchand!'

Ramchand almost jumped out of his skin.

He went to Mahajan, twisting his hands together nervously.

'Yes, Bauji?' he asked Mahajan in his politest voice.

'I'll give you Chander's address, and I'll give you the directions,' Mahajan almost barked at him. 'You go right now and see what that loafer is doing. Ask him if this is his father's shop, where he can come and go as he pleases. Tell him I have asked to see him.'

Ramchand's taut body sagged with relief. He had been sure Mahajan had discovered that he had not cleaned the shelf he had been told to two days before. At the same time, he felt a little sorry for the absent Chander.

Mahajan gave Ramchand directions. Ramchand listened attentively. 'Now repeat the directions to me,' Mahajan said, his voice still angry. 'I want to make sure you have understood all I have said to you. I don't want you to get lost. Then I'll have to send another person to look for you. Soon all of you will be wandering on the streets. Sometimes I wonder whether I am the manager of a sari shop or a lunatic asylum.'

Ramchand repeated the directions a little nervously. One never knew what little word might inflame Mahajan further when he was in one of his unreasonable moods. Mahajan listened and nodded and then Ramchand set off thankfully, not believing his luck. Years of being jailed in the shop, and then suddenly he was having one outing after another. First the Kapoor House, now this. This wouldn't be thrilling, of course, but it was something.

*

Chander's house was quite far from the shop, in the poorer interior of the city. Ramchand walked steadily for half an hour. The further he went into the interior, the more crowded and dirtier the surroundings became.

He turned into a narrow lane at the corner of which a small Hanuman temple stood, hoping this was the temple Mahajan had meant when he had given him directions. Mahajan would be furious if he went back and told him that he had got lost and hadn't been able to find Chander's place. Ramchand turned anyway, and passed the small temple. He could hear a pundit chanting inside and bells ringing furiously. The street was very narrow, a mere crack, as if the old buildings had just split open a little to let people pass. At present, it was full of people trying to squeeze their way past each other. Ramchand found himself edging through this crowd.

A woman with vegetable bags in her hands and a shining excited face rushed past him, knocking him aside with her elbow. Ramchand suddenly stumbled, and instinctively put out his hand to balance himself. His hand accidentally brushed against the breast of a woman who was hurrying by in the street. The woman, dressed in a cheap, bottle-green salwaar kameez and a black nylon chunni, stopped. She turned to him in fury, 'You bastard, mother fucker, can't you see where you are going?' She almost spat the words at him. Ramchand was so shocked that he could neither move nor speak. He just stood there staring at her dumbly. He had been about to apologize. He tried to speak but no words came out. There was something savage about her hardened face. It was deeply lined, though she could not have been more than thirty, even less perhaps. Her body seemed taut with rage. Ramchand continued to stare at her, his mouth slightly open.

Their eyes locked.

She glared at him and trembled with fury, till other people moved on and she was swept away in the crowd. Ramchand stared at her back till she disappeared. Then he walked on. His heart thudded with a vague fear and he felt jittery. He wandered around in the streets for a while, completely disoriented and then tried to get a hold on himself. He stopped at a tea stall. If he had been sent on an errand, he might as well make the most of it, he thought. A hot cup would calm him down. He had one and then had some fresh pakoras that the tea stall owner was frying. They were hot and fragrant and Ramchand felt drowsy as he sat munching them and warming himself in the sun. Then he had another cup of tea.

After half an hour he got to his feet feeling much better, and went on his way, asking people for directions. In the end he found himself again in the street with the Hanuman temple on the corner. He walked on till he was standing in front of Chander's house and was shocked. It was more a hovel than a house. It was a ramshackle structure that looked like it could collapse at any moment. Shop assistants were poor, but they were not as poor as this. Besides, Chander didn't even have any children to support.

And though Ramchand had considered the street he lived in to be the dirtiest he had ever seen, at least the dirty water flowed easily in its open drains. Here, going by the stench, the drains seemed to be blocked, filled with a slimy black sludge.

Ramchand knocked on the door and stood waiting, hoping this was the right house. The door looked ready to fall to pieces. He knocked again and heard raised voices within. He was surprised. He had never heard Chander raise his voice before. He was one of the quietest and gentlest men Ramchand had ever known. Then the door flew open and Chander stood there, looking furious. He calmed down when he saw Ramchand.

'What is it?' Chander asked him, in a slightly apologetic voice.

Ramchand was about to speak when his eyes took in the room behind Chander. Inside, a frail woman lay huddled in a heap in a corner. Red hand imprints stood out clearly on her face. Her hair was dishevelled; her green salwaar kameez was in disarray; her black chunni lay on the floor. Tears ran down her face. A corner of her mouth was bleeding a little. He recognized her as the foul-mouthed woman in the street, the one who had yelled at him. But she looked different now, weaker and broken. The lines on her face seemed even deeper, her eyes more hollow than before. She didn't move or speak. Ramchand averted his eyes.

'They are asking at the shop when will you come?' he said timidly. Chander suddenly seemed like a stranger.

'I'll come. I'll come tomorrow. I am very unwell. Explain to Mahajan. I will definitely come tomorrow,' Chander mumbled. His breath smelled strongly of alcohol and his eyes were bloodshot.

'Okay,' Ramchand said awkwardly. He didn't look at the woman again, even though he was deeply conscious of her, conscious of her as if she was the only living creature in the universe.

'I'll see you tomorrow then,' he said to Chander, turned and walked away. The woman remained huddled in the corner, along with a battered tin trunk.

All that day, Ramchand remained restless.

* * *

In the evening he slipped off alone, not wanting to talk to anyone on his way back. Even though it was early for dinner, Ramchand stopped to have a bite to eat at Lakhan's before he went back to his room. Lakhan was just stoking the tandoor when he got there.

'Sit down, Ramchand, this will take some time.'

Ramchand sat down. There was only one other man sipping tea in another corner of the room.

The tandoor got going at last, and the embers cast a red glow over Lakhan's tired looking face. Ramchand usually avoided conversation with him, afraid that he would start talking of his dead sons. But today he was still thinking of Chander's wife. He wanted to find out if she was all right. Even after he had walked away so callously. Well, what could he have done? She was Chander's wife, after all. He couldn't interfere in Chander's domestic matters. But he still longed to ask someone if she was okay and whether she had stopped crying. So he looked at Lakhan's face, on which pain had left permanent lines, and called out to him, 'How are you?'

Lakhan looked up. He said in a quiet voice, 'It is my son's birthday today. The elder one's.'

'Oh,' Ramchand said and that was all.

He had a cup of tea and ate two rotis with sabzi. He had been having too much tea, he knew that. He didn't smoke or drink. Tea was his only addiction, an answer to everything, to every headache, every thought, every confusion, every scolding from Mahajan. He knew he shouldn't have so much tea. It gave him acidity sometimes.

Lakhan went around the dhaba, attending to things, talking to his helpers, moving mechanically, his eyes opaque like a blind man's. When he came close to where Ramchand was sitting, Ramchand screwed up the courage to ask, 'Is your wife all right?'

At these words, Lakhan's mask-like face crumpled up in an instant.

'No, she isn't. It has been over fifteen years, but she refuses to forget. I come here and make more daal, stir vegetables till I forget, garnish them with coriander, make mint chutney, cook much more kheer than necessary, trying hard to forget, but she . . . she just sits inside weeping, kissing their photographs, remembering each and every incident in their lives. She talks about the time when the elder one took his first step. We were so surprised. We took him to the Golden Temple that evening, to get the True One's blessings. And the time the younger one had some rasmalai. A kid took him to a God-knows-which sweetshop and he had rasmalai there. The same night, he had constant vomiting and diarrhoea. The poor kid couldn't even keep a sip of water down in his stomach. His mother and I rushed him to the hospital. We were almost dead with anxiety. Even after he recovered, we were so careful for such a long time. One of us would get up at dawn to boil water, so that it would be cool enough for him to drink when he woke up. She keeps remembering all these things. So many memories. She doesn't forget and she doesn't let me forget. You know how it happened?'

Ramchand's stomach tightened. He did not want to know. But it was too late to withdraw now. Lakhan continued in the same low, monotonous voice. 'If we had known that morning that the day would have such a terrible end, we would have at least prayed to Waheguru. We would have prayed for Guru Nanak's blessings. But then, what would have been the point? It was in God's own house that He let it happen to our children. Or maybe He was helpless too. Sometimes we get angry with Him, sometimes we even stop believing in Him, but then we get scared. What if the souls of our children are in His care, and our disbelief stops them from being one with the Great One.'

By now Lakhan Singh was completely wrapped up in the past. He continued, 'That day they hadn't gone to the Golden Temple to pray, though. It was just that it was a very hot day, and they hated being cooped up here. We were all getting irritable. I snapped at the elder one because he was singing loudly, that too a song I especially disliked. I thought it vulgar. The hotter he felt, the louder he sang, just to irritate me. The younger one refused to listen to his mother. And in fact,' here a half-smile appeared on Lakhan Singh's face as he remembered the last day of family squabbles, 'my wife and I also quarrelled. The boys had taken their baths, and then what the younger one did was, he took out a new navy-blue turban that I had got for him and started wrapping it around his head. He was only sixteen and turbans were still new to him. I told him, "It is so hot and the turban is so new and starched. Why don't you save it for a special occasion? It will just get ruined with your perspiration." He turned to me and said, "Because I feel like wearing it. I feel like looking good." I just laughed, but his mother said God should have given her daughters instead. At least they would have been more considerate of a mother's feelings, that too on a hot June day. I had to keep going out to the dhaba to see to customers. Well, they kept teasing their mother, making demands for sherbet, asking her why she had to marry me, why hadn't she married a rich man so that they needn't have worried about turbans being old or new. She'd giggle at one thing they said, get irritated with the next, and finally she was ready to pull out her hair, they were bothering her so much, so she said to them, "Since both of you are all dressed up, why don't you go out somewhere so that I can have peace at least for an hour or two." They immediately said they would go to Company Bagh. Their mother said, "No, it is too far away." So the elder one said, "We'll go to Darbaar Sahib then." My wife got really angry then. "So, to you there is no difference between the Golden Temple and Company Bagh, hunh? One is the holiest shrine to us Sikhs, and the other is a public garden, but does it make any difference to these two animals? Oh, no. All you want to do is loaf. Go now." So both of them went to the Golden Temple.'

Here, Lakhan Singh paused. Ramchand could feel the older man's grief physically, but he still did not say anything. He waited for Lakhan to go on. He knew the rest of the story though – the Sikh fundamentalists holed up in the Golden Temple . . . Indira Gandhi's orders . . . the Indian army's siege on the temple . . . they had brought boots in, Sikhs had never recovered from this fact – Sikhs who washed their feet before entering the holiest of their temples . . . the battle between the fundamentalists and the army . . . the countless heart-breaking stories of how innocent people, visitors to the temple, 'devotees', the newspapers had called them, had also been trapped inside . . . Sikhs had just been killed outright, lined up and shot at . . . Eyewitnesses who had escaped somehow reported this, but the army did not admit it officially . . . there were reports later of heaps of bodies being carted away in army trucks . . .

All these fragments came back to Ramchand. He expected Lakhan Singh to recount once more the atrocities that had been committed that day. But Lakhan didn't. In a voice dangerously close to tears, he said, 'My children, they tied back the hands of my children behind them with their own turbans, made them stand in a row with others and then shot them. Along with many others. We didn't even find their bodies. Satwinder Singh, who got away, told us.'

Ramchand sat still as a statue. He did not ask who Satwinder Singh was.

'It was so terrible, especially as my younger son was wearing that new turban. That navy-blue one – crisp and long. And they must have tied the poor boy's hands behind him with it. They must have felt horrible during the last moments of their short lives, the last moments when they knew they were going to die. Oh, so handsome they were. I often told them they looked like monkeys, but they were really very good-looking. And they *had* to die? Why, oh why, didn't they go to Company Bagh that day?'

*

That night when Ramchand took up the *Complete Letter Writer* he could not concentrate at all. He had reached the chapter 'Clubs, Societies, etc'. He started on 'A Letter Requesting Payment of an Overdue Subscription to a Club'. He half-heartedly looked up subscription in the dictionary. *Act of subscribing.* He looked up subscribe. *Pay (specified sum) esp. regularly for membership of organization or receipt of publication, etc.* His eyes could not focus on the words. They followed the shapes slowly and his mind tried to make sense of them. He could feel a headache building up. What was the point of knowing what subscription meant? He had left Chander's wife lying in a broken heap! He didn't know what he could have done, she was, after all, Chander's own wife. But he felt disturbed nevertheless.

And after that, he had even been inadequate in the face of Lakhan's grief, only wanting to run away because he couldn't face Lakhan's traumatic memories.

He had finally interrupted Lakhan in mid-sentence because Lakhan looked like he would never stop. Then Ramchand had asked abruptly for another cup of tea. Lakhan had at first looked bewildered, then hurt, and then his face had assumed its stony mask-like quality again. He had got up quietly and glided away to order a cup of tea for Ramchand, later disappearing into a back door. Ramchand had gulped down the remaining tea, which was almost cold now, holding the glass with unsteady hands. He had thrown down rupee notes on the table to pay for his bill and had then left hastily. He had meant to eat more, perhaps have another cup of tea, he had still been hungry when he left Lakhan's dhaba. But after walking away from Lakhan, he had not felt inclined to go to any other eating place or food stall, and had made his way back to his room quietly.

Why did he always run away? Why couldn't he at least listen, offer consolation, try to make people feel better? Why did he always begin to feel suffocated and inadequate? He was just an uncaring, selfish coward! He had seen it written clearly on Lakhan Singh's unhappy, waiting-for-something face.

Ramchand threw himself on his bed with the *Complete Letter Writer* still in his hands. How could Lakhan guess that he had to leave because he had to, because he had been feeling so terrible that he couldn't breathe?

What a grubby, mean little life he had! Or maybe *he* didn't have a grubby, mean life. Life *was* grubby. Grubby, mean, flabby and meaningless! Grovelling, limited, scared! Sick, sick,

sick! And he was the same too! Just to be alive meant to be undignified, Ramchand thought, his stomach aching with acidity. Because it wasn't just about your own life eventually. What was the point of trying to learn, to develop the life of your mind, to whitewash your walls, when other people lay huddled and beaten in dingy rooms? Or had dark, dingy memories like rooms without doors and windows, rooms you could never leave.

Ramchand opened the *Complete Letter Writer* again, concentrated all his attention on it and tried to block out every other thought from his mind.

The other thoughts tried to squeeze their way back into his head.

Ramchand followed the words in the book desperately. He read the whole letter in one go.

> *The Three Turrets,*
> *Borsfield,*
> *Kent*
>
> *Miss R. Plunkett*
>
> *Dear Madam,*
> *I regret to note that your subscription to the Victoria Tennis Club*
> *is still outstanding.*

Ramchand sighed, sat up in his bed, picked up the dictionary and looked up 'outstanding'. *Conspicuous, esp. from excellence.*

In some confusion, Ramchand read on. *Still to be dealt with; (of debt) not settled.*

He sighed. The meaning brought him no satisfaction.

> *By the club's rules (no. 7), all subscriptions are due on 1 Jan, of*
> *each year and no member is allowed to play on the courts after*
> *1 August, if her subscription is still unpaid.*

(What if his hands were tied behind him, and he knew that he, Ramchand, was going to be shot? How would it feel?)

In the circumstances, I should be glad if you could forward to me your subscription (twenty pounds) by return.

Yours faithfully,
M. Jessop

God alone knows what pounds are now, Ramchand thought in despair, and slammed the book down on his table.

The rage that had been building up inside him just would not quieten down. He finally laid his books, pen and notebook aside, and, for the first time in the past several weeks, spent the evening just lying on his bed staring vacantly at the ceiling.

11

The next Sunday, Ramchand had opened the back window and was sitting on his trunk, with the essay book open in his lap, looking blankly out of the window. He couldn't let himself fall into depression again, he told himself sternly. The world was what it was, and that was no reason to stop learning how to read and write. He, Ramchand, would solve nothing by lying about in an idle stupor. He told himself all this, but his mind kept wandering from the essay book.

It was late afternoon. The shadows were getting longer, the evening chill was already announcing itself in the afternoon air.

In the courtyard below the landlord slept on a charpai, his face covered from the light with one of Sudha's blue chunnis. Ramchand knew this chunni well and loved it. It was a length of soft cotton fabric with tiny yellow flowers on it. She wore it often.

Sudha sat in a corner, her day's chores done, the dinner cooked, ready to be warmed again and eaten in the evening, flipping through the latest issue of *Sarita*.

Vishnu and Alka were laboriously working away at homework, stopping occasionally to fight over an eraser or a pencil.

Manoj sat just below Ramchand's window, with a box of crayons lying open by his side. He had drawn a picture and was colouring it in now, completely oblivious to the rest of the world. He loved getting top marks in everything, so he never let the colour run out of the lines. Ramchand peered down at the drawing sheet that Manoj held in his lap. It was the same drawing he always drew, the same drawing he was taught at school. Manoj never drew anything new. His hands created the same scene over and over again – the safe one, the old one, the one that had been taught to him, the one that got him top marks.

A straight horizontal line halfway across the sheet for the horizon, mountains in the upper half – neat triangles that he drew with a ruler, like upside-down ice-cream cones. Then a hut – a box-like structure with one window, a slanting roof and a brick chimney, a long spindly tree and then a blue strip for a river.

In the end he'd draw a sun in the sky, a simple circle with alternating long and short rays emanating from it.

The only human touch in the drawing was that since Manoj often forgot to draw the sun in the beginning, he had to draw it over the sky, when the rest of the drawing was already finished and coloured in. When he filled the sun in with a yellow crayon, the yellow of the sun would mingle with the blue of the sky beneath.

It resulted in a sun with an uneven texture and a greenish tinge, a sun that looked slightly sick, as if it was going to ythrow up at any moment all over the bright, crayoned world below.

*

Ramchand had decided by now that the letters were completely useless. However, one portion of the book had struck him as lucid and potentially useful. There was a page that listed opening sentences to use to begin a letter with. There was a wide range:

> I am very much obliged to you –
> It was very good of you to –
> I am sorry to say that –
> In accordance with your request –

Enclosed please find –
It is with considerable pleasure (regret) that I –
I have to point out that –

The last two he especially loved. He imagined walking up to Mahajan, combining both, and telling him, 'It is with considerable pleasure (regret) that I have to point out that you are a horrible, fat-faced, money-minded, selfish pig whose wife must be the most miserable and unlucky woman on this earth,' or following it with some other suitably worded insult.

The more ridiculously elaborate and formal the sentences, the better Ramchand liked them. He would try to memorize them, and failing that, he'd try to read them out aloud without halting.

But apart from this, he decided, the letter-writing book wasn't much good. It wouldn't do to be impressed by things just because they were in English, he thought wisely. Most of the letters seemed to be written to and by frivolous, idle people – people much like some of the customers who came to the shop.

And Ramchand didn't want to learn any more about them. In any language.

He knew enough!

*

One day Shyam and Rajesh came in together, as usual, beaming all over their faces. They had just been to a temple or at least to a puja – there were long tilaks on their foreheads. Shyam also held in his hands three identical cardboard mithai boxes with Bansal Sweet Shop written on them.

Bansal Sweet Shop was very far away, on Lawrence Road, and was one of the most expensive sweet shops in Amritsar. They went straight up to Mahajan and handed him two boxes with explanations that no one could hear and smiles that everyone could see. Mahajan smiled too, his rare, out-of-practice smile. Hari was agog with curiosity. 'Look, Mahajan is smiling,' he blurted out in surprise.

'Shh . . .' said Gokul and Ramchand to him in unison.

'I think they are celebrating something,' Ramchand said.

'How brilliant you are, Ramchand,' Gokul said sarcastically. 'I would never have guessed.'

Hari giggled. 'Maybe last night, Lord Brahma came down to the earth from the heavens and finally gave Mahajan a real, human heart,' he said. 'Maybe that's why they are celebrating.'

Ramchand couldn't help smiling at this. Chander, who was also sitting with them, didn't say anything all this while, looking out of the window moodily.

Then Shyam and Rajesh came to where all the other shop assistants were sitting. Shyam undid the thread that was tied around the remaining box. He opened it and offered the box to all of them. It was full of delicious looking pieces of barfi. 'Please, please have a sweet.'

Gokul said, 'Tell us the good news first. Then we'll have one.'

'My daughter, you know, eighteen years old, by God's grace, she is going to be Rajesh's daughter-in-law soon,' Shyam said.

'What slyness!' Gokul remarked in mock-anger, taking a piece of barfi. 'You have done everything and now you are telling us. You do not consider us close enough . . .'

Rajesh laughed and draped an arm around Gokul's shoulders, 'Arre bhai, we have done nothing. No function. Just a puja. We are not like all these big people after all, who will keep having functions the whole week before the wedding. Arre, we have just formally agreed to it. The wedding will take place next year. The pundit says the stars are not right and it won't be auspicious till next year. On the wedding day of course all of you will be invited. Now will you have the barfi?'

Hari asked, 'Why did you give Mahajan *two* boxes of sweets?'

Gokul frowned at Hari, but Shyam answered, unfazed, 'One for him and one to be sent for Bhimsen Seth.'

Hari nodded, satisfied. Ramchand took a piece of barfi too. It melted in his mouth.

Rajesh jumped up. 'It is not complete without samosas and tea. I'll arrange for that.' The whole group cheered up at this. They'd have a nice little snack and, this time, even Mahajan would have to refrain from commenting. After all, marriages were sacred business.

Soon they were all tucking in merrily. Mahajan left them with a benign smile. If a customer came, however, they knew one of them would have to get up and attend to her.

They all laughed and congratulated Shyam and Rajesh. Only Chander remained a little silent and aloof.

Later, when the crumbs had been cleared up, the empty tea glasses had been fetched by the boy from the tea shop, and the excitement had subsided a little, Hari asked Gokul, 'Why does Chander always look so miserable?'

They were now back in their places. Shyam, Rajesh and Chander on one side of the shop; Ramchand, Hari and Gokul on the opposite side.

'I mean, at least when you are having barfi and samosas with good, hot tea on a cold winter day, I think you should look happy,' Hari said with conviction.

'Everyone is not a pig like you. Your happiness depends on nothing but food,' Gokul told Hari.

'And what is wrong with that?' Hari retorted. 'I say, it is a short life, and you never know what happens when. So just eat, sleep, watch films and have fun. While you can. And what more does Chander want? He has a job, no? Enough money for meals, no? Then?'

'You are still young, Hari,' Gokul said wisely. 'You know

nothing of life. Chander has many problems at home. If a man does not have a good family life, what is the use of a job or anything like that?'

Hari considered this. Then he said, 'Even I don't have a good family life, Gokul Bhaiya. My father always scolding me, my mother always after my life . . .'

'Don't be so stupid, Hari,' Gokul said. 'Your father just scolds you when you try to watch two films instead of one every Sunday. And your mother, it is wicked to say that your mother is always after your life, when she packs food for you and stops you from coming to the shop in unwashed shirts.'

Ramchand grew a little morose at this.

Gokul continued, 'You fool, these are not family problems. Doesn't my Lakshmi nag me so much? And doesn't my Munna howl all night without the slightest reason. Hari, all this is part of every family. But Chander has serious problems.'

'What problems?' Hari asked, very curious by now.

'His wife is not a good woman,' Gokul said evasively.

Ramchand remembered the foul-mouthed woman who was Chander's wife. But he also remembered the woman lying in a huddled heap in Chander's house.

'Means?' asked Ramchand, a little warily.

'Oh, there are no other men,' Gokul said hastily. 'Nothing like that. We would have known if there had been. At least till now there haven't been. But who knows with a woman like that? I didn't really want to spread this about her, but now that you are asking, I'll tell you.'

There was a dramatic pause, then Gokul said, 'She drinks.'

Hari gasped at this. Drinking was bad enough, but a *woman* drinking.

'And she has none of the symptoms of being a woman belonging to a respectable family. Doesn't take a bath every morning, doesn't do puja, doesn't wear sindoor in her hair parting. What sindoor? Doesn't even comb her hair. Just roams about. And the language she uses! Tauba, tauba! I can't tell you how I pity Chander. Because she wasn't like this when he married her. I know, I have heard that from a lot of people living around in that area. She changed. Some say she is mad. Had a miscarriage or went for an abortion or something like that and then went mad. But how can that be? Things like miscarriages and all keep happening to women. If all of them reacted like this, what kind of a society would we be left with?'

Hari looked solemn now.

'And that is not all,' Gokul said. 'She has created a lot of trouble for him. She is rude to anybody she feels like. She stops strangers on the streets sometimes, full of drink, and insists that they owe her money. Whenever she sees the pundit of the Hanuman temple close to their home, she calls him a hypocrite and pretends to pick up a stone to throw at him. You know, the way one does to scare away stray dogs. Now tell me, how can Chander be happy?' Gokul sighed. 'A woman should know her place. Maybe she has had difficulties, maybe she has had problems, but it is a woman's duty after all to take care of her husband and his home first, and later think about herself.'

Hari was drinking all this in eagerly. Ramchand listened in silence, remembering the red hand imprints on the face of Chander's wife.

Gokul said, 'And some people say there is nothing wrong. She is just one of those nasty, evil women – a devil in the guise of a woman. Women in that neighbourhood shield their children and especially their babies from her evil eye. She never prays. Never even smiles.'

'Why doesn't she smile?' asked Ramchand in a low voice.

'Says Chander gives her no money, there is nothing to eat at home and what not,' Gokul said in impatient dismissal. 'She doesn't even get any work at people's houses, cleaning or cooking. She is so foul-mouthed. What decent family would let her inside the four walls of their house?'

Every coin has two sides – the sentence suddenly came back to Ramchand. Maybe even more than two, he thought grimly.

12

Rina Kapoor's wedding would always be remembered in Amritsar as the Grand Affair where forty different kinds of desserts were served.

There had been so much talk about it that Ramchand was dying of curiosity. When Mahajan went to the Kapoor House himself to settle the bills, he was graciously given an invitation card for the wedding.

Mahajan came back and showed it to Shyam and Rajesh, 'An invitation to the Kapoor wedding,' he explained, unable to keep the pride out of his nonchalant voice. Shyam and Rajesh had been visibly impressed, examining the expensive-looking card from all angles. Then, with Mahajan's permission, they passed it around. 'Imagine how much each card must have cost,' said Gokul. 'It is shiny, like the paper of those foreign magazines.'

It was. When Ramchand took the invitation card in his hands, he was very impressed. It wasn't just expensive-looking, it was beautiful. The card was made of thick, firm silver paper and had a large, flamboyant 'Om' embossed on the front in a brilliant blue. Inside the letters were printed in English, cordially inviting everyone to grace the auspicious occasion with their benign presence. Ramchand ran his fingers over the letters, happily noting that he could read almost all the English words on it. He noted the date, time and venue.

Hari was very excited, 'All the top people of Amritsar are going to be there. Will you go, Bauji?' he asked Mahajan.

Mahajan shook his head sadly, 'I won't be able to. My nephew is getting married on the same day. Must be an auspicious day, there are weddings in many families on that day. I won't be able to go to the Kapoor House. You know, my nephew's father, my brother, is dead, so I have to be there.'

Everyone nodded with a look of understanding sympathy.

Hari cleverly put in, 'You are like a saint, Bauji. Always duty before pleasure.'

Mahajan looked pleased and went downstairs, while Hari nudged Gokul slyly and everyone laughed.

*

On the day of Rina Kapoor's wedding, Ramchand thought about it all morning. Mahajan had taken the day off for his nephew's wedding. 'Must be stuffing his fat face with pakoras and samosas and sweets, while we work on an empty stomach in this tomb-like shop,' said Hari. Since he had been eating alu tikkis all day from a paper bag and hadn't done any work, determined to make the best of Mahajan's absence, no one paid him any attention. However, Gokul did tell him that it was important to respect both your instrument of work, if you were a craftsman, and your place of work. He said it could be very inauspicious for Hari to call the shop where he earned his living a tomb. At this Hari muttered rude things under his breath against the shop and against Mahajan and against 'that bloodsucker Bhimsen Seth', and then went out to buy warm groundnuts. Gokul began to say all sorts of uncomplimentary things about Hari, more out of habit than any real rancour.

Ramchand was still wondering about the wedding at the Kapoor House. He hardly heard what Gokul was saying.

In the evening Ramchand had a stroke of good luck. Gokul had been complaining of a headache all day and by evening he said he was feeling a little feverish. When Ramchand was wrapping up some saris that an irate customer had pulled out while looking for a sari with a thin border, Gokul asked him, 'Ramchand, will you do something for me?'

'What, Gokul Bhaiya?' Ramchand asked him, concerned, noticing the pinched, drawn look on Gokul's face.

'Do you think you can take my bicycle home with you today? And bring it back tomorrow? Because my head is almost bursting. I think I might have a fever coming on. Though the headache might be entirely because of that idiot Hari and his monkey chatter.'

Ramchand smiled. He knew that, despite his sharp tongue, Gokul had a soft spot for the cheeky Hari.

Gokul rubbed his temples with both his forefingers and said, 'I think I'd better take a rickshaw and go home. Is that all right with you?'

'*I* will take the bicycle, Gokul Bhaiya. You don't have to worry about anything,' Hari offered, with the air of one making a sacrifice for a friend.

'Certainly not, Hari,' said Gokul. 'I want my bicycle in one piece tomorrow. Will you take it, Ramchand?'

Ramchand agreed readily. Soon after, Gokul departed gloomily in a jolting rickshaw, groaning and complaining. Hari wandered off, looking disappointed. He had been hoping he could borrow the bicycle and ride to a kulfi stall a couple of miles away that sold creamy, cold kulfi with almonds and pistachios embedded in it, served with soft, white falooda.

It was when Ramchand was done for the day, had gone out of the shop and touched the gleaming handle of Gokul's bicycle that he knew he just had to go and take a peek at the Kapoor House. Just a little peek! The temptation was too great to resist.

He rode Gokul's bicycle all the way to the Kapoor House in Green Avenue. The sun had set. The bazaar was closing. Shop owners were downing their iron shutters and making for their homes. Ramchand was enchanted by the evening.

The sky was not completely dark yet. A faint, smoky golden haze left over from the day still hung in it. Streetlights were on; vegetable and fruit vendors had hung oil lanterns over their little carts and stalls. Piles of red tomatoes, purple brinjals and green capsicum shone in the light from the lanterns. Excitable housewives and middle-aged men were haggling at each of these stalls, knowing that it was easiest to get good bargains at this time of the day.

Ramchand rode on, a quiet excitement and a sense of well-being flooding through his heart.

*

He reached Green Avenue and turned into the lane where the Kapoor House was situated. And he was mesmerized by what he saw. At the entrance of this lane, a gateway made of flowers had been erected. Marigold, roses, jasmine flowers and green leaves were entwined in invisible threads to completely cover an iron frame that made the gateway.

The overpowering smell, however, was that of the marigolds, and it brought back a whiff of a memory. For a moment, Ramchand was transported to his barely remembered childhood, to the memories of a smiling face with a big red bindi and a leaf-shaped nose-pin, the smell of marigold petals in his hands and the sound of big brass bells ringing on happy Monday mornings.

He stood there dreamily for a while, his mind uplifted into a euphoric daze and then he cycled on. Every wall, every tree, every bush in the neighbourhood had been decorated with fairy lights. They twinkled and glimmered at Ramchand. For a moment, he felt that *this* was real, and the stuffy, dirty, inner city was just something his own diseased mind had conjured up. When the gentle breeze shook the leaves on the trees, all the tiny lights trembled slightly.

Even the road had been cleaned. Ramchand peacefully rode right up to the house.

The house itself was lit up brilliantly. All the entrances were draped with strings of flowers. In the park opposite the house, huge red and white canopies fluttered grandly in the slight breeze. Beautifully dressed people wandered around, flitting between the house and the tents. Even though it was early, long, sleek cars had already begun to line the road.

Ramchand stopped and got off the bicycle. He wheeled it along slowly, enraptured by all he saw. Suddenly, somebody stopped him.

'Hey, who are you?'

Ramchand was suddenly brought down to earth.

It was a security guard.

Ramchand looked at him with resentment. He knew he wouldn't have been stopped if he had been well dressed and prosperous looking. Then he saw that the security guard had some sort of a weapon tucked in his belt, and Ramchand began to stutter. 'I – actually –'

Big drops of perspiration immediately appeared on his forehead.

The guard was waiting. Another guard came up and stood beside them.

Ramchand tried again, desperately looking around for something to say. Then he finally said, 'You see . . . Rina Memsahib –'

The guard who had appeared later quickly said to the other, 'Better take him to Rina Memsahib and ask her. She might get angry otherwise.'

Without a word, Ramchand was steered towards the gate of the house by the hefty security guards. He started to sweat profusely. What would happen now?

*

Rina stood in front of the long mirror, feeling satisfied. She had been very apprehensive about what the Amritsar beauticians could do with her on her wedding day. Finally, her anxiety had driven her to fly in a beautician from Delhi. The beautician was a thin woman with cropped hair, and ran a beauty salon affiliated to a five-star hotel in Delhi. She was addressed as Dolly. Dolly had worked on Rina's clothes, hair and face for the past five hours and had now gone to take a ten-minute rest, before coming to work on Tina.

'Thank God!' said Rina, addressing her sister, who was sitting on the bed behind her, in a pale green lehnga that was far more expensive than it looked. 'I was so afraid that these people here in Amritsar would ruin my looks. Imagine my wedding pictures, showing my cheeks red with rouge, three necklaces hanging around my neck, shiny scarlet lipstick and garish eye shadow.'

Tina nodded. 'Yeah, they are such fools. No standard.'

Rina was, indeed, looking different from most brides. The lehnga she wore wasn't from Sevak Sari House. It was designed especially for her by a famous fashion designer based in Bombay. In designing the rich maroon lehnga, the designer had delicately incorporated silk, net, brocade and real gold thread to produce a magnificent outfit.

Instead of the usual numerous strings of gold, she wore a single handcrafted gold necklace, exquisitely made and beautifully embellished with rubies and diamonds. Matching earrings flashed at her ears, and a matching tikka hung from her centre hair parting, lighting up her forehead. Expensive kaleere hung from the chooda that was made of real ivory. Two days ago, a Rajasthani mehndi-wala had made a lovely henna design on her hands, reaching almost to her elbows. She had also covered Rina's delicate feet and ankles with the same design. The exquisite henna patterns were made of flowers, peacocks, leaves, palanquins and other motifs that the Rajasthani woman had learnt from her own grandmother.

Today, the mehndi shone brilliantly.

Dolly had applied matte make-up to Rina's face. Her eyes were expertly highlighted. Her hair was slicked back into an elegant knot behind her neck, just the right shape for a pallu to be draped over.

Yes, Rina felt satisfied.

She had prepared for her wedding day in her own way, ignoring most of the instructions her mother and other female relatives had given her.

There was a knock at the door. Tina went to the door and opened it. The maid stood outside, dressed in a bright fluorescent pink sari with a gajra of jasmine flowers in her hair. 'There is someone downstairs who says Rina Memsahib invited him. The guards want to confirm it with memsahib.'

'Tell them to wait in the hall. I am coming downstairs,' said Rina, her attention on the mirror again.

This was very irregular, and the maid knew it. But she did not dare to say a word, for Rina Memsahib had quite a temper. When she was angry, she could say cold, hard words dripping with sarcasm and didn't mind who she insulted in the presence of others.

Usually, brides sat coyly in a room, surrounded by giggling girls and having their pallu and jewellery adjusted and re-adjusted by matronly women, who did this along with a stream of advice for a young bride.

But none of this for Rina Kapoor! She prided herself on being a modern, enlightened young woman. She had insisted on being alone, with only her sister and the flown-in Dolly for company. She also had asked all the domestic help and the security guards to come to her if in doubt, instead of bothering her mother, who was busy receiving the wives of VIPs. The maid nodded and left.

After a few minutes, when Rina had finished adjusting her jewellery and her pallu till she was completely satisfied, she swept down the stairs and went to the hall, where Ramchand stood trembling flanked by the security guards and the maid. His ears were red and he felt immensely humiliated. The maid chewed her nails and stared at him with open curiosity. A heady smell of jasmine flowers pervaded the huge hall.

'Yes?' Rina Kapoor asked, knowing well that she looked striking.

One of the guards spoke, his hand still tightly gripping Ramchand's elbow. 'Memsahib, he was downstairs. He says you invited him.'

'I am your sari-wala,' Ramchand quickly blurted out in fear. Rina looked puzzled for a moment, failing to recognize him, but finally an amused smile began to play on her lips.

'And I invited you, did I?' Rina asked, still smiling. Ramchand did not reply. He did not like the way she was smiling. But then she surprised him by turning to the guards suddenly and saying, 'Yes, I did invite him.'

At this, the two guards left Ramchand standing there and quietly slunk away. Rina looked at Ramchand. He stared back at the gorgeously decked-up bride, completely dazzled. She gave a quiet laugh, turned and went back upstairs, the hem of her lehnga sweeping the marble staircase regally.

*

And so it came about that Ramchand ended up enjoying Rina Kapoor's wedding thoroughly. He didn't speak to a single person. He just wandered around taking in everything, sipping a glass of a cool green drink he didn't know the name of. He nibbled at paneer pakoras that hired waiters in smart black and white uniforms were carrying around on trays. He also had many delicate looking things that he didn't know the names of, delicious little things that you picked up with a toothpick stuck in them. Finally, when the baraat came, he stood at the back of the welcoming crowd, craning his neck to catch a glimpse of the groom on the horse. At the head of the wedding procession there were wildly dancing relatives, then came the groom on his horse, with a little decorated silk umbrella over his head.

For a long time, the dancing and the welcoming continued, gifts were exchanged and Ramchand watched tirelessly.

Then the baraat was welcomed into the red and white shamianas for dinner. Ramchand heard someone say that the mahurat for the actual wedding ceremony was for very late at night, and only close friends and family would stay on for it. Ramchand thought that he'd better eat now, with the baraat and then leave soon. It would take him a good half an hour to cycle back.

So he entered the fluttering red and white shamianas too. More delights were in store for him. Guests were being welcomed with a sprinkling of rose water. The tents had been used to create a large hall. Chandeliers sparkled at you when you looked up. Ramchand couldn't get over it. Chandeliers in a tent! Flowers had been strung around everywhere. Rina had refused the usual red throne-like chairs on which a couple sat before and after the actual wedding ceremony. Instead, an old-fashioned swing as big as a small bed, covered with red silk, stood in the place of honour. A makeshift water fountain completed the decor. The guests were offered delicacies on silver platters.

The dinner was even grander. Wine and meat were not served, for the Kapoors were strict vegetarians and teetotallers. The food, served in intricately carved metal dishes, was lined up on long tables covered with crisp white tablecloths. The dishes had little fires burning under them, fires just small enough to keep them warm. Ramchand was mystified. How did they do that? The china plates that the guests were given were warm and clean and dry, accompanied by pretty white paper napkins with floral blue borders. Ramchand wondered what one did with these beautiful pieces of folded paper. He decided to wait and see what the other guests did. He was so intimidated by the spread before him that he couldn't taste everything. He helped himself liberally to fragrant pulao and a few other things that he couldn't identify.

Ramchand was surprised to see so many people he knew. Or rather, so many women who bought saris from Sevak Sari House. There was Mrs Gupta, in that beautiful emerald green sari she had bought a few months back, with her new glimmering daughter-in-law in tow, who was covered in jewellery. Mrs Gupta was introducing her to everybody. The daughter-in-law was greeting everybody warmly. There was a fixed smile on her face. And there was Mrs Sandhu, though she was wearing a shimmering pink salwaar kameez. Well, but she was a sardaarni, so that was natural. She was talking volubly to another woman who looked like a sardaarni too. The two passed Ramchand on their way to the table to refill the table, and Ramchand overheard Mrs Sandhu say in an anxious voice, 'And, you know, there is so *much* syllabus, such fat books, and Manu is getting dark circles under his eyes. He works so hard. I hope he gets through. His life will be made. Just if he gets through these exams, he can live comfortably for the rest of his life . . .' Her voice trailed off as the two women passed out of Ramchand's hearing. Mrs Sachdeva was there in a plain beige silk sari that he still remembered her buying. Oh, that awful episode! She was wearing glasses and was talking learnedly to a tall, bald man who somehow did not look as if he belonged to Amritsar. Maybe he was a visiting professor. And there was Mrs Bhandari with her handsome husband, in that peacock blue-green brocade that she had bargained for till even thick-headed Mahajan's head had begun to ache. Ramchand stared at everyone. He was a little surprised to see all these women and their saris here. Somehow, to him, it was astonishing that the women and the saris existed beyond the shop, beyond his sphere. The shop, his whole existence, where things began and ended for him, was only the starting point for these people. While he just sat displaying saris to customers, they bought them, wore them and *did* things wearing them.

He looked around. Hari had been right. The cream of Amritsar was present here. Ramchand suddenly became aware of his scruffy shoes, his smelly feet, his silly striped shirt and his uncombed hair. He began to eat more hurriedly. He knew that it was unlikely that any of these people would remember him, but just in case somebody did, and mentioned it to Mahajan . . . He shuddered to think what would happen.

At the end of the dinner, he was shocked to see people wipe their dirty hands on the beautiful paper napkins, and then, regardless of the blue floral border, crumple them up and throw them away. Really, these people had no sense. Maybe this was the done thing, but couldn't they see how thin and fragile the paper was, how intricately made the little flowers were, how soft the napkin was to touch. He slipped his own napkin into his pocket.

Finally, the forty desserts were served. A hush fell over the gathering when dinner was cleared away and the forty desserts were set out on the tables, in big dishes. Ramchand tasted three, and then, feeling full, excited and a little confused, cycled back home.

*

Three days after Rina Kapoor's wedding, Ramchand had a surprise. It was a quiet morning and he was sitting in the shop talking to Hari. Hari had watched *Gadar* for the second time, and he was telling Ramchand the whole story, scene by scene. Ramchand was completely absorbed.

In the middle of this, Rina Kapoor came into the shop, alone.

Ramchand was astounded. Brides never ventured out alone for months after their wedding! They had to be present at post-wedding ceremonies, there were invitations to lunches and dinners, special pujas had to be performed. He had heard of how things worked in families. But this was surprising. And she was wearing a plain yellow salwaar kameez instead of bridal finery. She wasn't decked with jewellery either. She was just wearing diamonds, not the multiple strings of gold that newly wed brides wore. He usually disliked all that glitter, though he thought that Sudha had looked beautiful even when she was a newly wed woman indiscriminately covered with all the jewellery she owned. But then, Sudha was different.

Ramchand sat dreaming and gaping. He saw Rina's large alert eyes dart around the shop quickly, and stop when they spotted him. She headed straight towards him without hesitation. Ramchand panicked for a moment. She had kept quiet on her wedding day, maybe she had come to complain about it today. She would denounce him to everybody. She would tell Mahajan that he, Ramchand, had dared to turn up at her wedding uninvited. She would insist that he be sacked right now.

These thoughts made Ramchand's palms sweat. Meanwhile, she came and stood opposite to him, quietly, looking straight at his face.

'Namaste,' Ramchand stuttered.

'Namaste,' she said in a low voice, with the same amused look on her face that he had seen last time.

'Saris, memsahib?'

She smiled again, enigmatically. 'Okay, show me some saris,' she said, sounding as if she was giving in to a request of his.

Suddenly, Mahajan appeared at the top of the stairs and rushed towards her energetically. 'Madam, I saw your car and driver down below. Please sit down. Why did you bother to come all the way? You should have just called up and we would have gladly sent anything you needed. Ay Hari, get some Coca-Cola for Madam. With a straw. Make sure the glass is clean. Sit down, I'll show you saris myself. Ay Gokul . . .'

Rina held up a haughty hand. It immediately stopped the stream of words gushing out of Mahajan's mouth. He looked at her respectfully, his face silent and enquiring.

She pointed to Ramchand. 'What is his name?' she asked.

'Ramchand, madam,' answered Mahajan.

'Let him show me the saris. In peace,' she said pointedly. Mahajan took the hint and went away, looking puzzled.

Ramchand was completely confused. She had come alone, she had been married only three days, people didn't buy more saris after just three days of their wedding, she smiled without any reason, she looked as though she knew something about him, a secret about him, that he did not know himself.

Ramchand turned to the shelves and then remembered he hadn't asked her what kind of saris she wanted.

'What sort of saris, memsahib?' he asked her.

She threw her head back and laughed, a throaty laugh that went well with her voice.

'Silk saris,' she said, after composing herself.

Ramchand took out the saris and showed them to her. Rina hardly looked at the saris, just throwing quick, perfunctory glances at them. Instead, she talked to Ramchand. She asked him questions about himself, where he lived, how much he earned, was he married, etc. Ramchand answered politely. But then she started asking him other things, his opinions on different issues, his tastes, his emotions. Ramchand quickly grew uncomfortable. It was the first time that a woman was asking him such personal things, and that too such a magnificent woman, and it flustered him completely. He went red, he grew awkward and garrulous, he said things he didn't mean, he left sentences incomplete midway, hoping she'd understand what he meant.

She continued to look amused. Hari came up with a tray, bearing a clean glass of Coca-Cola and a straw in it. She accepted the glass and put it down on the floor by her, but left it untouched. She seemed to listen intently to him. This bothered Ramchand because he knew he was blithering away, speaking utter rubbish.

In the end, she thanked him graciously, picked up a blue and black silk sari randomly, gave him an intimate, amused smile again, paid for the sari and left in the long sleek grey car.

Mahajan came up to Ramchand when she had left. Ramchand expected him to be annoyed because Rina had sent him away, but he was beaming all over his face.

'Very good, boy, very good. You must have made a good impression on them when you went to their place. That's the way to keep customers coming back. Very good, very good.'

He spotted the untouched glass of the cold drink.

'Didn't she have that?' he asked Ramchand, pointing towards the glass.

'No, Bauji, she did not even have a sip.'

'Then you finish it up, Ramchand. Finish it up,' Mahajan said, still looking happy. 'You deserve it.'

Ramchand smiled, and Mahajan went downstairs, rubbing his hands together gleefully.

No one was watching. Ramchand took up the glass that she had held with her beautiful white hands, put his mouth to the straw, and drank it all up, blushing furiously.

PART TWO

I

Spring had come and gone quickly, as spring often does. The balmy, fresh air scented with the spring flowers had given way to the dry, dusty heat of May.

Children had put away their kites because the rooftops from where they had exuberantly sent their kites flying into the sky during the spring months now baked inhospitably in the hot summer sun.

The air in the fruit markets became fragrant with the heady smell of ripe mangoes, and housewives set hard to work pickling the raw ones. Huge jars of pickled mangoes discreetly appeared on sunny terraces and courtyards, put out in the sun to process.

Days became longer, and tempers grew shorter. People longed for the rain to come, but there wasn't a cloud in the blazing, clear sky. Water evaporated from the drains, leaving behind a sludge that stank. The few ponds at the outskirts of Amritsar dried up too, and lethargic buffaloes sunk deeper into the squelchy mud in the ponds, only their eyes showing as the cool mud slithered over their hot, black bodies.

The roads became dusty, and the faces of cyclists and pedestrians took on a permanently weary look. There were frequent power cuts every day. All over Amritsar people grew tired and cross, or sluggish and resigned. Mothers snapped at noisy children, mothers-in-law fought with young daughters-in-law, junior workers in shops, offices and factories got yelled at by their superiors all over the city.

Quiet families slept on dark, still terraces at night during power cuts, their shared memories swirling overhead in the hot air along with the swarms of mosquitoes. Old women sat on charpais, fanning themselves with jute fans and murmuring prayers with rosaries held in perspiring, wrinkled hands. An air of oppression hung over the whole city. Even the wealthy – and there were many in Amritsar – were driven to a frenzy by the brief forays they made out of air-conditioned houses and cars into the hot, dry, baking world outside.

In the afternoons only unhappy, perspiring vendors with ice cream carts, rickshaw pullers slumbering in their rickshaws in the shade of trees and panting stray dogs with their long tongues hanging out could be seen on the deserted roads that smelt of hot tar.

*

Chander's house had a tin sheet for a roof, and it became as hot as fire after the May sun had beat down on it even for an hour. The sun turned the little house into an airless furnace. It was here that Chander' wife sat one hot morning, her thin body soaked in sweat.

Her name was Kamla, even though everyone in Sevak Sari House always referred to her as just 'Chander's wife'. Once Kamla was a child, with a straggly plait of hair hanging down behind her neck, a thin body and big, inquisitive eyes. She lived in a small house in Jandiala, a tiny, nondescript town, little more than a village, about twenty kilometres from Amritsar, with her mother, father and a brother. Her brother was older than her, he was thirteen when she was only eight. Her father worked in a small factory – a factory that manufactured a local brand of washing powder called Chamki Washing Powder.

After her father left for his factory, and her brother went to the tailor's shop where he worked as an apprentice, Kamla's mother went to work in people's houses, to cook and clean for them. Sometimes Kamla went with her and helped her a bit.

At the age of eight, Kamla owned only two frocks. Both the frocks were old ones outgrown by the children of her mother's employers. One was a red and blue check, with pockets in the skirt and the other was a bedraggled pink, with some torn white lace at the collar and at the hem.

Kamla was supposed to do all her chores on her own, though her mother washed Kamla's brother's clothes, made tea for him and cleaned up after him. But she told Kamla that girls must learn all household work, and the sooner they started, the better it was for them. So, in serious imitation of her mother, once a week, the eight-year-old Kamla would squat near the tap and scrub both her frocks, rinse them, wring them dry till they were almost knotted up, and then would hang them out in the sun to dry. She personally liked the red and blue check better, even though the lace of the pink one always made her feel grand, like all those girls who lived in big houses and went out in cars and bought those chocolates in purple wrappers. Still, she did like the red and blue check better. It had pockets you could put things into, it looked newer than the pink one, and it looked much, much brighter and more cheerful. Kamla wore both frocks strictly by turns – one day the pink, the next day the red and blue check.

It was on the day of the red and blue check that Kamla's mother died. Kamla was alone at home with her mother. It was evening, and they were preparing to cook dinner.

Kamla had just learnt to peel potatoes. She was sitting on the floor peeling them with a blunt knife, because her mother still didn't trust her with the sharp one, and talking to her mother at the top of her voice. Kamla's mother had climbed up on a stool to get a jar of pickle from the top of a cupboard.

'And then, Ma, Ganga said Mina always cheated. She said the stone was at the edge of the chalk line, but Mina moved it with her foot. But, Ma, I *saw* her. She didn't. Do you think *Ganga* could be lying? I don't think so. Ganga never lies, but maybe she was mistaken. She is always so sure of herself. Ma, I think . . .'

Her mother stood on tiptoe on the stool, trying to reach the jar. She kept nodding, Kamla kept chattering on, without bothering to wait for her mother's replies.

'Ganga's sister, who got married, came back and gave her a silver bangle, Ma. A *real* silver bangle. It is so pretty, it has got tiny ghungroos on it, they tinkle when she moves. And Ganga keeps moving her arm about *on purpose* while talking, just to show off to us . . .'

Then Kamla's mother finally managed to get her fingers around the jar. She grasped it gingerly and pulled it towards her, saying, 'Here it is. Now, I think, for dinner, along with the potatoes and chillies, we can . . .'

Here, she tottered on the stool, her face a little startled, her eyebrows raised, still clutching the glass jar tightly. Then she suddenly slipped, the stool fell over on its side with a thud, there was a loud crack, and Kamla's mother fell silent. A pool of blood formed slowly under her head. The glass jar of pickles had broken too. A film of mustard oil began to spread towards the blood. The two mingled. Pieces of pickled lime and carrots were strewn around in the blood-oil puddle like pebbles. Kamla sat there quietly, her mouth slightly open, frozen, staring at her mother, with a half-peeled potato in her left hand, the blunt knife in the right and curly potato peels on the floor.

Her brother found her sitting there in the same position when he came home two hours later. He took in the sight, the shock making the bile rise in his throat. He took the knife out of her hand, and sent her to call their aunt, his father's sister, who lived close by.

At first Kamla wouldn't move, then, with his voice choking

with tears, her brother gave her a gentle shove, 'Go, Kamla, go. Go and fetch Bua. Tell her what has happened. She will come here. Then I'll go to the factory and fetch Pitaji.'

Kamla went by the familiar route to her Bua's place almost in a daze. After she got there, she kept repeating that the pickle jar broke. Finally, she started crying. Bua shook her shoulders and asked her what had happened. 'The pickle jar fell down,' Kamla repeated, 'and Ma with it.'

Bua came back to Kamla's place with her. The next few days passed in a daze for Kamla. Her father and brother seemed distant, busy making arrangements for the cremation and the puja. Meanwhile Bua was very busy too, seeing to the meals and beds of the relatives who had come to mourn. Kamla had to help her all day, cutting vegetables and folding bedclothes while her eyes and heart ached every moment. Her Bua told her, 'Now, after your mother, you'll have to look after the house. You'll have to take care of your father and brother, okay? Behave like a big girl now.'

Kamla nodded.

She began to go to work in place of her mother. Like Kamla's mother, Bua also earned a living by cooking and cleaning at big houses. Now she took Kamla under her wing and took her to the places she herself worked in. Kamla was quick to learn – she was nimble while sweeping the floors, she reached with the broom under beds, almost lying down on the floor to reach the far off corners, she cleaned behind sofas and under carpets. She cleaned kitchen shelves well, rubbing at oil and gravy stains with wet rags till they disappeared. She cleaned out kitchen sinks, carefully removing bits of food crumbs and salad leaves that blocked the jali over the sink drain. She chopped onions, ginger and tomatoes and left them in neat piles, covered with steel plates, for the housewife to use when she cooked lunch. Her employers were pleased with her and soon she began to bring in a hundred rupees a month.

She also did all the cooking single-handedly for her own household.

She continued to alternate her two frocks strictly, till she outgrew them and graduated to wearing salwaar kameez.

When she turned fourteen, her brother married, and his wife, anxious to secure her position in the house, took over the kitchen, relegating Kamla to the status of an assistant.

Bhabhi decided now what was to be cooked, she kept an eye over the provisions and cooked things her own way. Kamla went back to chopping, cutting, cleaning and doing the odd jobs that Bhabhi asked her to do.

*

At sixteen, when she married Chander, Kamla had been a pretty girl with lively eyes, cheerful most of the time, but given to occasional strange sulks that her family never understood. She had moods when she wouldn't talk to anybody. Then she'd just hum to herself or embroider flowers on plain leftover poplin that her brother sometimes got from the factory of ready-made garments that employed him as cutter and tailor. When she was in one of these moods, she wouldn't answer any questions, not even with a nod or a gesture. It annoyed her family very much, but it was pretty harmless, so they let it pass most of the time, putting it down to the instability of adolescent girls. She'd be all right after she got married, they reasoned.

Kamla could cook very well by now, and went to three different houses to work, cooking daals and vegetables, boiling rice and cleaning utensils efficiently every day.

Now she earned four hundred rupees a month. Apart from this, she got cast-off clothes occasionally, one meal a day at the big house painted white and one cup of tea at the pretty house with magenta bougainvillea climbing its gate. From each of the houses she would also get an extra twenty rupees every Diwali, and a few sweets. Sometimes she'd even bring home a couple of left-over chapatis with two pieces of oily dark-green mango pickle wrapped in them.

One day when she was sweeping the floor of one of the big houses, Kamla spotted a pretty red glass bead on the floor. It shone and had two holes at its opposite ends to string a thread through. Kamla's right hand that held the broom went still. With her left hand she picked up the bead, still squatting. She held it up to the sunlight streaming in from the window. It glinted. Kamla smiled.

Her employer, a good-natured woman who spent most of her time watching the films played on the local cable channel, looked up from the television and asked her, 'Ay, Kamla, what are you smiling about?'

'This bead, Bibiji, it is very beautiful. Too beautiful.'

The woman smiled. 'Oh, that? That is just a cheap thing. My daughter bought a boxful of them to make necklaces for her dolls. She has finished now. The silly things she does. Never studies. I don't know what will become of her. These days even to get married you need a BA degree.' Then, coming back to the bead, she asked Kamla. 'The rest of them are still lying around. They'll just clutter up the place for years now. Do you want to take them home with you?'

Kamla nodded. The woman got up slowly, went to a cupboard and brought back a cardboard box. She gave it to Kamla.

Kamla opened the box. A mass of luminous red beads filled the box, their glass surfaces smooth and shiny.

'Thank you, Bibiji,' Kamla said happily, clasping the box to her chest, her eyes shining.

'Happy?'

'Yes.'

'Then mind you scrub the clothes well today. The white shirt wasn't cleaned well yesterday.'

'That was a turmeric stain, Bibiji. They never go out, no matter how hard you scrub.'

*

That evening, Kamla was stringing the red beads together with a needle and thread when her father returned home from the soap factory. Usually he came back tired and quiet and rarely spoke to anyone till his daughter or his daughter-in-law had made him a cup of tea. But today he put down the three-storied steel tiffin box that Kamla packed for him every day, and called the whole family together. Her brother had just got back a few minutes before. He came to his father anxiously, hoping it was no financial crisis, followed by his wife who was now cradling a baby in her arms. Kamla sat where she was, with the needle, thread and the beads still in her lap. Then Kamla's father told his assembled family that today he had fixed up Kamla's marriage with the son of a man who worked with him. Kamla's brother smiled, her Bhabhi came and hugged her and everyone looked happy. Kamla smiled indifferently. She had been expecting this to happen any day now. It didn't affect her one way or the other. Every girl was brought up to know that marriage had to happen one day, and Kamla was quite prepared for it.

Then her father and brother began to discuss the arrangements for the wedding while Kamla and her Bhabhi retreated to the kitchen to make tea. Kamla was silent, as it was only proper to be silent, and her Bhabhi gushed on about many things that Kamla barely listened to.

Later, when everyone had settled in for the night, she went back to stringing the glass beads in the light of the bulb. Marriage happened to everyone, red beads rarely came one's way.

However, the storm broke a week before her marriage, when she found out that the man who was soon to be her husband, the man she had never seen and wasn't particularly interested in, lived and worked in Amritsar. She'd have to move there.

Kamla dissolved into tears the moment she heard this. She wept and told her father she wouldn't marry. Her Bhabhi tried to console her, but Kamla pushed her Bhabhi's comforting arms away. Her father told her gently that she shouldn't say such things. Everything had been finalized and she should just make up her mind to be a good wife.

Kamla calmed down; she knew he was right, but she continued to worry. She had assumed that Chander, for she had heard that was his name, lived in Jandiala too. She had never been outside Jandiala, and the prospect of living away from her family, all on her own, in a strange new city, was frightening. She had had very little contact with the outside world. Except for the people she worked for, the only people she knew were her family and the relatives who visited them. Her father had been careful to isolate her from the evils of the big world. He had always been afraid that in the absence of a mother, Kamla might run wild or pick up bad ways.

The small house was her real world, the safe world that she returned to every day after work. There were two small rooms. Her brother lived with his wife in one. They had recently had a baby boy and needed a room to themselves. The other was little more than a hole in a wall, with just enough space for her father's single bed and a pitcher of water. Kamla slept in a corner of the kitchen. She had a string cot there covered with a green bedspread that sometimes doubled for a shawl. Under her cot, she kept a tin trunk that contained all her worldly possessions.

This was her world, with all the familiar objects comfortingly in place. And now it would all disappear to be replaced by new things. Instead of excitement, this prospect only brought fear.

Her parents as well as Chander's parents would continue to live in Jandiala.

She would be all alone in Amritsar with a stranger. In a new, strange house.

She lay awake night after night, repeating these two sentences to herself over and over again in her mind till her head ached. Then one night she got tired of worrying. Nothing could be done about it, and anyway, girls had to adjust. She turned over in her bed and went to sleep.

*

And so, one fine morning, Kamla got married to Chander.

Later, the thing she could recollect most clearly about her wedding day was the smell of laddus everywhere.

Yellow, sweet laddus piled into neat pyramids on steel plates, being offered to gaudily dressed guests, being stolen by the children in the neighbourhood amidst suppressed giggles, being given to gods as offerings and being packed in red cardboard boxes to be given away to relatives.

A little girl even smuggled in a laddu for Kamla to eat on the morning of the wedding, when she sat in the inner room, the one where her Bhabhi and brother slept. Kamla was dressed in red, examining her henna-decorated palms. The day before her Bhabhi and some girls from the neighbourhood had mixed mehndi in a small steel bowl. Then her sister-in-law had, with the tip of a matchstick dipped in the mixture, made perfect circles in the centre of both her palms and had filled them in. Then the girls had taken turns, giggling all the while, to fill in each of her fingertips with mehndi. The mehndi had stained her palms a nice, dark orange. Her fingertips flamed too, but she wished her sister-in-law had thought of a more imaginative design. When the little girl brought in the smuggled laddu wrapped in a dirty hanky, Kamla took it absently, but was too nervous to do more than nibble on it. There was a smell of laddus everywhere, in the air of the house, in the worn green bedspread on her string cot, in her clothes, in the tiny smoky kitchen, in her hair.

The only other clear memory she had was that of tearfully requesting her aunt to let her wear her red glass beads around her neck on the wedding day.

Her aunt had firmly refused.

'You will not wear these, Kamla. What will people think?'

'But, Bua, they match *exactly* with my kameez,' Kamla said, almost hysterical. She was wearing a plain shiny synthetic red salwaar kameez that her brother had got cheap from his factory. She had bought a plain chunni, got it dyed a matching red and had then herself sewn golden gota at its edges to make it look bridal. Later Bhabhi had also sewn on some cheap golden-coloured sequins that she had bought. Kamla looked very pretty with the glittering chunni draped over her head, but she was still hankering after the string of glass beads.

'I badly want to wear it. Please, Bua.'

'No, Kamla, you will just wear the thin gold chain that your mother left behind and the gold earrings that your father has got made especially for your wedding. It may not be much, but it is enough for people like us. What will people think if you wear glass beads on your wedding day?'

'Bua, if I wear my own glass beads and go to Amritsar, I'll feel better. I'll feel I am still me,' said Kamla, incoherently, close to tears.

'What rubbish is that? Of course you are you. See, Kamla,' Bua said, her voice gentler now, 'all girls get jittery on their wedding day, but you be good now. Calm down and listen to your elders. You are going to become a responsible housewife now. Don't act like a child.'

'But, Bua . . .'

'Enough, Kamla, don't create trouble now. Be a good girl and be grateful for all that your father has done for you. Your father might be poor, but you are not a road-sweeper's daughter that you will wear glass trinkets on your wedding day.'

Bua was not to be persuaded and Kamla gave in.

She remembered little else about the day.

Kamla came to live in Amritsar with Chander, bringing all her belongings in her old tin trunk. She had packed the two new saris that her father had bought, the few salwaar kameezes and saris that her employers had kindly given her, all her underclothes, blouses and petticoats, her comb, her mirror, the new sindoor and bindi packs and the homemade sanitary napkins.

All this was packed under Bua's supervision and according to her instructions.

After Bua left, Kamla had opened the trunk again and had packed more things in surreptitiously.

So she also brought to Amritsar her precious string of red glass beads, her two childhood frocks – one pink and one red and blue check – in case she had a daughter, the new tube of Fair and Lovely that she had saved up for the last two months to buy, an imported brass safety pin and an old Chinese silk scarf that one of the ladies in the big houses had once given to her. She also brought with her the firm belief that turmeric stains did not go, no matter how hard you scrubbed.

2

Kamla had started out on her new marital life in the same way that all the girls she knew of did. She wasn't expected to go out and work now that she was married. She was expected to bear children soon, and Chander told her there was no point in starting on a job that she'd have to leave soon anyway.

'You can always start to work when the children grow up a bit. Till then we can manage. I am not *that* poor,' he had said to her.

So every day, Kamla cooked meals, washed clothes and cleaned her new home, a tiny, one-roomed house with a tin sheet for a roof. Chander said they would move into a better place soon, as soon as he had saved up some money. And there was the Diwali bonus coming up soon.

Chander did not have much money, and had long working hours. He went to the cloth factory where he worked early every morning and came back late at night. She had to scrimp and save a lot, but she was used to it. Things hadn't been much different at her father's house, except that she had never been alone there. Kamla became an economical housewife. She darned holes in old clothes, repaired and strengthened their seams, hemmed frayed edges. She carefully stored used cooking oil instead of throwing it away, and reused it a couple of times. She recycled every little bit of scrap cloth and paper that she could. She prepared all the meals without using too many spices, left garlic out completely and at the end of every month found that she had saved a little by all her efforts.

But somewhere down the line, something had gone wrong.

She had begun to brood, had begun to be tired of her life. Chander drank often and beat her up. This was pretty common, she knew. Men often beat up their wives. It was a matter of routine, nothing personal. It shouldn't have worried her.

But it did. It turned her temper sour. She would do her housework alone in the house all day, scrubbing, chopping and cleaning with a frown creasing her forehead, encased by the gnawing solitude of the small house, its tiny window bringing in only a gloomy grey light.

The whole day would pass in working at chores that seemed to grow more pointless each day, and watching the light change from dull grey to a slightly brighter grey at noon, and then dull grey again, when evening fell. Darkness would follow. Then she'd switch on the small bulb on the wall. Exposed wires ran from the bulb to the switchboard.

She'd cook dinner and start to wait for Chander. He'd stagger in, drunk, after midnight sometimes. Either he'd quietly fall into bed and go to sleep, or he'd pick a fight with her and beat her. Later, he would comfort her and caress her, but with a slurred voice and clammy hands.

Six months after her marriage she received the news that her father had died. Her brother had called up the factory where Chander worked. He had left a message with Chander's boss, who wasn't too pleased that Chander had given out the phone number to his relatives. Chander had immediately returned home, told Kamla the news, and before she had fully absorbed it, put her in a Punjab Roadways bus that jolted all the way to Jandiala. He gave her a twenty-rupee note to take with her.

She had got off the bus expecting to see her brother or one of her relatives there, but there wasn't a single familiar face in the crowd at the bus stand. With great trepidation, and for the first time in her life, she took a rickshaw alone, all by herself, and went to her father's house. Chander joined her a day later.

A month later, her brother lost his job at the Chandrika Readymade Garments factory. They had got in some new machines and needed fewer skilled cutters and tailors now.

He spent a frustrating two months looking for another job, but all the factories were full up already. He moved to Jalandhar with his wife and young son. His wife's brother had promised to help him get a job there. After moving to Jalandhar, he never contacted Kamla again, fully absorbed in his new life. Kamla pretended to herself that she didn't mind, but she did realize that she had forever lost the only home she had ever known.

Now Chander's house would be her home for the rest of her life. Every day of her life would begin and end there. Kamla became lonelier and quieter.

*

And then Kamla got pregnant. She previously had no particular idea about maternal longing and saw pregnancy as another thing that happened to you, like marriage. She had been completely indifferent to the prospect of being a mother.

She had never imagined that it could make her so happy. Her world seemed to change overnight. It became newer, fresher and the gloom that had settled on her for the past year lifted. She smiled to herself sometimes while she worked. She began to look forward to having a child of her own. She knew she would never be bored or listless or lonely again once the child came.

She began to be more interested in things around her. She would stand at the door sometimes and watch the dirty white cow that lived in the street nose for food in the garbage pile opposite their house. Or she would watch the neighbourhood children draw chalk patterns in the middle of the street to play hopscotch in, scattering like disturbed sparrows every time a bicycle squeezed its way through the narrow street.

Or she'd intently listen to women fighting over the Municipal Corporation tap. A few days after her wedding, Kamla had accidentally discovered the secret of the tap. She had woken up feeling claustrophobic at dawn. The room reeked of alcohol and sweat, and she had rushed out of the house, swathing her shawl around herself. She had turned on the brass tap hopefully, and there had indeed been some water there, with which she had splashed her face before going back in. No one knew the tap leaked water at that hour, and she had kept her secret. Now she always filled her green plastic bucket at four in the morning, so that she wouldn't have to stand in a queue in the sun with hordes of other women at nine in the morning. When the tap spluttered to let out a thin trickle of water into her bucket, she stood near it, a shadowy figure in the darkness, feeling grateful to the Municipal Corporation for this lapse.

Kamla began to settle down. When she sat on her doorstep sometimes and looked out at the busy people, the chattering groups of women with full lives, she wondered if she could try and make friends with some of them. Maybe they'd talk to her, even though she was an outsider. Maybe she would be able to become part of the community. And after all, who would her child play with if she didn't try? She should start now.

But none of this worrying and planning turned out to be necessary after all. In the third month of her pregnancy, Kamla had a miscarriage.

Chander was away at work at the time, and Kamla panicked when she found the red clots between her legs and realized what was happening. She rushed out, walking to the main road with quick steps. She took a rickshaw alone, all by herself, for the second time in her life, and told the rickshaw-wala to go to a government hospital, the cheapest hospital he knew of. She sat with her legs clenched together, weeping bitterly throughout the bumpy ride to a hospital about two kilometres away.

She felt angry with her mother-in-law for being absent, she felt furious with her own mother for being dead, and she hated Chander for leaving her alone every day. She wept and wept, hating everyone, the feeling of wetness between her legs increasing frighteningly every moment.

In the hospital everything was cold. The antiseptic smell was cold. The faces she saw were cold. People were dressed in a cold, mourning white. The wetness between her legs was cold. The metal stretchers painted white, carried around by blank-faced, indifferent attendants, were cold.

Terror followed her through the crowded hospital corridors. She made her way through the sickening smells of medicines and blood and through the sights of mangled people waiting for treatment. Patients and their relatives who had come from adjoining villages slept, ate and talked in the waiting area, in the corridors, they even spilled into a small storeroom full of stretchers. Some had urgency on their faces, others had faces that had become stiff with waiting. With tears running down her cheeks, she asked urgently who she could see. No one took her seriously till an attendant saw traces of blood at her ankles, below her sari. Then she was shown into a large ward full of groaning people. A man was gathering old, bloodstained bandages into a basket. Kamla felt like throwing up.

In the ward she was quickly made to lie down and was examined by a rude doctor – a thickset woman with a wide jaw whose breath smelt of onions.

Kamla was admitted and discharged from the hospital on the same day. Intense pain and complete terror blinded her to what was going on around her. Hands touching her . . . blurred faces hovering around . . . coldness . . . These were the only things that registered. Before she left, still understanding very little of what had happened, just aware of a pain in her abdomen that intensified whenever she moved her legs, the doctor told her briskly that she had lost her baby and would never conceive again. She didn't explain further, muttering something about ignorant village people before impatiently moving to the next patient.

Kamla paid the bill with the money she had been saving out of the household expenses. She came back in a daze, in another rickshaw, looking at the alien city around her with unseeing eyes. That evening, she waited for Chander impatiently.

He came late, even more drunk than usual. She told him everything, gulping to steady her voice – a voice that didn't break down once, though it trembled often. She longed to cry but she wanted to tell him first. Then she'd cry and cry on his shoulder and he would comfort her.

He listened intently with a glazed look on his face.

Then he told her that he was devastated. He didn't mention her miscarriage. Instead he rambled on in a slurred voice about how they would soon be on the streets. It was after he had continued to ramble on in this strain for about five minutes that Kamla gathered what he was talking about. Apparently, he had lost his job. The factory where he worked had been incurring losses and was closing down. He hadn't been paid the last three months' salary. He had no money. In fact, he owed people money.

And then Chander told her in an even, toneless voice, his slurred speech suddenly becoming clear, 'You have been very unlucky for me, Kamla. Ever since I married you, I have been having nothing but bad luck.'

There was a pause. Kamla stared at his impassive face in horror and disbelief.

'You are unlucky even for your own family,' he said, his words senselessly washing over her ears.

Then he raised his voice, 'You have a black heart, a black heart, a black heart,' he repeated, close to breaking down, tears in his bloodshot eyes. 'You killed your mother. You ate up your own father. Your brother lost his job. Now you have eaten up my child. Soon, you will also devour me.'

Tears trickled down Kamla's face, her lips still and silent, her eyes stony.

'I should have known. The first day you stepped into this house, you brought ill luck with you. On the very first day after our marriage, I dropped my mother's photograph while moving it from the shelf to make space for your things. The glass broke. Do you remember, Kamla?'

She shook her head dumbly.

'You don't even remember,' he said in disgust. 'The glass broke and cut my finger. I should have known then. It was inauspicious. It was a bad omen.'

Then Chander started to cry, and fell to the ground with his hands folded. He wept, he called aloud to the gods, asking them why they had ruined his life by marrying him off to a black-tongued witch. He slobbered. Saliva covered his folded hands. He was completely drunk.

Kamla continued to stare without saying a word. Her tears dried up. Then she absently got a tumbler of water for him. She watched him drink it up in one go, watched his throat contract and expand as the water went in, waited till he had drained the glass. Then she took the empty tumbler from him. She laid it aside without washing it and went to lie down on the string cot. She was asleep in an instant, utterly exhausted.

The next morning, Chander was cold and silent. Kamla didn't get up to make tea or cook anything. She just sat on the bed, sunk in silence. Chander didn't ask for food either.

But before leaving, just as he was about to go out of the

door, he turned to her and said savagely, 'Your child was dead. Your husband was dying. But you slept like a queen all night.'

Kamla said nothing.

*

Chander often kept a bottle of cheap rum at home. Though he usually drank sitting outside small liquor shops with some of his friends from the factory, he thought it was a good idea to keep a bottle at hand, tucked under the charpai or standing in a corner with the broom. Occasionally he would get up at night and take a few gulps from the bottle.

Kamla started by taking swigs from this bottle. She would drink just a little bit, and to make up for it, she would fill the bottle up with water, making sure she dried the outside of the bottle and the cork with one end of her sari pallu.

Then she started to take a few coins from the pocket of Chander's shirt when he hung it up before going to sleep. She'd wait till he was snoring and then creep up silently to the hook where his shirt hung. She would fumble in his pocket and take the smallest coins, so he wouldn't miss them. If he grunted or turned in his sleep, she would go still as a statue, and wait till she heard his snores again.

When she had collected enough, she would go and buy a bottle of country liquor from a local liquor maker. Chander would spend all his days away from home, looking for work. It didn't occur to Kamla that she could also look for the kind of work she had done before her marriage. She spent all her energies on planning how to procure the next bottle.

She developed a cunning that she never knew existed, hidden tucked away inside her somewhere. She managed to supply herself with country liquor even while their finances dwindled alarmingly and they came down to having just one meal a day.

Chander would return home frustrated each night, usually drunk, and he would fight with her, slapping her face and throwing her against the wall before flinging himself on his bed. He didn't notice the drunk state Kamla was usually in, he didn't notice her secret smile when her head struck the wall hard – a smile that would have scared a normal, sane man. This happened day after day, till her forehead got hardened with bumps.

The news that Chander had got another job at some sari shop hardly registered in her stupefied, drunk mind. Chander accused her of not being happy for him. She just looked back at him unblinkingly. Chander couldn't guess where the pretty, cheerful girl he had married had disappeared to, and who this stony-eyed monster was.

One day Chander came back early from the shop. The months of stress, drinking and missed meals had taken their toll. He had felt dizzy and had almost fallen headlong down the steps. After taking a look at his ashen, weak face, Mahajan had told him to go home early.

Chander came back to see the door of his house swinging open on its hinges. He entered his house and discovered Kamla sitting on the floor with the bottle in her hand. Chander was speechless. She looked up at him and then went back to her bottle. Genuinely shocked that a wife of his should be actually drinking, Chander beat her up more harshly than usual. Then he went to sit at the Hanuman temple, trying to keep his tears from flowing on to his cheeks.

After that Kamla had begun to drink openly. She became bleary eyed and foul mouthed. She stopped cleaning the house, she stopped praying to the small clay Shiva idol in the corner – the one to which she had once so lovingly offered flowers every morning, she stopped taking baths. Her saris became filthy, the house stank and Chander's face took on a haunted look. She soon had dark circles under her eyes, her face became pale and worn and her hair started to fall in thick lumps. And she wept and drank, and Chander beat her every day, usually breaking down himself later.

The more Chander shouted at her, the more she smirked at him. The more he beat her, the more she drank. She fell quiet and he rarely heard her speak of her own accord.

She had the destiny of many others like her, yet for no known reason (she wasn't even educated), she had trouble accepting it. She was beginning to realize that there were other things, apart from turmeric stains, that did not go away no matter how hard you scrubbed. She was full of bitter poison. And when this poison mixed with alcohol, rage and recklessness filled her.

Then, with the alcohol-laced anger coursing like fire through her blood, she would sally forth into the world with red, angry eyes, abusing and swearing at everybody. A resigned beating at night from Chander would fail to dilute this poison and soon made her even more of a savage animal.

She snarled at cars on the road if they didn't slow down long enough for her to cross. She snapped at those men on the streets who, taking advantage of her drunken state, tried to paw her.

Once she even shouted at the pundit in the nearby temple who touched both his ears whenever he saw her, apparently praying for mankind's salvation despite the existence of women such as her. She shouted out what she thought of him and his little ways. She yelled that he was getting fatter on the coconuts and rice that devotees offered at the temple. Though the pundit always reacted with self-righteous indignation, he was also scared of her wild tongue that uttered such embarrassing things for the whole street to hear. She'd also pretend to be picking up a stone to throw at him, which would scare him and make the watching children laugh. Kamla became a disgrace to the whole neighbourhood.

Chander was relieved when he had got a job at Sevak Sari House, but he refused to tell Kamla where he worked, in case she decided to come and have a brawl with Mahajan.

Chander shuddered at the thought.

He had cut down on his own drinking now, though he couldn't help the occasional relapses. He was happy to have got this job and meant to keep it.

Soon Chander began to ignore Kamla completely. He left her alone, in whatever state she was in, and went about living his own life, buying most of his meals at dhabas and food stalls.

He and Kamla hardly spoke to each other any more.

*

Today, Kamla had had more to drink than usual. She sat alone on the floor of her dirty house, completely drunk, weeping and hiccuping.

The floor was littered with unwashed clothes. Dirty utensils in a corner had started to give off a rancid odour. Kamla hadn't taken a bath for the past three days and she smelt rancid too. There were rashes on her skin because of the heat, her hair was dishevelled and her eyes were wild.

Random thoughts ran around in her head. And out of these random thoughts, one coherent thought was emerging.

Yes, she knew whose fault it all was.

She wouldn't let them live in peace. The familiar anger coursed through her body and she struggled to get to her feet.

3

In Mrs Gupta's house, Shilpa, married happily for five months now, had just found out that she was pregnant.

When Shilpa had entered the household five months back, she had done so with all the usual apprehensions of a new bride. Her husband Tarun would be okay, he had a big factory and was tall, healthy and good looking. And anyway he and her father-in-law would be away at work all day.

It all boiled down to her mother-in-law, Mrs Gupta. Would there be the usual problems – the bullying, the power tussle, the kitchen politics?

And even if there weren't, how was she going to measure up to Mrs Gupta? For the lady had the local reputation of being wise, witty and a woman of the world.

And Shilpa had few illusions about herself. She had scraped her way through school and one year of college uninterestedly, awaiting the wonderful marriage that her parents would arrange for her as soon as possible. Not that school and college mattered – hardly any of the girls from the high up business families were interested in studying, but Shilpa knew she fell short on other counts. She didn't have the sharp wit or the talents of some of her cousins. She wasn't stunningly beautiful. Her hair was slightly thin, and worst of all, her English wasn't good. The biggest thing in her favour was that her father was a well-known, rich businessman. She had known they would find a brilliant match for her.

And they had, indeed! They had fixed up her marriage with Tarun Gupta. He was the elder son of the Gupta family and she knew that she couldn't have got a better deal. They were a well-known family and her cousins had said, after taking a look at him, that he looked a little like Salman Khan. She had met him once when he had come to visit her with his mother. They had talked desultorily for about five minutes, and both had then complacently and officially accepted each other.

The wedding had been a lavish one. All the big industrialists of Amritsar had been invited, including Ravinder Kapoor, who had told the Guptas that his own daughter, Rina, was getting married in three weeks' time. He wasn't very pleased about it, because it was a Love Marriage, and his daughter had chosen to marry a *Captain in the Indian Army*. Ravinder Kapoor still couldn't believe it, but he had tried not to let his disappointment show. As he told everyone, he had enough money for two families, even for six families. What mattered was that his daughter should be happy. She was a brilliant girl, you couldn't expect her to be the wife of a businessman and sit at home all day, he said proudly. Shilpa's parents winced at this but no one dared to contradict him. He said he'd make sure Rina maintained the lifestyle she was accustomed to, even after she got married.

At the wedding party, many deals had been finalized and many business contacts had been made by the guests. So, all in all, it was quite a success.

Shilpa's parents had given Tarun a white Opel Astra, and had got an interior decorator to do up the couple's bedroom at their own expense. The decorator had done it up in the latest fashion, copied from a magazine, in cream and pale pistachio green. The bedspread and the curtains were also in the same colours. Wall-to-wall carpeting, a luxurious sofa with the cream and green coloured cushions and a wrought iron table with a glass top completed the décor.

Shilpa's parents then also had a new air conditioner installed in the room. It sucked all the heat out of the room, leaving it neat and cold.

And all this – the room, the furniture, the air conditioner and the car, were in addition to all the cash, jewellery and clothes they had given to Shilpa, and all the gifts of clothes and jewellery they had given to her in-laws and to her husband. Yes, she had no reason not to be able to hold up her head in her new family.

But still, when it came to a mother-in-law, one never knew . . .

But Shilpa needn't have feared anything. Mrs Gupta was too shrewd to start an unnecessary feud with her daughter-in-law. She had seen too many bickering households where constant disharmony took its toll on all the family members.

Instead, she treated Shilpa, as she often told her friends at kitty parties, like a daughter.

She instructed Shilpa in everything – clothes, make-up, behaviour, recipes. She was kind and sweet to her, at the same time keeping a sharp eye and an iron control over how Shilpa looked, dressed and behaved. Shilpa recognized this, but accepted it. It was better than many other things that she had known to happen between mother-in-law and daughter-in-law.

Besides, Shilpa knew that sooner or later, the elder Mrs Gupta would grow old, and then the factory, the house, all the property – it would all be hers.

So the two settled into a fragile relationship in which the equation had to be balanced constantly, with a touch here, a gentle nudge there, a small disagreement here, and a gratified smile there. They began to understand each other, and though the wariness remained, and was indeed, to always remain, they spent their days together amiably enough. Once the husbands had been sent off to work, maids had come and left and meals had been cooked, they'd settle down to watch the reruns of the soaps on Star Plus. In the commercial breaks, they would make cups of tea and gossip.

Mrs Gupta had a competitive streak in her. She liked to be the best. In her circle of friends and relatives, she liked to have the best complexion, the cleanest house, the nicest clothes. And she passed on this competitiveness to the previously inert Shilpa, galvanizing her into a new life of self-improvement.

The duo had to outdo every other woman they knew. They tried new recipes, and then sent around food in little steel tiffin boxes to neighbours as a 'good gesture', accepting the compliments graciously. They tried out new combinations of homemade face packs while they watched *Kyunki Saas Bhi Kabhi Bahu Thi*. Mrs Sandhu had a glossy skin and they wondered what she used on it. They went for long walks together to keep their stomachs flat, eventually landing up at sales of Chinese goods, where they bought pretty Chinese lampshades to make their drawing room look exotic.

*

This morning, Shilpa had cooked pasta for breakfast. She had taken Mrs Singh's Continental Cooking Classes for four months before her marriage. She had been anxious to impress the Gupta family with her pasta.

Everyone had loved it.

Then she had cleared up the breakfast table while her mother-in-law supervised the maid who came in to clean every day.

At the last moment, just before leaving for the factory, Mr Gupta said he felt a little ill. 'Maybe I am coming down with something,' he said uncertainly. 'Maybe it is the flu that is going around. I don't think I'll go to the factory today.'

His wife hadn't looked too pleased. In fact, she had looked slightly disbelieving, but he had avoided making eye contact with her.

Mrs Gupta had sighed. His presence would hamper their usual routine, she knew, but nothing could be done about it.

Then the woman who came in to cook lunch and dinner, wash the dishes and do other chores in the kitchen, arrived. Mrs Gupta accompanied her to the kitchen.

Shilpa, meanwhile, made beds and dusted the delicate crystal and china ornaments in the house that no maid was allowed to touch.

After this, and after taking some tea for her father-in-law to his bedroom, Shilpa had retired to her own bedroom. She had tidied it up and then she sat down on the bed with a pile of her husband's clothes in front of her, and began to fold them, one by one. She loved to spend as much time in this room as she could. It was so comfortable. Her parents had spared no expense in doing it up.

*

It was while she had been sitting there sorting through Tarun's Arrow shirts that the doctor had called her mother-in-law to tell her the result of the tests. Mrs Gupta had rushed up to her daughter-in-law to tell her, beaming all over her face.

Shilpa was surprised, even though she had been half-expecting it. She smiled back at her mother-in-law and the two women hugged each other.

'I'll go and tell your Papaji now,' Mrs Gupta told her. 'We'll have to have a long talk about this later, Shilpa,' she said, patting her shoulder, giving her a fond smile.

'Yes, Mummyji,' Shilpa said, her shy smile accompanied by a blush. She was mildly glad at having achieved the next state expected of her.

Shilpa fervently hoped it would be a boy. That would forever consolidate her position in the family.

*

When Mrs Gupta went back downstairs to tell her husband, who was now sleepily watching a show on Zee TV, Shilpa went into a reverie. How did one behave when expecting a child? What would she be expected to do? A special diet of course, and a woman to come in and massage her legs gently every day. She had enough female cousins to know that. But what else? In her parents' family, they had the Godbharai ceremony. She wondered if they would have it here. If they did, then she'd get new clothes, a couple of jewellery sets . . . it had to be a boy . . . that would make things a lot easier for her . . . she didn't want a daughter . . .

She kept thinking with pursed lips, her hands deftly moving over the pile of her husband's clothes, till she heard a shout from below. It sounded as if it came from somewhere near the front gate. Shilpa got up, walked to the window, pushed away the green curtain with cream tassels at the border, and looked down.

An uncouth-looking woman with dishevelled hair, obviously belonging to a lower class, stood at the front gate. She wore a cheap purple nylon sari with big, white flowers on it. She was glaring up at the windows of the house with red, baleful eyes, looking a little like a rabid dog.

'You are responsible for all this. You are responsible for our misery,' she shouted loudly, very loudly, her ugly face contorted with anger. 'You think you can live in peace now?'

Shilpa felt bewildered. Who was this woman? Shilpa made sure she peered from a crack in the curtain, without letting herself be seen.

Then the woman standing below abruptly started swearing, shouting out every word that Shilpa had either never heard before, or that had been mentioned in hushed voices by the older women in her family as an example of the words that were *very* bad. Words that good girls never spoke. And here was this woman, shouting them out for all the neighbours to hear, shouting them at her in-laws' front gate.

Shilpa hurried downstairs anxiously to where her in-laws Mrs and Mr Gupta stood, looking agitated and uncertain. The driver was out. The servant had gone to the market to buy vegetables. The shouts outside rose even higher. The woman was even jangling their gate. Then there was a pause and a fresh stream of abuse.

'Guptas, hunh? Big Name, hunh? Just beggars you are. You are like the jackals that feed off the carcasses of dead animals. You are worse than us.'

'Do something,' moaned Mrs Gupta to her husband. 'Oh, please do something. *All* the neighbours must be listening by now. Who *is* she? What does she want? Do something.'

Her husband went outside and shouted at the woman from a safe distance. 'Hey, who are you? Go away. Go away.' Then, seeing that many neighbours were out, on terraces and balconies, listening for all they were worth, he retreated.

Kamla continued to shout. 'May God burn all of you up in that big house or that big car of yours. May you die thirsting for a sip of water.'

When he came in, his wife was on the phone, frantically dialling her son's number at the factory, her face drained of colour. She found the number engaged.

'Your son is also a villain. Will your grandson be also the devil? Do any of you have human blood in you?'

The woman continued to shout outside, her voice very unsteady and hysterical.

Shilpa's bewilderment turned to fear. She shifted from one foot to another, looking at her in-laws. Mrs Gupta fumbled at the phone again, almost in tears. 'Who is this woman?' she asked her husband. 'Saying such inauspicious things, that too today, when we have just heard the good news. We'll have to get a havan conducted to counteract her evil eye. Shilpa, don't you go near the door or the windows.'

Shilpa nodded, her face white with anxiety. Then she said to her mother-in-law, 'If Tarun's factory number is engaged, call him up on his mobile phone.'

'Yes, yes, why didn't I think of that,' Mrs Gupta said, dialling quickly.

Mr Gupta saw his wife tearfully tell their son about everything. Then she paused and listened hard to what their son was saying at the other end, nodding all the time. Looking only slightly relieved, she put the phone down and turned to her husband. 'Tarun says none of us are to go out,' she said, her speech uneven and breathless. 'He says the woman might turn violent. Maybe she is mad. He said to call the police. He knows somebody at the police station. He said he is coming home meanwhile.'

Their son's instructions were carried out rapidly. The police were called and the family sat waiting inside quiet as mice.

Meanwhile, the woman outside ranted and raved, accusations mingled with swearing and abuse.

About ten minutes later, a police jeep drove up. Two men briskly handcuffed Kamla and hustled her into the jeep. Just as they were about to drive away with her, Tarun returned from his factory, speeding anxiously in his new white Opel Astra, looking worried though unruffled. He shook hands with the policemen, thanked them, and gave them five hundred rupees each to express his appreciation for their swift response. Finally, the jeep drove away and the family heaved a collective sigh of relief. They went inside and looked at their servant resentfully when he returned with a bag of vegetables, as if it was his fault for being away. However, they said nothing but ordered him to make tea for all of them.

'Imagine!' said Shilpa, looking nervous, already cradling her baby in her imagination. 'How could she say such terrible things about you,' she said to her husband. 'You are the kindest, sweetest man in the world.'

Tarun gave her a gentle smile. Only when the tea came, and they sat in peace, sipping fragrant tea from beautiful china cups, did they finally calm down.

Then Tarun was told the good news, that he was going to become a father. He smiled and looked at Shilpa, and Shilpa blushed.

Tarun decided to take the rest of the day off, and when he was alone with Shilpa, he turned to her.

'Don't worry about anything,' he said, feeling terrible at the look on her shocked face. She was so soft hearted, he thought tenderly. Why did that terrible woman, whoever she was, have to come here *today*? Tarun touched Shilpa's face with one hand and lifted her chin up with the other. 'I will never let anybody hurt you. You are safe with me. Any sort of stress is bad for you and the baby,' he said with a smile. 'Forget what happened today, okay?'

Shilpa nodded with a tearful smile. All her apprehension vanished and she smiled up at him tenderly. 'I couldn't have wished for a better husband,' she said.

That night, he took her out to dinner to a new Chinese restaurant, whose Head Cook was a man from a village 50 kilometres away from Amritsar. She wore her blue sari with the intricate embroidered border, the first sari that her mother-in-law had given her.

Over dinner, Tarun assured himself that his wife wasn't overworked as a housewife and daughter-in-law. By now they had forgotten all about the unpleasant incident that afternoon.

While they were having dinner, Kamla was being raped by the two policemen who had brought her in. Then, one of the policemen, a married man, went home to his wife, while the other stayed back, drinking cheap rum and listening to film songs on the radio, hoping to have another go at Kamla in the morning before letting her leave.

Next morning, Kamla tottered out and went back home. Chander was waiting for her.

'So, now you will do this too,' he said angrily, hitting her hard across the face with tears swimming in his own bloodshot eyes. 'Staying away all night, drunk, God knows where. You should just kill yourself, Kamla, if you have any shame left.'

He left after saying this. There were dark circles under his eyes, and his eyes looked weak and angry and resigned at the same time. There were dark circles under Kamla's eyes too, but the eyes themselves were empty and hollow.

4

That morning the temperature in Amritsar rose higher than it had so far in the month of May. Ramchand went to the shop feeling drained of energy by the oppressive heat. He had grown his moustache back again. He had decided that he looked too jaunty without it. It lent a nice, humble air to his face.

The heat had taken his appetite away and he had grown even thinner since winter.

He began the day's work feeling listless. At noon, Mahajan came up fuming. Chander still hadn't turned up for work. Again! What was happening in this shop? Was this how a business was run? Anybody else would have sacked Chander a long time back! Ramchand was to immediately go to Chander's house and drag him to the shop, whatever state he was in.

Ramchand stood listening to Mahajan's tirade in a respectful silence, but he groaned inwardly at the idea of walking all the way to Chander's house in the heat. He wondered if he could make some excuse, but seeing Mahajan's present mood, he did not dare to. He shuffled down the stairs sulkily. When he stepped out, the sun hit him with full force.

He remembered the last time when he had gone to Chander's house. He hoped he wouldn't find Chander drunk again. Ramchand felt furious. Mahajan was such a fool! How could he expect Ramchand to drag a drunk Chander to the shop? But he couldn't refuse Mahajan. Ramchand reluctantly dragged his feet towards the direction of Chander's house.

The sun beat down on him, perspiration covered his face, his shirt got wet and stuck to his back and chest. Flies crawled on the floor outside the halwai's shop. The little tea stalls he passed sent out fresh waves of heat at him from their little stoves.

He dragged his feet in the dust, his throat parched. He had started out the day tired to begin with. The landlord had bought a new washing machine a few weeks back, and Sudha washed clothes in it enthusiastically at all sorts of odd hours. The washing machine was noisy; it wasn't one of the latest, sleekest, almost silent models. On many days it woke Ramchand up at six in the morning. Today had been such a morning.

As the areas he passed got poorer and filthier, the shops began to get smaller and less swanky than the ones in the main bazaar. However all the shops had signboards, and Ramchand began to read all of them out aloud, softly enunciating the words to himself, as he passed each one of them. 'Pappu Automobile Works, Deepak Medical Store, Durga Electricals, Jhilmil Orchestra for Weddings . . .' Ramchand read quite fluently now, without pausing and hesitating over each letter. In the past five months he had kept at his spelling and reading diligently. In his room his books, notebook and dictionary still lay on the table, looking even more battered than they had in the winter. The bottle of Camlin Royal Blue had broken and had been replaced with Chelpark Permanent Black. True, after the initial enthusiasm, the pace had slackened, but he hadn't abandoned his project. Little by little, he had pieced together the mysteries of words. Even now, he did not know the meanings of many difficult words, but he kept hoping.

In the dictionary, he had finally finished all words beginning with 'A'. It had taken him much longer than he had expected, a full five months, but he hadn't given up. He had been both relieved and jubilant when he had come to the last word. Azure. It meant *bright blue (colour)* as in *an azure sky*. He had taken a three-day break then, and last night he had started on 'B', working on Babble, Babe and Baboon.

He read the essays regularly, the *Complete Letter Writer* he read more rarely, as it made less and less sense to him. He had bought two more books, and read them regularly too, even though these days the heat had sapped his brain so much that he could hardly think straight. After Mahajan's chack chack all day, he rarely had the strength to go through the books after the shop closed. Neither had he painted his room yet. But he was glad, as he read another signboard, Mahesh Kiryana Store. At least he had stuck to *something*.

*

The two new books that Ramchand had bought over the course of the past five months had kept him very busy.

One day after reading 'Pandit Jawaharlal Nehru' (or 'Our Favourite Leader') in *Radiant Essays*, he had realized that the *Complete Letter Writer* and the *Radiant Essays* were getting a little stale and boring now. He had made another foray to the second-hand bookstalls to see if he could buy something new. The first book he had spotted in one of the bookstalls seemed promising, and he almost bought it the same instant. It was called *Improve Your English*, written by a Dr Ajay Rai.

On the jacket, there was a note about the book. Ramchand read it hopefully. It said:

> The importance of English is well accepted. Importance of good English only more so.
> - Ability to use and know effective English is the correct and proper prelude to your successful professional career as well as a dominant, commanding place in society.
> - Success in the use of computers is very closely connected to

the success in the use of English, since almost 90 per cent of all the information that is stored in a computer is in English.

Ramchand stopped reading right there. For one, he found the language a little too elaborate. And also the sudden introduction of computers into his already complicated efforts to study alarmed him.

When he leafed through the book, his suspicions were confirmed. The book was too difficult for him, at least at this stage. It had passages in it that one was supposed to read carefully. Then there were two sections following each passage – *Answer the following*, and *Correct and punctuate the following*.

Ramchand put the book back on the counter, a little dispirited. He found the passages very difficult to understand at first glance, and he didn't even know what 'punctuate' meant. He still hadn't reached the letter 'p' in the dictionary. Maybe one day, when he was more proficient, he could buy a book like this . . .

Ramchand turned his attention to other books.

There was a faded book that he was sure he could get cheap – a book called *Quotations for all Occasions*. Ramchand had always thought that quotations were something to do with fixing the price of wholesale fabric, but the book jacket explained that quotations were things of wit and wisdom said by great people. He didn't know what wit meant, but he knew he could do with some wisdom. Another thing that was in favour of the book was that the quotations were short. He needn't have a Sunday or a whole evening free before working on the book. It could be dipped into during empty pockets of time, and he could read at least one quotation while waiting for the rice to be done, or while warming water for a bath. Ramchand bought the book, haggling till he got it for twenty rupees, sure that it would help fill in empty moments with wisdom and with wit, which he was sure was a desirable thing.

The quotations were classified in alphabetical order. There were quotations in the beginning of the book about Ability. A few pages later, there were some about Adversity. The book went on to report the ideas and opinions of great men on everything from Flattery to Literature to Tact, ending with Youth, Yukon and finally Zeal.

The quotations evoked mixed, but passionate reactions from Ramchand. Some quotations he just didn't understand, and he skipped over them. Sometimes he skipped whole subjects that he either didn't understand at all or found uninteresting.

Some quotations he wholeheartedly agreed with, and others he vehemently and angrily opposed. While reading through 'Ability', he was impressed by this:

Ability is of little account without opportunity – Napoleon

How true that was, Ramchand thought sadly, wondering who Napoleon was. Maybe a foreign poet. How right he was! He, Ramchand, would have gone to an English-medium school if his parents had not died.

He read with some scepticism an idea attributed to somebody called Aughey.

Aughey, whoever he was, had commented on Adversity. Ramchand looked up Adversity in the dictionary. It meant *misfortune*. Ramchand shook his head and looked up *misfortune*. It meant *bad luck*. Ramchand sighed and read the quotation:

God brings men into deep waters, not to drown them, but to cleanse them.

Ramchand snorted at this. 'Yes,' he thought scornfully, 'and sometimes He just leaves them in deep waters till they are wrinkled and shrivelled like a washerwoman's hands and are no good to themselves or to anyone else.'

Ramchand skipped all the quotations under the heading of America.

He solemnly admitted the wisdom of most of the quotations under Borrowing.

Debt is a bottomless sea, somebody called Carlyle had said. And hadn't his father always said that to his mother, whenever they had been short of money, 'Never mind,' he'd tell his anxious wife. 'We'll manage on whatever we have. But I am not borrowing money from anyone. There is no end to it once you start. It can make life hell.'

And Gokul also echoed the same sentiments about borrowing money. 'It is a whirlpool, Ramchand. Don't you ever get sucked into it. Make do with whatever you have. Limit your needs according to the money you have in your pocket. Once you get in the hand of moneylenders . . .' Gokul had shaken his head. 'And even if you borrow money from friends and acquaintances and relatives, some sort of pressure is always there. It is better to wear old clothes and have one meal a day and have some peace of mind than to live on borrowed money.'

By February Ramchand had reached Darkness, after skipping Capital and Labour and wondering at the sort of nonsense there was under Cats.

There is not room to swing a cat – Smollett, Humphrey Clinker.

A cat may look at a king – John Heywood.

The things supposedly great men had said about cats didn't impress Ramchand much.

In April Ramchand bought another book.

He hadn't meant to, he had been just browsing through the books at a bookstall, but he had fallen in love with this book as he hadn't with any other. It was called *Pocket Science for Children*. It was a small book, made of very glossy paper. It contained colour pictures, beautiful illustrations and *so much* knowledge that Ramchand was overwhelmed.

Ramchand asked the price. It was for 150 rupees. He was dismayed. It was a huge amount to pay for just one book, but the shopkeeper said it was a foreign book and he wouldn't budge from the price. Even after bargaining his best, Ramchand only managed to bring it down to 120 rupees. But he couldn't go back without it, he knew that. Besides, he had bought *Quotations for all Occasions* about two months back. Surely it was all right to buy this now. He didn't think any more about it and bought it.

It was so absorbing and delightful that Ramchand had to tear himself away from it in the mornings to leave for the shop. And his first thought on getting back every evening was to start reading it again. Even Sudha was a little neglected in favour of *Pocket Science for Children*.

Inside its pages there were pictures of stars and planets, machines, plants and the inside of the human body. It explained, in words that Ramchand could understand now, how electricity was generated, how car brakes worked, why hot air balloons rose up in the air, why guitars had holes in them and why rainbows were formed in the sky. It explained how penguins, birds that Ramchand had never seen or heard of before, used wave movements to swim. Ramchand gazed at the accompanying picture of penguins with wonder. They looked like the solemn waiters in bow ties and black suits who had been serving food at Rina Kapoor's wedding.

The book also explained why diamonds sparkled and said, to Ramchand's surprise, that there were 640 muscles in the human body, and that human beings were fast using everything on earth and if they went on at this rate, there would soon be nothing left.

Ramchand loved this book above all the others that he possessed, even though he didn't like to admit it to himself.

After reading it, when he placed it on top of the fast-increasing book pile that now had *five* books, he began to feel the first stirrings of a book-collector's possessive pride.

He had his eye on *A Short History of the World for Youngsters* now, but it was for a hundred rupees, and he thought it would be better to wait till August before he bought it. He hoped no one else would buy it meanwhile.

*

Now, while Ramchand walked towards Chander's place, he felt satisfaction welling up inside himself as he read one signboard after another without faltering once. Sunder Ram Brass Band, Sukhvinder Hardware Store, Shiv Shankar General Store . . .

The signboards petered out a long way before he reached Chander's neighbourhood, though. Instead, there were just small houses, more like shanties, and dark, poky, miserable little shops. The neighbourhood had seemed bad enough when he had come here last time, but that had been in the winter. The summer somehow made it seem much worse. The whole place stank, the drains were festering with filth, the heat made the dirt even more unbearable.

When Ramchand reached the Hanuman temple, it seemed to him as if he had been walking for eternity. He turned into the street. There was an alcove in the long stretch of crumbling walls, and in this space the Municipal Corporation tap was installed.

Two women stood quarrelling by the tap, flailing their arms around and screaming at each other. Ramchand couldn't pass because other women and children who were watching the fight with interest blocked the street.

One of the women was screaming, 'You think this is your father's tap? We don't get water to drink, to cook, and look at this maharani. She is giving her young prince a bath.'

A skinny, naked boy of five or six stood between the two women. He was soaped all over, down to his bony knees and scabbed feet. Only his face was soap free; even his head was covered with soapsuds. He looked miserable.

His mother had a restraining hand on his shoulder in case he tried to run away.

'Just because you are content to have your children's head full of lice and their knees black as soot doesn't mean everybody is the same!' the boy's mother screamed back at the other woman.

The other woman had a firm hand clasped on the tap. She shouted back, 'You don't have to act as if you are a clean Brahmin or something. You throw your garbage all over the street!'

'What can I do? *I* am not on such intimate terms with shopkeepers that they will give me things like plastic dustbins for free.'

'You bitch!' the other screamed. 'What are you trying to say?'

'I am just saying I know what goes on after your husband goes to sell bananas every day. Don't make me open my mouth.'

The two women were screaming at the top of their lungs now.

'At least my husband doesn't go to other women. I also know lots of things about your household, so you keep your filthy mouth shut.'

The child looked even more miserable. He hadn't wanted a bath in the first place. The soap on his skin was drying now. His hair was beginning to form spikes and his body felt itchy. It was so hot that he was sweating under the layer of soap he was sweating. Sweat and drying soap were making him feel wretched, but his mother still had as firm a hold on his shoulder as the other woman had on the tap. Some children in the crowd laughed at him. He glared back at them.

There would be more fighting on the street later on in the day.

By now, Ramchand was wedged in the middle of the crushing horde of women and children, being pressed and pushed from all directions, and he had to struggle very hard to get past them.

He was relieved when he got to Chander's door. He knocked at the door wearily. No one answered. He knocked again, louder this time. Silence. Ramchand pushed at the door gently. When no one spoke, he grew bolder and opened the door. At first he thought there was no one inside. Then he saw her, sitting propped up in a corner of the room, head bowed, silent, holding the half-full bottle of rum that Chander had left behind when he had stalked out of the house in a temper.

Ramchand cautiously crept towards Kamla, shocked at the sight of a woman with a bottle in her hand. He had never before seen a woman drinking. He opened his mouth to address her, but stopped. It seemed stupid to call her Bhabhi. Bhabhis were decorous women who gave you tea, sometimes irritated you with a lot of information about their children and occasionally asked with sly smiles when you were planning to get married. This creature in a drunken stupor, staring with unseen eyes at the wall opposite – how should he address her? Then he saw her unkempt appearance, tear-stained cheeks, pinched face and decided that this was no happy drunk. He bent over her and lightly placed an arm on her shoulder. He shook her slightly. No response. A dead woman's eyes continued to stare into air. For a moment Ramchand panicked. Was she dead? But he could hear her breathe. He shook her slightly again.

The memory of the day when he had left her in a huddled heap after Chander had beaten her came back vividly to him, bringing with it a fresh pang of guilt. The image had often come back to haunt him, but he had always pushed it away to the recesses of his mind. But a persistent, though vague feeling of guilt had remained, a feeling that he had not even admitted to himself.

So he mustered up all his courage and sat down on the floor

beside her. Then he spoke to her softly, his voice trembling, 'What is the matter? Are you feeling ill?'

She continued to stare into space. Ramchand felt awkward, sitting next to a woman he didn't know. What if Chander came back and saw him? What would he think? But something on Kamla's face held him and he kept sitting there silently. Minutes passed. There was a waiting silence in the room. The room was getting hotter and Ramchand was completely drenched in sweat. But he still sat there, knowing nothing but that he should not leave, that he was needed here. A dread was building up inside him. He could neither leave, nor stay here. But he held on.

The tomb-like atmosphere in the house gripped Ramchand with its vulture-talons. It seemed far removed from the bustle of the street outside, from the busy city outside. It was an isolated world, where you could feel the air thick with despair, thick with unsaid words and unshed tears. It was like travelling into darkness and reaching the heart of it. Ramchand's mind went blank. His body went still. He waited.

After a while, she moved slightly, and a bone somewhere in her body creaked.

Ramchand spoke again, surprised at his own courage, 'You can tell me what is wrong. Maybe I can help you.' Even while he spoke, he hoped she'd remain silent and corpse-like, so that he could steal away after a while with a clear conscience. But the moment the words were out of his mouth, the woman came to life.

Then she did respond. She slowly turned her neck, without moving her body at all, and looked at him.

Her eyes were like dark, twin tunnels that led nowhere.

Ramchand recoiled from her gaze.

But he couldn't look away. Something in her face held him there on the spot, squatting silently.

Her dry, parched lips quivered, but no sound came out of

them. He saw that there was dried vomit on her chin. She wore a cheap, purple nylon sari with a pattern of big, white flowers on it. The pallu was slightly askew; Ramchand saw that there were flakes of dried vomit on the blouse too. She had downy hair on her forearms, and there was a long, old scar on the inside of her left elbow.

Then finally, she spoke. From faraway, came her croaking words.

'Help?' she said, barely opening her mouth to form the words.

Then he saw that both the corners of her mouth had cuts on them, sharp cuts going outwards from her lips like the ghost of a smile.

Then her dead eyes blazed at him. She drew up her upper lip in a snarl, like an animal. Ramchand watched in horror. And suddenly she did erupt with an angry snarl. '*Help?* You want to *help* me?'

Ramchand was frightened. He would have leapt to his feet and run away, except that he couldn't. He felt he had lost the power to move a single muscle in his body.

The coal-like eyes, the two bottomless pits, rooted him to the spot.

He continued to stare at her in a fearful silence, one palm resting beside him on the floor to support his weight.

She spoke again through clenched teeth. 'What can you do? Tell me, what can you do?'

Her voice rose to a scream. 'What can you doooo?' she wailed.

Ramchand was terrified now. He didn't know how to handle this. His pulse quickened. Why, oh why, couldn't he just get up and run? Run away from the woman and the terrible blackness of her eyes. And from the strange, filthy smells that surrounded her.

But he couldn't. He sat transfixed by her. Her body, her

attitude, the way she slumped against the wall, made her seem like an animal that was within inches of dying.

'You want to help me? You want to know what they did to me?' she said, her voice trembling hysterically, her breath reeking of alcohol. 'Do you know? Do you think they just raped me? And then let me go? Look at this.' She pointed to her lap.

Ramchand stared at her lap in incomprehension.

Then, horror dawned on him slowly. Horror that he had never imagined he was capable of feeling. He saw that most of the white flowers on the purple sari below her hips were not white. They were rust-red. Stale-bloodstain-red.

Her words, her eyes and the rust-red flowers suddenly clicked into place in Ramchand's head and he understood. They set him trembling violently.

'You'd think they'd be satisfied just raping me, wouldn't you? But the second one . . . he did this with a lathi . . . because I kicked him in the stomach.' At the last words, a trace of satisfaction appeared on her face, and the beginnings of a twisted smile.

Ramchand was terrified. Her words crawled into his ears like worms and embedded themselves in his brain.

The palm of his right hand, the one he was leaning on, felt strained, the wrist hurt, but he couldn't move. She had stopped that horrible smile mid-way and was sobbing uncontrollably now.

'With a lathi,' she repeated. Then she lifted the bottle to her mouth and drank.

And then Ramchand felt the wetness on his palm that still rested on the floor. He didn't move an inch, he didn't even move his eyes. Panic. Were those bloodstains on her sari old? Was she still bleeding? He was sitting so close to her. Was there a pool of blood around her that he hadn't seen? Was it her blood that was wetting his hand? He felt sick with dread.

He was shaking violently now, robbed of any coherent thought or action. He faintly realized that his face was wet, he must have been crying.

Then he slowly looked down at his hand. The fingers were strained, his knuckles looked white. He held up his hand before him.

It was only some rum she had spilled out of the bottle. He examined his hand, both the back and the palm.

Just rum.

No blood.

'You want to help me?' she was still screaming.

Ramchand heard himself crying and blubbering loudly now. He managed to get up to his feet and then ran out, as fast as he could in the crowded streets, and didn't stop running till he reached his little, dingy, safe room.

5

The same week, Rina Kapoor's novel was published.

If she had been a plain, unmarried girl from an ordinary family, it wouldn't really have made much news in Amritsar, a city that had much money but only one real bookshop. But since Rina was recently married, rich, glossy and permed, and wanted to draw the attention of the cream of Amritsar, she did. There was a spectacular launch of the book in New Delhi. There were press conferences and interviews in magazines.

Ravinder Kapoor threw a large party when his daughter came to Amritsar, and invited big industrialists, bureaucrats and even the District Commissioner of Amritsar to the party. Rina invited all her acquaintances from the University, both teachers and students.

At the party all kinds of delicacies prepared by a chef from Delhi were served, along with imported cheese and chocolates. Rina wore a sheer black chiffon sari that glittered with silver sequins. Her husband looked handsome with his erect carriage and his blue blazer, every inch a proud army man.

Everyone remarked on what a striking couple they made!

The next day, young, pretty housewives saw her picture in *Amritsar Newsline* with envy in their hearts.

Rina had first got the germ of an idea for a novel, finally, on the day of her wedding, when she had seen her trembling sari-wala standing by the security guards and had heard him lie about being invited by her to the party. How she had laughed with Tina about it when she had got back! And then she had started thinking about him, curiosity taking hold of her. She had even gone to see him, to speak to him, so that she could give a real identity to her sudden inspiration. She had started working on the first draft during the honeymoon itself, and had finished the book in five months flat.

The novel was the story of a shop assistant in a sari shop. The protagonist was called Sitaram. He was a funny guy, superstitious, clever and lovable. The other characters in the book were a sadhu who performed miracles, a mad dog and a middle-aged woman who was a kleptomaniac.

There was also a beautiful village girl who Sitaram was in love with. She had almond-shaped, kohl-lined eyes and wore jasmine flowers in her hair. She had a swaying walk and a bewitching smile, and found Sitaram slightly ridiculous but endearing.

Sitaram needed the help of the old sadhu and his magic herbs before he could woo her and win her finally.

It was a well-crafted book, it began and ended well, the chapters flew seamlessly into each other. There was a good streak of humour running through it. It received favourable reviews in the press. Mrs Sachdeva read many of these in newspapers and weeklies. She cut out the best ones and proudly pinned them up on the notice board in the English Literature department. Students crowded around the notice board admiringly.

*

A policeman is a very useful and important public servant, Ramchand read in the essay book, his heart heavy with pain. *His duty is very hard. Sometimes he is working in the day while sometimes he is on patrol at night. He guards our life and property. He helps in tracing out the culprits and get them booked. A traffic policeman also regulates the traffic in an orderly and smooth fashion.*

His day begins with a morning parade in police lines. This enables him to keep physically fit. He puts on a khaki uniform and a red and blue turban. Mostly, in all the states, the policemen wear almost the same uniform. His shoes are always shining. He possesses a well-built body. He is quite a tall person. He puts on a leather belt around his waist which indicates his number and district. He carries a thick rod called a baton.

Ramchand picked up his dictionary with an effort. His limbs felt heavy, made of lead. He looked up the meaning mechanically.

> *Baton: the most likely meaning was Constable's truncheon*
> *Truncheon: Short club or cudgel e.g. that carried by policeman*
> *Club: Stick with one thick end as weapon*
> *Cudgel: Short thick stick used as weapon*

It just meant a lathi, Ramchand thought tiredly. This time there wasn't the usual excitement of chasing a word around the squiggly dictionary till he had found the meaning. Just a lathi. Just cold certainty. *He did it with a lathi*, the anguished voice said in his head.

The smell of stale cooking oil and dry vomit came back to him.

A crow cawed outside. Ramchand looked at it. It was perched outside his window. It had very small eyes. Ramchand moved, the crow, with a startled caw, flew off. Ramchand went back to his essay.

His duty is to maintain peace and order in his area. He looks for evil characters like eve-teasers, drunkards, gamblers, pick pockets etc. He patrols his area at night also. He arrests thieves, criminals and locks them up in the police station.

Ramchand could not read any further.

The room was hot and oppressive. The open window did not help.

If he kept the window open, the blinding glare of the summer sun filled the room, making his head ache. The air from outside brought in fresh heat waves that stung the eyes and seared the lungs. If he kept the windows shut and bolted, the room became close and airless.

The fan whirred slowly. It had a regulator, a round black knob on the cracked switchboard, with five small lines arranged around it, like the rays of the sun that Manoj drew in his drawing book. There were five such lines, marked from one to five neatly in Roman numerals. The regulator however, was old, and had a happy disregard for the five neat markings. It swivelled around freely when touched and had no effect on the speed of the fan. Anarchy reigned in more places than one in Ramchand's room.

So the fan whirred slowly, in a monotonous rhythm of its own, slowing down even more when the voltage was low.

Ramchand felt an ache spread slowly over his forehead. No, he couldn't read further. The words just swam around meaninglessly, like irritating little black houseflies, in front of his eyes and inside his mind.

Kamla's eyes wouldn't leave him alone. Much as he tried. Nothing made sense. It was just those eyes that haunted all his waking moments and even his dreams. He couldn't concentrate on anything. When Mahajan had been speaking to him today, all Ramchand could see was a shallow face with a crude, crass, commercial mind, and he listened mutely to Mahajan, unable to take in or understand a single word he was saying. His headache had returned after months.

Two days had elapsed since he had been to Chander's house, but it seemed like a very, very long time ago. For the past two days, he had just been thinking. Like before. Not intelligible thoughts, but a noise that went on and on in his head, a noise of constantly whirling rotation, like Sudha's new washing machine.

He looked uncomprehendingly at the *Radiant Essays* he held in his hand, and sat down on the edge of his bed. And thought.

Confused thoughts. Of paan-stained teeth. Of silk saris and gold. Of peacocks that danced. And of white sari flowers that, unnoticed by the world, had turned a rust-red.

With finality, Ramchand got up and closed the book. With an impassive face, and slow, decisive movements, he gathered everything he had bought so enthusiastically a few months back – the *Radiant Essays*, *The Complete Letter Writer*, *Quotations for all Occasions*, *Pocket Science for Children*, the notebooks, the pen, the inkpot.

With a lump in his throat, he put them away in a neat pile on the uppermost shelf in the wall, a shelf he never used. A shelf where he wouldn't be able to see them.

He decided to get up and wash his bedsheet and his pillow cover. They had begun to look very dirty.

The pillow was depressed in the middle. The pillow cover had coconut hair-oil stains on it, and a few hairs clung to the stains. Ramchand peeled the cover off the pillow. It felt sticky against his fingers. He fluffed the pillow out by pummeling it this way and that with his fists. He whipped the sheet off the bed, its edges wrinkled where it had been tucked neatly under the sides of the mattress.

Soon Ramchand was squatting on the bathroom floor, scrubbing the pillow cover energetically with a bar of blue detergent soap, his whole mind intent on removing the stains. He didn't want to think of anything else.

6

It was later in that week that Ramchand learnt how Kamla had gone to the Guptas' place and had been arrested.

As always, it was Gokul who told him.

It had been a busy morning. Customers had been coming and going at an alarming pace. And today had been one of those days when many customers came to the shop, but few made any purchases. Most of them just looked at everything in a discontented way, made everyone run around, examined many saris, and then left after half an hour without buying anything.

To make matters worse, a quarrel had flared up between Gokul and Rajesh.

Gokul was stacking a collection of crushed tissue saris before putting them away safely in a cupboard. When he got up to open the cupboard, he suddenly stumbled and the saris he was carrying slipped out of his hands, scattering themselves all over the place.

'Arre Gokul, can't you watch what you are doing?' snapped Rajesh. Rajesh stood up to help Gokul and noticed a chiffon sari in the collection of crushed tissue saris. 'What is this?' asked Rajesh, picking out the chiffon sari. He was speaking in an unnecessarily sharp voice. 'First you don't sort them carefully and then you go and spill them all over the place. Where is your mind?'

Nobody even noticed, and certainly no one expected Gokul to react the way he did.

He said in a most dignified voice, 'My mind is always on

my work. Which is more than I can say for some people around here.'

'What do you mean, Gokul? What are you trying to say?' Rajesh asked quietly, his nostrils flaring slightly in anger.

'Just that,' said Gokul, and turned away.

'Look here, Gokul, you can't just say things like that and walk off. I know what you mean.'

'Good if you know. Then why are you asking me?'

'Let me tell you something, Gokul. We, that is Shyam and I, have been working here for a very long time. Long before any of you came here. If you think you can just talk rubbish at us and we'll take it, you are wrong.'

'I know you have been here a long time. Maybe that's why you have both forgotten what work is. I do more work than both of you do put together.'

By now everyone was listening.

Now Rajesh raised his voice, 'Enough is enough, Gokul. We have always been nice to all of you, and now you say things . . .'

Gokul interrupted him. His own voice slightly rose too.

'So you think you can just pat our heads, be nice to us when you feel like it, lord it over us and go to smoke bidis for hours while we work here like donkeys? *And* get paid more too?'

'You'll hear about this, Gokul, see if you don't.'

The two men stood facing each other belligerently.

Everyone was a little surprised. Both of them were usually mild-mannered, but today they had almost come down to name-calling.

However, the two had to calm down almost immediately because a gaggle of girls accompanied by a large, matronly woman came in.

The girls were noisy and giggly. From their conversation, Ramchand soon gathered that they were a group of first-year college students from the Government College for Women. They were all from nearby villages and tiny towns around Amritsar, and were sent to Amritsar to study only because the hostel warden of the Government College was very strict. Her reputation was that of a hard, unwavering and commanding woman who knew that morality came even before education. There was very little chance of any of the girls acquiring a boyfriend and compromising the family honour while they were under her charge.

It turned out that the regular hostel warden was ill, and this woman, the assistant warden, was in charge of the girls today. She looked tired and harassed. She told the sympathetic Gokul all about it. Two of the girls had wanted to buy saris for the Freshers' Party in the hostel, otherwise she would never have brought them into the shop, she said apologetically. Gokul nodded understandingly. Encouraged, she told him how difficult it was to control these wretched girls, especially since this was their monthly outing. After a month of being cooped up in the hostel building, they almost lost their heads when they came out. It made them dizzy and mad. One of them had almost got run down by a car because she was giggling so hysterically that she hadn't looked right or left before crossing the road. 'Tell me, if some accident had happened, who would have been held responsible? Me, of course.'

While she lamented, the girls ran amok in the shop. The assistant warden hoarsely explained that this particular group was the worst in the whole hostel.

'But when they are with the warden, even these girls are as quiet as mice. I don't know how she does it,' she added with a sigh.

The girls, who looked about sixteen or seventeen, smiled and giggled at the shop assistants. They burst into guffaws each time the older woman told them to behave.

Ramchand was glad to see that this time he wasn't the only

one who was getting self-conscious. Hari was blushing, with a sheepish smile fixed on his face. Gokul looked uncomfortable. Ramchand was about to smile, infected by the ridiculous high spirits of the girls, when he remembered the sooty walls and the purple sari. He wondered if Chander's wife had once been like this, at sixteen or seventeen, giggly and silly.

And the smile died out.

Hari kept smiling at the girls foolishly till Gokul gave him a good-natured thump on his head. 'Take that smile off your face and throw it out of the window, my boy. Or hide it under the mattress. Keep your eyes on the saris only. You don't want to get into trouble, do you?'

The girls asked to see expensive wedding saris and for impossibly fine silks and crêpes. Each sari they asked for probably cost more than their spending money for a year. Once the saris were shown to them, they pressed them on each other.

'You take it, how beautiful you will look in it.'

'No, no, how can I deprive my friend of such a beautiful sari.'

'You take this green one, with the beautiful gold border. How distractingly beautiful you will look when you write your Hindi Literature exam in it. Never mind if you will fail, at least it will always be remembered.'

'If you wear this pink satin sari, you'll look so enchanting that the hostel watchman will marry you. Then you can come and go as you please.'

'No, no, this purple Kanjeevaram silk is for me. It is just the right thing to wear while boiling potatoes at midnight.'

By now, the girls were doubling up with laughter.

The assistant warden said, 'Girls, behave. A written complaint will be sent to the warden if you don't behave. And who has been boiling potatoes? You know no cooking is allowed in the rooms. You get good food, and there is no need for you to cook anything else. And you know that no heaters or gas stoves or immersion rods are allowed. Now, who said that, come on, tell me? Who has been cooking?'

But the girls all looked away. One innocently said, 'No, madam, we were talking about how good it is that the hostel authorities boil the water they give to us to drink.'

That the drinking water given to the girls was boiled was just a tall claim made by the hostel authorities, so the assistant warden subsided.

'We were talking about boiled water, not potatoes,' said the irrepressible girl.

'Okay, enough. Now, if you really want to buy something, buy it quickly. Stop wasting everyone's time as well as your own.'

But the girls did just the opposite.

They made all the shop assistants run around, they draped the pallus of expensive brocades and silks on their shoulders, looked at themselves in the mirrors, nudged each other, giggled, and then in the end bought two of the cheapest saris in nylon and cotton that Sevak Sari House carried. They chose impossibly bright colours and left cheerfully, followed by the nervous, irritable assistant warden. While leaving, they all said namaste to Mahajan with folded hands in mock-politeness and were delighted to see his red face.

Their visit slightly dispelled the acrid, bitter smell that Gokul and Rajesh's quarrel had left in the air, but it did not make it disappear altogether.

Finally, at about one in the afternoon, the shop was empty for about fifteen minutes.

Ramchand went and sat beside Gokul. He waited for Gokul to speak first.

Gokul said after a while, 'I don't care what anyone says. High time someone told Shyam and Rajesh that they are not our bosses. They are shop assistants, just like us.'

Ramchand patted his shoulder. 'Forget it Gokul Bhaiya. Just forget the whole thing.'

Gokul said worriedly, 'Rajesh said "You'll hear of it." Do you think he'll complain to Mahajan?'

'I don't think he will,' Ramchand said reassuringly. 'Their own idling is bound to come out if he does. Mahajan notices it, you know. He just has to ignore it, but I am sure he doesn't like it. You know Mahajan. If Rajesh or Shyam bring this up with Mahajan, it just might give Mahajan a chance to tick them off gently about it. I don't think those two will do anything. You just relax, Gokul Bhaiya.'

Gokul looked at him gratefully. Then he asked, 'And what is wrong with *you*, Ramchand? Haven't seen you smile for days.'

'Nothing, nothing at all,' Ramchand lied quickly.

Gokul looked disbelieving, but let it go. Then he sighed and said, 'Maybe the stars are all wrong. Everyone is having problems. Chander is also going around with a gloomy face. He is completely tired of that wife of his, if you can call such a creature a wife.'

Ramchand stiffened. Then he asked, 'Why, what happened?'

Gokul didn't hear the note of urgency in Ramchand's voice.

'Yaar, she is getting worse and worse. I don't know how Chander manages to live with her. You know what is the latest she has been doing? First, she stayed out all night, *all night* mind you, and when she came back in the morning, she was shameless enough to look Chander in his eyes. Chander just slapped her and left. But later someone from the police station sent for Chander. He was very nervous, didn't know what he had done. We poor people can't afford to be mixed up with the police, you know.'

Ramchand nodded.

Gokul continued. 'He went to the police station. Some policeman was there. Chander doesn't even know who is a constable and who is an inspector. This policeman seemed very angry. He told Chander that his wife had gone to the Guptas' place, completely drunk. Imagine being called to the police station and being told that your wife has been drinking and making scenes. It is enough to break the strongest man. The policeman told him that she had *really* misbehaved there, and had even damaged some of their property, broken windows and smashed the glass of their cars or something. Those people are respected, you know. They didn't know *what* to do. Finally, they sent for the police. This policeman, along with another, quickly went there and arrested her. Can you imagine how Chander must have felt, standing there in the police station, listening to all this about his wife, whom he had married in good faith? Fortunately, the police just let her off with a stern warning and told her to go home, the policeman told Chander. But he told Chander that if something like this happened again, if Chander didn't control his wife's conduct, they wouldn't be so lenient in the future.'

'They were considerate enough to let her go immediately because she was a woman and maybe this was the first time she had done something like this. And yet she didn't come home till morning. Can you believe it?'

Ramchand shook his head.

'Obviously, Chander was furious. I tell you, we poor people just *can't* afford to be mixed up with the police in any way. If there is a next time, things might not be so easy for Chander. And how is it his fault? He does all that he can. He scolds her, beats her, but she is so stubborn. Chander felt so bad that he went to the Hanuman temple near his place to pray. He was so disturbed that he sat at the temple for two hours, then he went home and beat her up. What else could he do, tell me? What choice does he have? Though I doubt it does her any good. No wonder he is absent from work so often and gets into trouble with Mahajan.' Gokul paused to cough and clear his throat. Then he continued. 'The next morning, Chander came to the shop a bit early. Wanted to get away from her and the place he calls home as soon as he could, I suppose. I too was here about ten minutes before time. Lakshmi had to go to a relative – her cousin was going to deliver a baby – so she gave me my breakfast early and sent me off. She gets very irritable if she has to go somewhere with the children and I get in her way. But, you know, the more I hear about Chander's wife, the more I thank God for giving me Lakshmi as a wife. Just talks too much and gets worked up easily, otherwise she is a decent, good-hearted woman. I do think I am fortunate, don't you?' Gokul asked him with a half-smile.

Ramchand nodded. Gokul said, 'Anyway, so that day, both Chander and I were the first ones here. You wouldn't believe it, Ramchand. Chander, the poor boy, wept his heart out while he told me everything. I told him he should just leave the witch and marry again. He said he would think about it.'

Then Gokul noticed the look on Ramchand's face.

'Why are you looking so miserable?' he asked in a concerned voice. 'In fact, you are looking ill. Pale and ill. Maybe you need more fresh air. But in this shop,' he said bitterly, 'fresh air and two hour lunches are only for Shyam and Rajesh.'

Ramchand didn't speak. Gokul looked at him again. 'Ay Ramchand, tu theek hai? Are you all right? What is wrong?'

Ramchand again said, 'Nothing,' but this time he couldn't even manage one of his fake, watery smiles.

Now, Ramchand could guess what really must have happened.

He looked far away for a while and then asked Gokul in a troubled voice, 'But why? Why did she go to the Guptas' place? What does she have to do with them?'

Gokul said, 'See, what happened was, the Guptas and the Kapoors had opened a joint business a few years back. They had started this cloth-processing unit. Before Chander started work here, in this shop, he worked for them. However, the business started to run at a loss, and they finally had to close down the unit. They didn't pay wages to any of the workers for the last three months of work. Chander was completely out of money. Then I don't know what happened exactly. Either he fell ill, or his wife did, but they went through a pretty bad time. I have heard he even went to Mr Gupta and Mr Kapoor to ask for some money, at least lend him some money till he found another job. They were quite nice to him, but they said that if they gave him money, all the other workers would also turn up asking for their share. Chander said he wouldn't tell anyone, but both the men were firm. You can understand their point of view in a way. They are businessmen, after all.'

'I don't know the details, but from what I have heard, Chander and his wife really went through a very bad time for months, till Chander found this job here. Chander made a mistake though. One day, when he was drunk, he told his wife their names, the Guptas and the Kapoors, and where they lived. Bas, that is all she needed I suppose. He has forgotten all about it, because you have to get on with life, and these things happen all the time. That's the way of the world. But his wife, she is a complete witch. Mad woman that she is, she still holds a grudge against her husband's employers after all these years. Abuses them in anyone's hearing. And after all you know, both of them are counted amongst the biggest men in Amritsar. And who is she? Nobody. It is so unwise of her. At least she should have thought of her husband, no? While living in the same water, a small fish cannot afford to make enemies with the crocodile. But who will explain that to her? She is completely mad, I think. And she drinks. It is disgraceful, and so hard on Chander, isn't it? God alone knows what happens to her mind when she is drunk.'

Ramchand listened in silence. He thought of her, the woman

in the purple sari, of her collarbones sticking out, of the emptiness in her eyes.

And for the first time, he felt completely sick with himself, for being deferential towards Mrs Gupta when she came shopping, for enjoying Rina Kapoor's wedding, for being flattered by Rina's interest in him, for being the person he was.

*

Over the next few days, Ramchand became more withdrawn than he had ever been. Into his heart, crept a permanent feeling that everything was very wrong – a constant disquiet, a perpetual sinking feeling in the stomach. Sometimes he felt guilty. Maybe he should have spoken out. But why hadn't Chander's wife spoken up for herself? Maybe she wanted to keep it quiet. In that case, maybe he was right to keep quiet too.

His appetite vanished, sometimes he couldn't even bear the smell of food. He felt unwashed and dirty even after he took thorough, soapy baths and wore freshly laundered clothes. There was a constant bad taste in his mouth. His intake of tea went up, and he rarely spoke to anyone, just listening quietly when anyone addressed him.

He even lost the comfort of fantasizing about Sudha, or anyone else, for that matter. For when he lay down, shut his eyes, and started rubbing his crotch over his trousers, ready to be aroused and pleasured by daydreams, ready to find some physical relief from his misery, the only images he could conjure up were the vomit stains on Kamla's blouse and the bloodstains on her sari.

Then he would feel the pricking of tears in his eyes, and all physical desire would disappear.

*

And then, one morning, to his horror, Ramchand saw the door of the shop open, and Mrs Gupta came in, as usual accompanied by Mrs Sandhu. Apart from Ramchand and Gokul, everyone was busy attending to other customers.

Ramchand didn't want to wait on Mrs Gupta. He quietly got to his feet and shuffled into a corner, hoping not to be noticed.

So it was in front of Gokul that the two women plopped themselves down.

Gokul gave them his best smile.

'Aai hai, it is so hot,' Mrs Gupta said, taking out a scented, lace-edged, pink handkerchief from her handbag. She mopped her face carefully with it, skirting cleverly around the lipstick and dabbing her eyes gently so as not to smudge the eyeliner.

Mrs Sandhu's fair skin had gone red. She fanned herself with one end of her blue chunni.

'Shall I get some water?' Gokul asked solicitously.

'No, no,' Mrs Gupta said, groping in her bag and drawing out a ten rupee note. She held it out to Gokul. 'Just send for a bottle of chilled mineral water. Chilled. And only Bisleri, mind you.'

Gokul motioned to Hari, who had just finished selling a peach sari to a thin, harried looking woman and was looking pleased with himself.

Hari came over, swaggering. He rarely sold a sari all on his own.

Gokul gave him the note and the instructions. And in a lower voice, he hissed in Hari's ear, 'And be back in a minute. Don't go off to loaf or to buy pakoras.'

Hari looked injured. ' Have I ever done such a thing, Gokul Bhaiya?' he asked in a pathetic voice. 'Maybe I have,' he added, 'but not for a very long time now. These days, if you haven't noticed, I have become hard working. You'll hardly ever see me wasting time. And you know . . .'

'Shut up, Hari. No drama now. Go immediately,' Gokul told him and then turned to the two women again, smiling.

'Show us some thin saris, for summerwear. But nothing that creases easily, okay?' said Mrs Gupta.

'We want cotton, but the most superior quality cotton you have,' added Mrs Sandhu.

Gokul nodded and gestured to Chander across the room. Chander was looking weary. He could be heard throughout the shop arguing with a customer over the price of a zardosi-bordered sari. Chander nodded at Gokul and, continuing to argue, reached out to the shelf behind him and took out a few packed saris. One by one, he threw them accurately at Gokul. They flew over the heads of all the customers and Gokul caught them deftly.

He opened the packs one by one, extolling the virtues of each sari. Hari returned with a bottle of chilled mineral water. Ramchand remained huddled in the corner, watching silently, thinking of Chander's wife.

Did Chander know? Should he tell Chander, ask him if he knew or not? But how could he speak to Chander about something this intimate concerning his wife? He looked at the animated, chattering face of Mrs Gupta. Should he tell *her*? What would be the right thing to do?

He groaned quietly, drew up his knees and bent his head down, resting it gently on them. He felt like crying, weeping out loud, collecting all the people in the shop and telling them everything. Surely, someone would do *something*.

Would they?

Ramchand continued to squat on the mattress, his ten toes sinking inside it, gripping the softness firmly.

'Ramchand?' A voice startled him. He looked up.

Mahajan stood towering over him.

'What is this, hunh? The shop is full, everyone is so busy that nobody has the time to scratch his head even, and you are sitting here relaxing. You think you are sitting on a bench in Company Bagh?'

'Bauji . . .' Ramchand began.

'Okay, okay. Now don't give me any of your excuses. At least help Gokul if you have nothing else to do,' Mahajan said, turned abruptly and walked away.

Ramchand looked at Mahajan's unyielding, spiteful, flabby retreating back with fresh dislike.

He was about to shuffle closer to Gokul when he saw Mrs Bhandari come in with Mrs Sachdeva. It felt so unreal. He remembered a similar afternoon, or was it a morning, in the winter, when they had all come to the shop on the same day. He had attended to all of them.

But at least now he wouldn't have to show Mrs Gupta any saris. He came forward and smiled weakly at the two women who had just come in. They did not look at him. They ran their eyes around at the shelves before they sat down in front of Ramchand, murmuring to each other in low voices, unlike Mrs Gupta and Mrs Sandhu, whose shrill conversation could be heard all over the shop.

'Show us some new batik prints,' said Mrs Sachdeva. Ramchand nodded and got up to fetch them. He didn't feel like shouting to Hari, who was closer to the batik prints shelf, and have Hari grin and shout and throw him the packs.

He rummaged for a while in the shelf while the two women waited. Shyam caught his eye and frowned at him. It was considered criminal in Sevak Sari House to keep customers waiting. It was much better to drown them in a deluge of saris, till they *had* to choose one, even if just in order to escape. Ramchand hurriedly took out a few packs and went back to his place.

The women began the familiar routine. They felt the fabric of each sari with their fingers, they made comments to each other in low voices, they examined the borders critically.

Ramchand didn't say much. He did not try to push any sari forward or draw their attention to anything remarkable in a particular sari. He just sat there silently, handing them the saris one by one.

Shyam caught his eye again and raised his eyebrows questioningly, looking slightly annoyed. In Mahajan's absence, Shyam and Rajesh considered themselves to be in charge of the shop, as long as it didn't interfere with their tea-drinking and bidi-smoking sessions.

Ramchand deliberately looked away.

He tried his best to appear calm when Mrs Sachdeva picked up a brown sari and complained to Mrs Bhandari, 'See, this would have been perfect if the border hadn't been so wide, wouldn't it?'

Ramchand remembered the time when he had sat in the drawing room of the Kapoor House, listening to Rina Kapoor talk to Mrs Sachdeva. The Kapoors, who had been partners with the Guptas in the cloth-processing unit, who hadn't paid Chander, who had made Chander's wife so angry.

'Are you listening?' Mrs Sachdeva asked him sharply. 'I said, do you have the same sari, same colour and design, but with a thinner border?'

Ramchand shook his head.

She looked annoyed.

Ramchand looked at the creases in her forehead. What would she say if she knew?

She was supposed to be a learned woman. Then another thought struck him. Did Rina Kapoor know that her father did not pay wages on time? At least sometimes.

Should he go to her and talk to her? But he felt doubtful. Who would believe him? To Mrs Sachdeva, Ravinder Kapoor was probably just the doting father of her star pupil.

Ramchand squeezed and pinched the area between his

eyes. Everything seemed so dark and hasty suddenly. What could he do?

Now, Rajesh was frowning at Ramchand too. Ramchand felt a wave of resentment against him. Silly man, always talking, talking, talking, never even pausing to think what to say next!

Ramchand tried to collect himself together and pay more attention to the two exacting woman facing him. He took out some more saris.

'Oh, hello, Mrs Bhandari,' said Mrs Gupta suddenly.

Mrs Bhandari looked up, appearing to be surprised. 'Oh, hello. I didn't see you. Shopping?'

How silly, thought Ramchand, of course all the women were shopping.

'You know Mrs Sandhu?' asked Mrs Gupta, waving a hand towards her companion. 'Her husband is Chief Engineer in the Electricity Board.'

'Oh, that is nice,' Mrs Bhandari said vaguely. 'And I am sure you know Mrs Sachdeva. Head of English Department . . .'

Mrs Gupta interrupted her with a bright smile. 'Oh, yes, of course I remember her. Don't you think all of us met at the Kapoor wedding, you know Ravinder Kapoor's daughter's wedding?'

'Yes, that is right,' said Mrs Sachdeva. 'But, you know, that girl is so bright that even if you say Rina Kapoor, one would know who you are talking about. She has forged an identity of her own, you know, she is not just Ravinder Kapoor's daughter.'

There was an awkward pause in the conversation. Then Mrs Bhandari asked, 'So, Mrs Gupta, what is your news? What is happening? How is your daughter-in-law? Shipra, her name is, right?

'Shilpa,' said Mrs Gupta, beaming. 'Really, God is very kind.

Very, very kind. Touch wood. She is expecting, third month.'

Everyone smiled at this.

'Well, congratulations. We'll wait for the baby and then you'll have to give us a party,' said Mrs Bhandari.

'Oh, yes, sure. And she is such a nice girl, you know. So submissive and well mannered. And by God's grace, my son Tarun's factory is also doing very well. And my younger son calls up from the USA every week.'

Mrs Sachdeva looked at her, then turned her eyes back to the sari she had in her hands, saying in a very low voice, 'That is very nice.'

Mrs Gupta beamed.

Mrs Bhandari then turned to Mrs Sandhu.

'And how are your children?' she asked in a friendly voice.

Mrs Sandhu replied in a slow, placid voice. 'Oh, they are doing well. My elder son, Manu, Mandeep, his name is, but we call him Manu, he has cleared his entrance exams. He'll be able to get into the Amritsar Medical College. Finally, I can use the mixer-grinder and the washing machine without worrying about making a noise and disturbing him. All Waheguru's blessings.'

'Well, yes, academics are very important these days,' said Mrs Bhandari. 'My Rosie has gone to Delhi to do her MSc. I told her, do it here, but she wouldn't listen. There are such good matches coming for her, but she says she is not in the frame of mind to marry now. She says marriage and money aren't everything in life.'

Mrs Gupta sniffed. Mrs Sandhu said with a fond smile, 'But believe me, Mrs Bhandari, today's youngsters want everything. No matter what they say, they do want money. My younger son is just in Class Ten. And a new demand every other day. Now he is saying he wouldn't go to school till we buy him a motorcycle. What can one do?'

'Well, we are as bad, aren't we?' said Mrs Gupta, with a

conspiratorial smile. 'Just the other day we bought a new microwave oven and now I feel like buying an outdoors barbeque set.'

'What to do? You can't help it,' said Mrs Sandhu. 'You do need money, bhai, no matter what anyone says.'

Mrs Sachdeva suddenly said in a smooth voice. 'True, money is very important. To maintain a standard of living. But there must be other things in life apart from money. Now look at Rina Kapoor. Doesn't lack anything in life. She has money, beauty, a solid family backing. But she has carved out a niche for herself by writing a book, by earning her own reputation. Have you read the book?' she asked Mrs Gupta and Mrs Sandhu.

Both of them shook their heads, and Mrs Gupta said, 'Who has the time? For you it is your job, but we have to look after so much at home, you know.'

There was tension in the air.

Then Mrs Sachdeva suddenly smiled a friendly smile. 'By the way, Mrs Gupta,' she asked in a friendly voice, 'your daughter-in-law is pretty young, isn't she?'

'Yes, she is twenty-one.'

'And what has she done?' Mrs Sachdeva asked casually.

'You mean?' Mrs Gupta faltered.

'I mean, her qualifications?'

'Well, she did take admission in BA. But she couldn't finish it, you see, the marriage got fixed up in the middle of it.'

'Oh,' said Mrs Sachdeva, and then fell silent.

Mrs Gupta looked disconcerted for a moment, then she said, 'But, well, she knows all the things worth knowing. She is not one of those girls who knows the capitals of all the countries in the world but doesn't know the name of the daal they are eating.'

Mrs Bhandari immediately replied, 'There is no reason why a girl shouldn't know both. Now, my Rosie is an excellent

207

cook, apart from being a brilliant student. I miss her so much.'

Mrs Sandhu said pityingly, 'I know, it must be terrible for you. Especially since she is your only child.' Then, as an afterthought she added, 'I am really glad that both my sons are so obedient. At least most of the time.'

Throughout the conversation, Gokul and Ramchand sat tired and helpless, watching and listening to the women, who held forgotten saris in their laps, waiting for them to remember what they had come here for. But this did happen sometimes. Women ran into acquaintances at the shop and carried on long conversations with each other while the shop assistants waited. There was nothing you could do about it.

Gokul was still sitting patiently, his mind far away. He was thinking whether he should buy a new stove or not – Lakshmi had been clamouring for one for the last two months.

Ramchand had been listening to the conversation carefully, completely unimpressed this time. Such a harmless life these women seemed to live, but as the *Radiant Essays* said – every coin has two sides.

In the world they conjured up, Chander's wife featured nowhere. He stared at the four women.

He felt a void where some kind of an understanding or knowledge should have been. And then a helpless pain in his heart. Yes, he could actually feel it in the left side of his chest, where the heart was supposed to be.

Then suddenly, Mrs Bhandari caught Gokul's eye. Then she looked at the brown sari in her lap. She gave a little laugh and said, 'Just look at us. We have forgotten completely about our shopping.'

'Happens rarely,' laughed Mrs Sandhu.

All four women went back to the saris.

Mrs Sachdeva and Mrs Bhandari were the first to make up their minds. They chose one sari each, both with traditional batik prints, one in mauve and the other in sky blue.

They went back to their low mutterings as they decided. Ramchand stared impassively.

He heard Mrs Sachdeva say, almost under her breath, 'These women . . . all the same . . . nothing in their heads except money and nonsense . . . why must we even talk to them?'

Then he missed something that Mrs Bhandari said. But he did hear her last sentence. 'After all, we live in the same city . . . one keeps running into them . . . one has to be civil.'

Mrs Sachdeva nodded, then motioned to Ramchand to pack the two saris.

They smiled and waved at Mrs Gupta and Mrs Sandhu before they left.

The two waved back. But as soon as they disappeared through the glass door, Mrs Gupta turned to Mrs Sandhu and said, 'Really, these women, I don't know what these two have such a superiority complex about. Mrs Sachdeva has no children and her husband is also just some professor somewhere. She is a nobody. And Mrs Bhandari, even though her husband is a D.I.G. in the police, well, her Rosie is twenty-seven, I think. And unmarried. Good matches indeed! Nothing is happening, so she will go to Delhi, get some fancy degree, and then show off about it. And talking about us like that, just sour grapes, you know.'

Mrs Sandhu was her usual placid self. 'Never mind,' she said, 'what is it to do with us? They are probably frustrated. We should just thank God for all he has given us.'

They left shortly after buying an expensive sari each instead of the cotton saris they had come for. Mrs Gupta's was one of the crushed tissue saris that had been exclaimed over delightedly by the college girls a few days back, and Mrs Sandhu's was an onion pink silk with filigree work.

As soon as they left, Gokul said, 'These women can be real headaches. If they are not bragging about their houses, it is their husbands. And if isn't the husbands, it is the children.

Ramchand, do you think I should buy one of those new Clix gas stoves?'

'I really don't know anything about gas stoves, Gokul Bhaiya. I have a kerosene stove,' said Ramchand in a low voice.

The kerosene stove, the purple sari, the flowers . . . Ramchand went to the tiny toilet adjoining the storeroom at the top of the shop, locked himself in and then cried for a while. Then he wiped his face with his hanky, came out, and went back to his place in the shop.

7

Yes, Ramchand had decided. He was going to do it. And he felt it was the most important decision of his life. He couldn't bear his own falseness any more. He, who felt nervous even when showing customers beautiful saris, was going to gather all the moral courage he had, dig it up from all corners of his mind and soul. And he *was* going to do it. The very next time Mrs Sachdeva came to the shop with Mrs Bhandari. After all, Mrs Sachdeva was a learned woman and Mrs Bhandari's husband was the D.I.G. of police. Besides, more importantly, they were women. Surely they would understand the urgency.

Ramchand went around looking drawn and ill. He was thinner than ever and now his eyes looked sunken, his shoulders had begun to look bony through the thin cotton shirts he wore these days.

After the decision, came the waiting. For the next few days, every time the glass door of the first floor opened, Ramchand looked up with a start, his heart beating a shade faster, and subsided when he saw it wasn't Mrs Sachdeva with Mrs Bhandari. But many days passed, and neither of the two women appeared. Ramchand expected them every day, for both of them were frequent shoppers. As he had heard Mrs Sachdeva tell Mrs Bhandari many times, when you went to a good college to teach every day, you couldn't keep repeating saris.

Then, one day, when he was looking out of the window, anxiously watching the fruit-juice seller fix the wheel of his cart – Ramchand was afraid the pile of oranges might topple over as the cart shook and heaved – he heard the sound of the door open and turned his head sharply. And there she was. Mrs Sachdeva. But Mrs Bhandari wasn't accompanying her as usual.

Ramchand was a little disconcerted. He had wanted to talk to both of them together. But he collected himself quickly. He saw her move to the empty space opposite Chander and hurried forward, 'Please come and sit, Madam. What would you like to see?'

So she came and sat opposite him, producing a small velvet pouch from her bag. She opened it reverently to reveal an exquisite jewellery set – a thin gold necklace set with tiny green stones and matching earrings. She showed it to Ramchand, pointing out the green stones to him.

'See, it is like this. I want the same green as this, exactly the same, in pure chiffon. Plain or printed doesn't matter, I just don't want any borders with very loud colours.'

Ramchand nodded absently. He took out some green chiffon saris. Then he said to her, 'Would you like to come near the window? You'll make no mistake about matching the exact colour then. Here, under the tube lights, you might make a mistake. Things look different in the daylight.'

She looked pleased at the considerate suggestion.

She went to sit near the window and Ramchand followed her with an armful of saris in varying shades of green.

They sat down. Now, nobody would be able to hear what he had to say to her. Mrs Sachdeva pursed her lips, a small crease of concentration in the middle of her forehead, and started examining the saris one by one, her eyes darting from jewellery to sari again and again.

This was the moment. Ramchand's pulse quickened, his breath became shallow, but *this* time, he wasn't going to run away. He was going to do something.

'Madam, I want to talk to you about something.' His voice sounded unnatural and strained even to his own ears.

She looked startled.

'About something very serious,' Ramchand said.

'What is it?' she asked suspiciously.

'Can you see that man at the opposite end,' he said, pointing towards Chander.

'I see no man there,' she said.

'The shop assistant, madam, the tall one.'

'Oh, *him*,' she said, nodding. 'Yes, what about him?'

'His name is Chander. I want to talk to you about his wife,' said Ramchand.

Mrs Sachdeva looked at him as if he were mad.

Then, faltering a little sometimes, stumbling here and there, but keeping his head clear, Ramchand, with his ears redder than ever, but also with more courage in his heart than ever, told Mrs Sachdeva the whole ugly, sordid story, putting together the pieces as well as he could, completing it like a jigsaw puzzle.

Mrs Sachdeva stared at him speechless.

Then, as his words sank in, the lines on her face were disturbed. They seemed to move a little, the way ripples move in still water after a stone has been thrown in. She tried to interrupt him, but he held up his hand, trying to be firm and strong, and said, 'Please, let me finish.'

And he did, while Mrs Sachdeva got more and more agitated. Ramchand could see unshed tears in her eyes.

In the end, Ramchand felt drained. He wasn't surprised to see Mrs Sachdeva look agitated. He would have been too, if such a story had been sprung on him.

But Ramchand was completely unprepared for the fury that now burst forth from each pore of Mrs Sachdeva's red face.

She glared at him. 'How dare you?' she said in a low, angry hiss, her voice trembling. 'How dare you, a mere shop assistant, bring me here to this corner and tell me filthy stories about the kind of women you seem to know.'

He was about to speak but she didn't let him. 'The Guptas are respectable people. They happen to be friends of the Kapoors. Do you know what you are saying? And do you have any proof of all this? And why are you telling *me*? What have *I* got to do with all this dirty business?'

Her indignation was making her stutter. Her voice sounded tearful even through the anger.

'Memsahib, please listen. Maybe the Guptas didn't know this would happen, but they did get her arrested. And the policemen did . . .'

'Oh, shut up,' she said, speaking through clenched teeth in a low voice. She was anxious that no one in the shop should overhear this conversation. 'I don't want to listen to all that vulgar rubbish again, that too in Hindi. Why are you bothering *me* about all this? It is no concern of mine.'

Ramchand answered with despair in his voice. 'Because you are a respected woman, and your friend Mrs Bhandari's husband is the . . .'

'Oh, so that is it. There have been some horrible, filthy things going on, and now respectable people are to be dragged into it? Let me just tell you one thing, you try this once more, and I'll speak to the shop manager about this. This just might cost you your job, do you understand?'

With this, she gathered her jewellery carefully into the little velvet pouch, pushed away the green saris on her lap and walked out of the shop on trembling legs.

*

Two more months went by. July came but Amritsar remained dry and dusty. The monsoons were late. One hot, dizzy day, when Ramchand climbed up the familiar wooden stairs of the shop for the umpteenth time, pushed the big glass door open and went in, he saw everyone sombrely standing in small groups, talking in low voices. Shyam was looking pensive, Rajesh was nodding to something that Mahajan had just said to him, Gokul was silent, Hari was whispering something urgently into Gokul's ears. Nobody had opened the windows yet, and the shop was stiflingly hot and still.

The next thing Ramchand noticed was that Chander was absent, and panic surged through him. Chander hasn't turned up again and they would send him to his house again to fetch him, Ramchand thought. He would refuse, he thought in blind terror. No matter what happened, he *wouldn't* go there again. He would feign a headache . . . he would say he felt ill . . . he wanted to go home . . .

But nobody said anything to him. They continued to stand around, talking in hushed voices.

Gokul caught Ramchand's eye and beckoned to him. Ramchand went up to him slowly, a feeling of dread in his heart.

'What happened?' he asked Gokul. 'Why is Mahajan looking so solemn? Where is Chander? Has he been sacked? Why are . . . ?'

'Sssh,' said Gokul, his dark eyes solemn. 'Nothing is wrong with Chander. But Chander's wife, you know, Kamla? I told you about her.'

Ramchand waited.

'Well . . . she has been killed,' Mahajan said. 'It happened last evening. So Chander won't be coming to work today.'

'What?' Ramchand whispered.

His world spun around him.

'Killed? But who . . . ?'

Gokul turned to Hari again, who was asking him something, still in a whisper.

Ramchand couldn't make sense of anything. He tugged at Gokul's shirt sleeve.

'Yes?' Gokul asked him.

'Did Chander . . . I mean . . . who killed her?' It sounded

absurd to his ears, talking about something like this logically, sanely, in broad daylight, standing in the middle of the shop, in view of everyone.

'No, Chander didn't kill her. You wait. I'll tell you everything later,' Gokul said mysteriously, his hair looking even thinner and greyer today.

At that moment, a plump woman came in with her plump daughter-in-law asking to see printed cotton saris. Each shop assistant moved back effortlessly to his place. Gokul dealt with the woman even more politely and efficiently that he usually did. Mahajan caught his eye, gave him an approving nod and went downstairs.

It wasn't until later in the morning, when there was a brief lull in the stream of customers, that Gokul told Ramchand everything.

According to Gokul, Kamla had tried her tricks once too often. She had got disgracefully drunk. Then she had gone to *the Kapoor House*, no less.

And there she had stood outside the gate, shouting at the top of her voice. When the Kapoors sent out their chauffeur, gardener and servants to restrain her, she let out a stream of abuse at them, and then went on to abuse the whole of the Kapoor family. Passers-by stopped to listen. Finally, seeing no other way out of this embarrassment, Ravinder Kapoor himself came out.

At the sight of him, Kamla picked up a stone and hurled it at him. It catapulted through the air in a defiant semi-circle, and struck his forehead. The sharp edge of the stone made a deep gash. Blood seeped through the gash and then dripped down to Ravinder Kapoor's white silk kurta. He stood there with a look of shocked disbelief on his face.

Kamla's fate was sealed at that very moment. Ravinder Kapoor couldn't help it. It was a matter of his prestige in the city. He could not let a common woman go scot-free after that.

Yes, it was a matter of his prestige, a matter of honour.

This had happened the morning before. At seven in the evening, four men broke into Chander's house. Kamla was alone at home then. One of the men held Kamla while the other three proceeded to break every single thing in the house, down to the earthen water pitcher. They threw out all the utensils in the house. They emptied jars of rice and daal into the garbage heap outside, they even broke the fragile wooden door. They smashed the old, smoky glass of the window. They broke the bulb and emptied the kerosene stove. By this time, a crowd had gathered outside and the four men made sure everyone saw what they were doing. No one dared protest.

All this they did mechanically, without any anger or pleasure on their faces. In ten minutes, the already shabby, unhappy house was completely and efficiently destroyed.

Then the men beat Kamla up.

They systematically broke her collarbone, they kicked her till two of her ribs broke. The back of her head split open when they threw her against the wall. Her blood left a bell-shaped mark on the discoloured wall.

Then they dragged her outside and paraded her in the neighbourhood with her hands tied behind her back so everyone could see what happened to those who stepped beyond their limits.

She could barely walk, she had to be dragged and pushed into moving. Finally, they pushed her back into her home, locked the door, sprinkled the small house liberally with kerosene and set it on fire.

Chander had gone home from the shop last night to find the charred remains of his house and his wife.

It was a brief story. Very like a scene from a Bombay masala film. Just a brief story, told in very few words. But the words washed over Ramchand again and again, like unforgiving waves of an ocean returning again and again to crash on the shore.

The shop stood still. Ash trembled at the tip of an incense stick. A fly tried to fly out through the glass of the closed window. People turned into statues. Saris were suspended in time. And the lane below that he could see out of the window was a picture, a snapshot caught in the wooden frame of the window. It wasn't real. Like the picture of the thatched cottage that had hung in his room ever since he had moved into it. Only, the text had changed. Instead of the line . . . *Home is where the heart is*, now the words said . . .

. . . *With her hands tied back . . . they tied the hands of my sons behind them with their own turbans . . . she tried her tricks once too often . . . the charred remains . . . it is with considerable regret that I say . . . Kamla's fate was sealed at that very moment . . .*

He went about in a shocked daze for the next half an hour, just repeating the story to himself, and mixing it up with other things in his head. He was vaguely aware that everyone was still talking about it in low voices.

And then Ramchand saw Hari's face break into a sly smile. Then Hari said, 'You know, I am not sure, but I heard from somebody in that area that they paraded her naked before doing It.'

And then . . . then Hari threw his head back and laughed.

His even teeth gleamed; the inside of his mouth was very pink.

A fraction of a moment after Hari laughed, everyone was surprised to hear Ramchand – for no apparent reason – making a sound like a half-gasp, half-scream, and then turn towards the door, and rush out of the shop. They heard him crashing down the last few steps of the wooden staircase and then the clatter of his running feet. Then there was silence.

Hari laughed.

Hari *laughed*, Ramchand thought in shocked disbelief.

Cheerful, carefree Hari laughed.

His friend, Hari, laughed. Ramchand blindly stumbled out

of Sevak Sari House with only one coherent thought in his mind. He was never returning here. He was now standing under the signboard, out in the street. Here too, there were people. More and more people, milling around in the streets, strangers with impassive faces. You could not know what lurked beneath the placid normal exteriors.

Ramchand could barely breathe, but he didn't slow down. He pushed and elbowed his way through the crowds. So that was her name – Kamla, he thought. He hadn't known her name until today. Ramchand was drenched in sweat by the time he had left the lane where the shop stood. He wanted to get away, get away for ever from the claustrophobia of the shop and the laughing, bizarre Hari.

He slowed down when he got out of the lane. Now that he was away from the shop, he didn't know what to do. He felt too full of emotion to go back to his room straightaway.

It was a new emotion – a strong emotion, a mix of irrational fear and an unfamiliar anger.

It filled his heart and mind.

It furred his tongue.

It replaced the confusion and the detachment that he felt most of the time towards his life and towards the world around him. It was potent, but also pungent. There was a metallic taste in his mouth.

He wandered through the bazaar aimlessly, looking for a chance to give vent to this emotion. For the first time in his life, he felt like picking a fight with someone. At the same time, he felt tender and protective towards all defenceless things. He felt strong.

A stray, mangy dog that lay with its head on its front paws looked at him understandingly. The streets seemed littered with droppings from vegetable carts.

Ramchand tried hard to stop himself from crying. He hated to cry in front of anyone.

An hour elapsed. Ramchand continued to roam the streets with suppressed energy in each cell of his body. He was unable to control his feet – they went where they pleased, they took him to the same streets, the same temples, the same shops over and over again.

And then Ramchand's eyes fell on the familiar sight of Lakhan's dhaba as he passed it. The busy entrance, people arriving and leaving quickly, the mingled smells of pakoras, baking rotis in the tandoor and tea, warm and comforting and inviting. The only people who didn't seem to feel comforted ever in Lakhan Singh's dhaba were the man himself and his wife. A strong, physical wave of sympathy rose in Ramchand's confused heart for the tall sardaar and his melancholic wife.

He stepped into the dhaba impulsively, still panting slightly, his brain threatening to burst out of his skull.

He looked around for Lakhan but couldn't see him any-where. Two men were chewing on rotis dipped in daal. There were mounds of sabzi on their plates. A young man, one of Lakhan's new helpers, was serving them. There was nobody else around, except a boy washing glasses in a corner, whistling tunelessly to himself. Ramchand went up to the boy and asked him where Lakhan was. The boy waved his soapsud-covered arm vaguely. He told Ramchand that Lakhan was in his house behind the dhaba.

Without pausing to ask anyone for permission, Ramchand bravely walked through the back door of the dhaba that led to Lakhan's living quarters.

He found himself in a small room where Lakhan's wife, a slight, swarthy woman with grey hair at the temples sat on a chatai, counting the day's earnings. She wore a cream-coloured salwaar kameez, with a pattern of tiny, almost invisible green leaves on it. She had her head covered with a grey chunni that did not match her clothes. In her ears she wore big, round, plain gold rings. They were the sort that every woman of her age and background wore. In fact, she had worn them for so long that now the pierced holes in her ears had become vertical slits.

She was a very efficient woman. Into a life in which chaos and pain had been thrown so haphazardly and suddenly, she tried to bring order by counting money, by buying same-sized onions at the wholesale vegetable market, and by keeping the quiet, laughterless house spick and span. Yes, she liked everything to be in order. At times, Lakhan got very tired of her relentless efficiency.

Lakhan sat on a low, wooden stool nearby, writing up accounts in a thick ledger. The room was sparsely furnished. A table, a few low stools and a divan covered with an embroidered blue bedspread. There was a picture of a benign looking, white-bearded Guru Nanak on one wall. On the opposite wall were two blown-up colour photographs of two young men, little more than teenagers. One smiled full into the camera, neatly dressed in a navy-blue turban and a blue-and-white check shirt. He was leaning against a tree, his body looked lean and lanky.

The other looked younger. He had a sullen face and his turban was a little askew as if he had just recently learnt to tie it. Both the pictures were framed and garlanded with fresh marigold flowers.

The old couple was surprised and a little angry to see Ramchand burst in on them. But before they could say anything, Ramchand spoke in a rush. 'I have come to say that I am sorry about your sons. It shouldn't have happened,' he said abruptly, without any preamble.

A stunned silence followed his words.

The elderly couple stared at him bewildered, and he stared back at them, looking a little mad. Perspiration had made his hair stick together in damp little bunches and his eyes were full of tears. He should have been feeling ridiculous, but he felt strangely relieved.

The silence was broken by what was first only a whimper and then rose into a full-throated wail. Lakhan's wife had started to cry. Lakhan put his arm around her and tried to calm her down. Ramchand looked at the pictures again and rage welled up in him. He cringed. What constant injustice! What a warped way of living! How wrong it all was! He felt reckless, strong enough to do anything, fight anyone for justice, for truth.

'I didn't come here to upset you,' he said, with a note of urgency in his voice that they did not understand. 'Just don't worry, I will do something. These things can't just go on happening. Everything will change one day.' And his voice sounded convincing to his ears. 'I will do something,' he said again. Lakhan's wife calmed down a little, though she continued to cry quietly for the remaining part of Ramchand's visit. Lakhan and his wife did not say much. They looked at him sadly, with tired eyes. Lakhan's wife got up after a while, drying her eyes with one end of her chunni and came back with a glass of milk for Ramchand. Meanwhile, Lakhan Singh and Ramchand sat together in silence. Ramchand finished the glass of milk, and then left after a while, still in the same wild-eyed state in which he had arrived.

Lakhan and his wife sat in a perplexed silence for a while after he left. Then, Lakhan sighed and started working at his accounts again. But his wife couldn't go back to counting the money. She sat still for the rest of the evening, with her hands folded in her lap, doing nothing.

*

When a badly shaken Chander had managed to salvage some of his things from the burnt down house, he found Kamla's tin trunk intact. He opened it to find, among other things, two little frocks, one pink, one red and blue check, a string of cheap red glass beads that were wrapped carefully in a Chinese silk scarf, and an imported safety pin. Chander was very surprised. He had never known that Kamla had possessed any of these things. They seemed useless, he wondered why she had kept them.

8

The nightmare wouldn't go away. It was here to stay. It was the same old him, going back to the same old room with the peeling walls, the same lanes, the same people. Yet, suddenly, everything had turned profoundly menacing. The familiar people looked malevolent. They would throw their heads back and laugh at anything. He alone was normal. Or was he? Was it he who was mad?

Ramchand suddenly felt someone was following him. But when he quickly turned back, it was a stranger. Who was he? Ramchand stared at him suspiciously. The man looked uncomfortable, and nervously hurried past him. Ramchand hurried too, rage and fear jostling each other inside him.

For the first time in his life, he felt that his mind was clear. That he had seen finally what he had always hoped to get a glimpse of. But the feeling brought no comfort to him. He remembered Kamla again. Every detail of the time he had squatted by her side in the dirty house came back to him vividly – the blackened walls, the kerosene stove, the low ceiling, the tin trunk, the purple sari, the flowers on it . . .

And the eyes. He would never forget the eyes. He started to run. People turned to stare at him, but he was beyond caring. Hari's laugh still rang in his ears, and he ran and ran, driven and chased by that laugh. He reached his lodgings and ran up the dark staircase. The moment he was inside, he bolted the door and then locked himself inside with the same lock and key that he used to lock up his room every day from the outside.

Ramchand knew why he needed to lock himself in. For the first time in his life, he realized that it was only weakness that kept people strong. Strength weakened you. And so, in the first moments of complete strength and clarity he had ever known, he felt debilitated, helpless, defenceless.

In the middle of his fumbling with the lock and the big iron key, there was a power cut. It plunged the room into complete darkness. Ramchand felt more afraid of the dark than he ever had in his life, even in his childhood. He groped his way towards the window facing the street and opened it. There was complete darkness outside. The power cut wasn't just in his neighbourhood. As far as he could see, there wasn't even a pinprick of light. As he watched, dim candlelight appeared in certain places as people in their comfortable homes, surrounded by their families, rooted by tradition, led by the family elders, calmly lit candles that shone weakly through thin curtains. A few shadows flitted behind some of the curtains. A dog barked somewhere.

He turned and opened the other window too. He saw that Sudha had lit two candles – one in the kitchen and one in the living room.

But before he could think of lighting one too, a fresh bout of panic seized him and he sat trembling on the edge of his bed.

Darkness smothered him. He couldn't breathe. He had no name, no language. He did not know where and why he lived. He began to tremble in fury. Terror filled the little room. Ramchand was enveloped in a sense of timelessness. He didn't know anything. He knew everything. These thoughts did not just run through his head, they ran through his body, the way a shiver does. 'You cannot keep demons out. They all have a foot in the door,' he thought incoherently.

There was a sound outside, someone wheeling a bicycle

and light footsteps. The faint sounds fell on Ramchand's nerves as frightening assaults. He could not control his trembling. He was mad, yes, mad. No other explanation.

Ramchand ran to the bathroom and threw up, once, then again after five minutes. He had eaten little, but the litres of tea he had drunk erupted out of his mouth as a sour brown liquid that trickled down into the hole of the Indian-style toilet. He washed his face and came back in the dark. He did not look for the candles or the matchbox. On his way to his bed, he tripped on the uneven floor and fell, his bony frame making a loud crack. He did not get up. He lay there curled up as tightly as he could and vomited again, just a little bit of vomit. More old tea trickled to the floor. Tears came pouring down Ramchand's face. He wanted to scream loudly, as loudly as he could. But he couldn't. Because you couldn't scream. Not really, not like this, in darkness, in your room, without any real reason. You couldn't cry either.

His books, his notebook and his Oxford dictionary stood on their tiptoes on the uppermost shelf. And the Indian Beggar, the Policeman, Phyllis, Peggy, Penguins and Pandit Jawaharlal Nehru (or my favourite leader) all leered down at him in unison.

He lay weeping on the floor and it was almost morning when he dropped off to sleep out of sheer exhaustion. In his troubled sleep, Ramchand had a dream. A vivid dream, with the lights, shadows, darkness and colours, all in place.

He dreamt that he was alone in the sari shop. It was twilight and he was all alone. Surrounded by saris and silence. But there were shadows behind him – shadows that moved but slid away as soon as he turned around to look at them. No matter how quickly he whipped around, they were faster than him. Small, prickly, invisible *things* crawled out of the white mattresses and crawled up his body. They didn't bite or hurt him, but they were there, nestled against his body snugly. And he didn't know who or what they were.

Then, the saris began to flap, and they began to unwind, all of them. The ones that were rolled up and the ones in transparent cellophane packs. Soon, the room was full of swishing and flapping sounds of cloth. A few saris grew very long, even longer than the longest in real life, much, much longer than the grand old-fashioned nine-yard saris. They flew out at him and whipped themselves around his neck, almost strangling him. A navy-blue sari floated in front of the window, like a curtain. It had no border, no embroidery, no patterns on it. It was perfectly plain, like a new, crisp, navy-blue turban.

Finally, a parrot green sari (the sort he had once unsuccessfully tried to sell to Mrs Bhandari), floated from the shelf towards him. He watched as it drew closer.

It then descended over his head, engulfing him like a shroud, its black border suffocating him.

Throughout the dream, a dead woman's eyes followed him.

*

The next day, he woke up feeling violently angry. He didn't get angry; he just woke up like that, on the hard floor, wanting to hit somebody. It was such an alien, new feeling for Ramchand that it took him a while to get used to it. Like wearing a stiffly starched new cotton shirt.

He did not go to work. Instead, he just paced his room, his mind completely upside down, occasionally kicking out at the walls.

One particularly violent kick sent flakes of plaster falling in the room below. The landlord emerged and shouted, '*Raaamchand!*'

Ramchand opened his window, looked down and, for the first time in his life, shouted.

'*Shuuut up!*' he screamed back at the landlord, and then spat for good measure.

227

He caught sight of Sudha's upturned, astonished face. She stood in the courtyard with a plateful of shelled peas in her hands, wearing a pretty multi-coloured sari with a floral pattern.

Ramchand slammed his window shut. He didn't eat anything all day. He didn't even have tea. He swallowed a lot of water in large gulps and continued to feel restless.

*

At five in the evening, he got dressed slowly and went out. Then he made his way to the shop. He walked slowly, softly, padding along like a leopard stalking its prey.

When he got there, the first to spot him was Mahajan. 'So, you have arrived finally. What happened to you? Are you completely mad, Ramchand? I tell you, if things go on like this . . .'

'You think you are so smart, don't you, Mahajan?' Ramchand said suddenly in a quiet voice.

Mahajan was really, truly, shocked.

'What? How dare you speak to me like this?' he spluttered.

It was only with supreme effort that Ramchand kept his fists clenched by his sides.

'I dare because I dare,' answered Ramchand. 'And you are not God, you know, after all.'

Mahajan was about to shout back at him, but he paused. This was very unusual. Ramchand had always been so timid and obedient. He backed off a little, his face turning wary. Something was wrong. Ramchand was in a strange mood. Mahajan thought he would go and fetch Gokul. Ramchand usually listened to Gokul. But there were customers upstairs. He would have to be discreet. He'd go up and fetch Gokul, to be on the safe side. You never knew with young men. They sometimes suddenly turned violent.

When he spoke, though, his tone was still authoritative, betraying none of his apprehension. 'You wait here, I am just coming.'

Mahajan rushed up the stairs. What *had* got into Ramchand? He went to where Gokul was sitting, and was whispering into his ears, when he suddenly saw Ramchand come up and enter the glass door. Mahajan groaned.

Ramchand came and stood in the middle of the room, glaring at Mahajan, and began to slowly, deliberately, crack his knuckles, as if daring Mahajan to do something to stop him.

Mahajan stood transfixed. Gokul looked worried. The others hadn't noticed yet. Ramchand looked around, still cracking his knuckles. His eyes turned to Chander's corner. Chander was free for the moment. He sat by Hari. They were both laughing and talking. Ramchand turned his glare on them. When they didn't notice, he turned to the only chair in the room. It was a small chair kept especially for elderly women whose joints ached and made it impossible for them to sit on the floor. It happened to be vacant right now. Ramchand picked it up, held it up over his head, and then, with all his might, flung it at Hari and Chander.

They yelled and scrambled to their feet. All the chatter in the shop died. Every head turned to look at Ramchand. Most women got up, afraid, ready to leave if a fight broke out.

'Ramchand, son, calm down,' said Mahajan, almost affectionately.

Ramchand couldn't bear his oily voice. What he wanted to do most at that moment was strike. Just strike, break, destroy. His eyes were red.

'He is drunk,' Gokul whispered to Mahajan.

'And I can hear you, Gokul!' Ramchand screamed in fury.

The longer he stood there, the louder he shouted. Some women began to leave quietly. Others, torn between fear of this madman and the acquisition of a beautiful sari, remained. When Mahajan saw a few women leaving, he began to get angry. Customers leaving? What would Bhimsen Seth say?

'Ramchand,' he said, sternly now. 'Leave immediately, or I'll have to take some serious action . . .'

Then Ramchand did the unthinkable. He lunged at Mahajan and grabbed him by his collar. He began to shake him in fury. Mahajan looked shocked, his eyes goggling as his frame shook.

'You shut up,' Ramchand screamed, his blood boiling, his eyes bloodshot. 'You just keep your mouth shut or I'll cut your tongue up into little pieces and tie it up in your own handkerchief and give it to you.'

At this, all the customers fled for their lives, leaving behind whatever saris their feminine hearts had desired. The shop was empty in a minute except for the shop assistants. Ramchand still had Mahajan firmly by the collar.

Gokul and Hari rushed forward to intervene, their faces serious but shining with excitement. Hari put his arm around Ramchand's shoulders and tried to calm him down. Ramchand turned on Hari and tried to get his fingers around Hari's throat, fighting like a madman to get rid of the arm around his shoulder.

'And you, Hari!' Ramchand yelled. 'Don't laugh, don't you ever laugh again. Ever, you understand? If I ever see you laughing, I swear by all the gods I know that I'll break every tooth in that grinning mouth of yours.' Ramchand tried to push Gokul's arm away, but Chander came to help, trying to pin Ramchand's arms to his side.

'Oh. Chander is very brave now, isn't he?' Ramchand screamed. 'Chander, if you had any heart, any courage, any belief, you wouldn't have been sitting here gossiping like an old woman.'

And then Ramchand spat. His spit landed on a gorgeous turquoise sari embroidered with real silver thread that someone among the fleeing customers had been about to buy. The glob of spit gleamed tremblingly on the delicate silver pattern.

Then Ramchand wrenched his arm free, and ran out of the shop, not looking back once.

9

When Ramchand returned to his room, feeling slightly sobered up after the scene, it had begun to rain. It looked like the monsoon had finally arrived. People looked up at the sky in happy anticipation. Ramchand climbed up the stairs dejectedly, and went into his room. He walked straight to the back window and opened it. In the courtyard below, Sudha was taking the washing off the line in a hurry. She wore a blue salwaar kameez. The hem of the kameez was edged with lace, and it fitted her very well. The raindrops made dark little holes in the blue fabric, like little bullet holes. Her hair got damp and her chunni fluttered in the breeze. Ramchand calmed down at the sight of her, but only slightly.

However, the few raindrops proved to be a false signal. Even as Ramchand watched, the few clouds in the sky disappeared and the sun shone down again, as hot and cruel as ever. The monsoons were still not here. Sudha reappeared with an armful of the washing. She hung it up on the line again, looking slightly morose.

Ramchand's brain seemed to thud against the insides of his skull. He rubbed some balm on his forehead and lay down on the bed. The vapours from the balm stung his eyelids.

*

Ramchand spent the next twelve days like this, locked up in his room. A strange twelve days. He had crashed into a broken vacant state, all rage gone. No rage, no worries, no happiness, no ambition, no doubt, no grief. He felt completely blank.

He did not step out even once, he had no contact with the outside world, he did not even keep track of day and night. He just spent all his time lying on his bed or sitting by the window without bothering to open it, thinking of nothing.

He skipped most meals, remembering to eat only when the gnawing void in his stomach became acute. Even then he wouldn't cook much. He'd boil rice, without bothering to make any daal to go with it. Then he would chew up large quantities of boiled rice with pieces of mango pickle out of a jar. Occasionally, he would walk to the stove in a daze after such a meal and make strong tea, without any milk, to wash down the meal with. Usually, after such a meal, his stomach would get distended, he'd get acidity and usually end up with a bad stomach-ache.

He lost count of the date and days. He didn't brush his teeth or shave, though he'd take sudden cold baths when he felt like it. He grew a rough stubble; his hair became sticky and oily, and clung to his scalp, making it itch. His toenails grew, their surface became rough. He didn't touch his books or his notebook. No one came to visit him.

Dust settled on every surface in the room – on the floor, on the desk, on the shelves, on the tops of all the jars, on the mirror, on the tin trunk, on his neat pile of books.

He watched a spider make a web between the table and the wall. He watched it with uninterest, completely detached, while the spider purposefully and industriously spun on. A lizard on the wall stared at him unblinkingly most of the day, breaking out into energetic chases whenever it saw an insect.

The days grew so hot that even the floor of his room radiated heat. There were frequent power cuts, but Ramchand did not get up to open a window or light a candle during any of them. He remained where he was, and remained there even after the power came back on. On most days, the voltage was very low, so that most of the time, the fan merely crawled lazily around its axis. After it grew dark, sometimes Ramchand would switch on the bulb. When he did, the bulb gave a very dim light. When he didn't, the room grew dark and cavernous. During the still nights, he could sometimes hear the scurry of mice in the room.

The air in the closed room grew stale. Heat and dust swathed the room like a heavy blanket, and Ramchand remained inert under their weight. On the thirteenth day, when Ramchand woke up feeling cold and shivery, he had his first coherent thought. 'I wonder if I am running a fever.' This was the first complete, sensible sentence that had taken shape in his mind for the last twelve days.

How could he feel cold in July? It was July, wasn't it? Ramchand felt a stab of fear and he got out of his bed. What time was it? What month was it? Where had he been? What had he been doing? For how long? And why was he feeling so cold? It had been very hot till yesterday. Ramchand felt completely disoriented.

He got to his feet and walked gingerly to the front window like an ill, old man. He slipped the bolt of the window with rusty fingers and opened it. It seemed like an eternity since he had last looked out of the windows.

Now he did.

And saw that outside, the morning sky was covered completely with low, dark, cool clouds. The light was unusual, with a smoky, purple tinge to it; it made the ordinary landscape appear strange, turning the most familiar things into extraordinary, beautiful objects. A chilly gale, the strongest that Ramchand had ever seen, was whipping around fiercely in the old city like a happy madman. It whipped crazily through trees, it swept away old newspapers from rooftops, it whirled away any washing left on clotheslines by careless housewives. The morning had an enchanted, unreal feel about it. The temperature had fallen dramatically. In the street below, plastic bags, dried fruit peel, leaves, coils of hair that women removed from their combs every day and threw down the windows carelessly and bits of paper danced all around the street, this way and that, in the frenzy that the gale had created. A stray pup crazily chased first one thing, then another, finally pursuing in a mad happiness a blue plastic bag that the gale tantalizingly kept just out of the pup's reach. The pup chased the plastic bag, children chased the pup, squealing in excitement. The old buildings of the city seemed enveloped in that blue-purple light, looking like a film set of an old film. An uncertain half-smile appeared on Ramchand's unshaven, dirty face. He felt caught up in the beautiful, powerful gale. He stood there at the front window for a while.

Then he turned around and looked at his room in surprise. The room was a complete mess! Everything was in disarray and a thick layer of dust coated every surface. Ramchand felt confused and dazed. What had happened to him? How had he let himself and his room get into such an appalling state? True, he had been upset, but still . . .

Then, as a sleepwalker does, he went to the door and was surprised to find it locked. He didn't remember locking it. He looked around for the key. It was on the table. He unlocked the door and pushed it open. The wind burst in through the door, immediately stirring up the whole room into a flurry: blowing the dust settled on the floor across the room, rustling up clothes and the stale air in the room. The spider scuttled crazily across the floor to a corner.

Ramchand went to the back window, unlatched it and pushed it open. It creaked and opened. Now that both the windows and the door were open, the room rustled and swished even more thankfully in the strong wind that blew in.

In the landlord's courtyard, Sudha sat in a sheltered place, mending summer holiday clothes busily, with a needle and black thread. She held the shirt she was mending tightly to keep it from flapping. Tendrils of hair that had come loose from her bun framed her plump face, fluttering wildly. She wore a white and red salwaar kameez. Her red chunni fluttered too, like her hair, as she bent over the blue shirt in her lap.

The children were running around in the courtyard trying to fly a kite. The cool, windy day had made them bring out their old kite that had been lying on top of Sudha's cupboard throughout the summer. It was a red kite, decorated with blue and yellow. Manoj held the kite. The younger boy, Vishnu, held the big ball of string. Alka, their sister, just danced around them excitedly, her green frock flapping around her brown knees. Their faces were flushed with excitement. However, now the gale was too strong and they had given up, content to merely run around holding the kite, emitting whoops of delight now and then. Ramchand called out to Manoj. The boy stopped running and looked up curiously.

'What is the date today?' Ramchand asked him.

The boy looked puzzled. Then he went into a whispered consultation with his siblings. Ramchand heard them argue. They apparently disagreed, for Alka suddenly thumped Vishnu on his back and he pinched her above her elbow.

Then Ramchand remembered it must be the middle of their summer holidays. The children couldn't be expected to keep track of the days. Manoj then held up his hand, motioning Ramchand to wait. Ramchand nodded. The boy disappeared inside to appear with a pocket calendar. He consulted it with an important, business-like air, for a moment looking startlingly like his father, and then shouted up at Ramchand.

'July 27!' he yelled, in English. His mother gave him a proud smile from across the courtyard. She didn't know a word of English herself. She didn't smile up at Ramchand, though, as she usually did. She probably remembered how, without any provocation at all, he had spat down into her courtyard.

July 27! Ramchand leaned against the wall weakly, shocked. He last remembered only the 14th or so. And the shop! With horror, Ramchand remembered his behaviour on his last day at work. He had made a scene, he had shouted at everyone, he had flung a chair at somebody, he didn't remember at whom. But he did remember that he had shaken Mahajan by his collar. And had sworn at him too. Ramchand grew weak at the knees. Mahajan must be furious, of course, or else he would have sent somebody to check up on him. He had lost his job! And it was the 27th! Almost the end of the month! And he was supposed to pay next month's rent on the first of August! And nobody would ever forgive him! It all came back to him in a rush.

What had he done! People died to get a good job all their lives. They went from one city to another with their families, their bedding and their utensils, desperately looking for work. They did back-breaking work at construction sites and starved when the building was finished. They slaved for long hours in factories till they grew old and were thrown out. Or else they worked as craftsmen, learning to weave or make jewellery, and went half blind when they were in their forties.

And here he was – he had thrown a perfectly good job away. How would he survive now? What *had* he done?

He walked to the bathroom in a daze, washed the dust-covered tube of Colgate toothpaste and his toothbrush, and then brushed his teeth carefully, making a lot of foam. Then he went to stand in front of the small mirror on the wall. A gaunt, thin face with the beginnings of a beard looked back at him. He lathered on soap on the strange, new hair with his shaving brush, and shaved very carefully, leaving his moustache intact. The shape of the moustache seemed somewhat altered, but it would do. He looked around for fresh clothes. When he couldn't find any, he opened his tin trunk and rummaged around in it till he unearthed an old brown shirt and a clean white pyjama.

He took a bath, scrubbing himself carefully, scrubbing his rough heels with a pumice stone, cleaning his toes with an old toothbrush and vigorously rubbing the bar of soap into his smelly armpits.

Then he towelled himself dry and put on the fresh clothes. He was about to drape his damp, striped towel across the back of the chair as he usually did, before he noticed that the back of the chair was covered with dust. He picked up the rag he used as a duster and wet it from the bathroom tap. Then he carefully cleaned the back of the chair and hung his towel around its back to dry.

He looked around for his watch. It was lying on the table and showed that it was ten in the morning.

There wasn't a moment to lose now. It was probably already too late. He would clean up the room later, when he returned.

Ramchand rubbed in some Parachute coconut oil into his freshly washed hair, combed it neatly, with a side parting, and hastened off to the shop. The wind ran its fingers gently through his oiled hair as he hurried through the familiar lanes.

*

'Ingratitude! That's what I call it. After all these years. Plain ingratitude.' Mahajan's moustache was quivering with indignant anger. Ramchand stood before him abjectly with his hands folded. At first, Mahajan had refused to even listen to him. Then, he had let himself go for about twenty minutes. He had shouted, ranted and raved at Ramchand. Ramchand stood there with his head hanging down, not saying a word, hoping he looked suitably ashamed.

After the first angry outburst was over, Mahajan calmed down a little. Now he was just repeating all the points that he had already made earlier. Ramchand continued to look deferential. It was pouring outside now, the first real monsoon shower. Rain was coming down in torrents. Black umbrellas dotted the street. Even though the street was flooded with water, drains were overflowing and every pothole had turned into a puddle, people looked happy. The relief from the unrelenting heat showed on every face. Most shopkeepers sat at their shop entrances, sipping tea. Ramchand knew that by now, Manoj, Vishnu and Alka would be sailing paper boats in the puddles in their courtyard. They did it each time it rained.

Mahajan continued to lecture and scold.

Finally, Mahajan looked up at him and, putting on an astute look on his face, asked shrewdly, 'Tell me something honestly, Ramchand. Were you drunk?'

Ramchand looked up at him in surprise. Mahajan misunderstood the look. 'So, that was it, was it? And you thought I wouldn't know.'

Ramchand considered this. He had never tasted alcohol in his life. But if he said he hadn't been drunk, how could he explain his behaviour away? Wouldn't Mahajan be less offended if he thought that it had been under the influence of alcohol that Ramchand had grabbed him by the collar? How else could he explain away the rage that had possessed him?

So, Ramchand didn't disagree. He merely hung his head down again.

'Oh, so that was it,' Mahajan said, looking satisfied now.

Now, Ramchand thought it was safe to speak. 'Bauji, please forgive me. I don't know how I could have . . .' Here, Ramchand suitably faltered at the right place. Mahajan laid a hand on his shoulder. 'Well, this is the first time you have ever misbehaved. And the last, I hope. We all make mistakes in our youth. You can come to work at this very moment if you like.'

Ramchand fell at Mahajan's feet.

Every single person watching the scene looked gratified. Gokul even wiped away a tear. Ramchand was back.

*

They all had to disperse because customers were coming in again. Ramchand went to his place and sat down, his legs shaky. Soon, the shop was full of the familiar chatter and rustle. Ramchand attended to three customers over the next two hours and sold two saris. He went out to have lunch and ate two puris at a food stall. At first, the other shop assistants were a little awkward with him, but in the evening, Ramchand bought samosas for everyone, offering two on a plate to Mahajan, who accepted with a smile.

After that, everything was back to normal. No one mentioned the day Ramchand had burst into the shop and attacked everyone. As Mahajan had said, everyone makes mistakes when they are young.

In the evening, Hari suggested they go to Lakhan's dhaba. Chander had already left, and Hari and Rajesh were going to have dinner together at Rajesh's place.

'Ay, Ramchand. You will come with us, right?' Gokul asked Ramchand, a happy smile on his face.

Ramchand smiled at Gokul and nodded. Hari leapt up to them and said, 'Let's go quickly. I am famished.'

The three went to Lakhan's dhaba. Hari took a chair next to Ramchand, and when Lakhan came to take their order, Ramchand averted his eyes from him.

They ate sabzi and tandoori rotis and then ordered tea. When Ramchand felt the familiar feel of a warm glass of tea in his hands, he had to blink back tears.

Gokul and Hari bantered with each other and Ramchand smiled at both of them, contributing very little to the conversation.

After the meal, Hari and Gokul said goodbye to him. Hari winked at Ramchand and Gokul patted his shoulder. Then they both went their own ways.

Ramchand walked back the familiar route to his room, climbed up the dark stairs and unlocked his door. He pushed the door open and saw the dust-covered room. He looked for the rag he used as a duster and went to work, slowly wiping each surface, except for the shelf that contained his books. He carefully avoided that.

An hour later, the room was dusted and swept, and Ramchand lay down on his bed, staring blankly at a damp spot on the ceiling.

Acknowledgements

I would like to thank my family, my friends and all the people in and outside publishing who helped bring this book into the world.